ENLIVENED DECAY

THE PURIFIED

INARA GAGE

To those who battle the monster within, who wrestle with their own darkness every day, and choose to rise above it.
I see you.
I honor your fight.

PROLOGUE
A CURE?

Thi*s was it—it had to be,* Dr. Elias Mercer, a board-certified oncologist, thought as he watched the mixture of puréed chicken, vegetables, and chemotherapy drugs flow through the cannula into the decomposing body of his patient. Patient A, bound at the wrists and ankles by thick chains bolted to the floor, lay motionless as the solution entered his body through what remained of his nose.

This session of Purifying seemed more successful than any before. Patient A struggled less and for the first time, his blood-shot, rheumy eyes seemed to truly see Dr. Mercer rather than viewing him as prey. This was the twentieth round of experimental treatments, and Dr. Mercer was starting to notice real progress.

In the dim light of his fortified treatment room, he watched the bag of pale orange liquid hanging from an IV pole steadily drain. As the concoction entered the patient's rotting form, the peeling flesh of his face appeared slightly less necrotic. Patient A even turned his head slightly, making direct eye contact with the doctor before slowly gazing at the ceiling, his decayed, bloodied clothing beginning to tighten against a frame that was once skeletal.

Dr. Mercer's epiphany came during a sleepless night in his office. Ever since the outbreak, he'd wondered if these creatures, dubbed "Ronas" by survivors, could be reconditioned. What if they were fed real food, treated with chemotherapy to repair their damaged systems, and had their dependency on human flesh reprogrammed? The next day, determined to find out, he began his dangerous experiment.

The apocalypse had transformed his medical office on the outskirts of Fort Collins, Colorado into a refuge. Its location outside the city center had spared it from the worst chaos. After losing his wife and daughter, Dr. Mercer had retreated here, fortified the building, and restored power using his background as a master electrician.

The plan to capture a Rona involved a makeshift trap: a tarp, rope, and a tranquilizer concoction brewed in his pharmacy. From the second-floor window, he spotted his target—a large man wandering the parking lot below. With calculated precision, he lowered the tarp, drawing the creature's attention. Silent and predatory, the Rona stepped onto the tarp. Dr. Mercer quickly hoisted the creature up and through the window, injecting it with the tranquilizer before retreating. Once the thrashing ceased, he secured the Rona with chains and transferred it to one of his treatment tables.

The first few treatments were disheartening. Patient A thrashed violently, deprived of human flesh. But after ten rounds of nutrient-rich food and chemotherapy, the results were undeniable. His struggles subsided, and his rotting skin began to regenerate. By the twentieth round, his flesh was peeling less, revealing patches of bright, healthy skin beneath.

Then, it happened.

As the last of the orange liquid drained into Patient A, a low gurgle emerged from his throat. "Good," he rasped.

Dr. Mercer froze.

Could it be?

He spun to face Patient A, whose bloodshot eyes now glistened with a faint clarity.

The creature, a former human, was regaining his mind.

Each day brought more progress. The pungent stench of decay diminished. Patient A's peeling skin gave way to fresh layers, his body beginning to look more like a burn victim healing rather than a rotting corpse. His movements became deliberate, his gaze more focused.

"Thank... you," Patient A stammered one night.

Dr. Mercer studied him, careful to maintain his distance. "Are your memories returning?" Patient A slowly nodded. "Who were you before you got infected?"

"Charlie," he whispered, his voice a rasp, words forced through a ruined mouth.

"Do you still crave flesh?"

"I... do," Charlie admitted, turning his gaze to the ceiling. "But it's... dwindling."

The doctor's heart raced. For the first time, he felt hope. "You realize I can't release you yet. Not until the cravings stop completely."

"I do."

***

Over the following weeks, Charlie's transformation became more remarkable. His lips regenerated, his cheeks filled out, and his skin turned pink and vibrant. By then, his cravings had nearly disappeared.

The doctor leaned closer, brimming with anticipation. Charlie had become proof that his cure was working. The disease that had torn apart the world could be reversed.

The next phase was clear: more patients, more testing, and ultimately the salvation of humanity.

One night, Dr. Mercer sat in the room while Charlie was

being fed through his tube. Charlie's lips were almost fully healed now, giving him a disturbingly human appearance.

"Do you remember how you got CoRona?" Dr. Mercer asked, his voice steady despite the grim subject.

"I do," Charlie replied, his tone eerily casual. "My wife must've caught it. She was going through chemo, no immune system to speak of. Maybe she crossed paths with someone sick and didn't realize it. She came home, we went to bed like usual, and I woke up to her chewing on my arm."

Dr. Mercer felt his stomach turn, but he kept listening.

"I got away before she could eat me whole," Charlie continued. "Back then, I didn't know that a bite was enough to doom you. I was driving to the hospital when the symptoms hit. Blood poured from my ears, nose, mouth—everywhere. That's the last thing I remember from... before."

Dr. Mercer hesitated before asking, "And do you remember anything about being... a Rona?"

Charlie nodded slowly. "I remember everything."

Dr. Mercer leaned forward, his curiosity outweighing his caution. "Do you still crave flesh?"

"It's not that I crave it," Charlie explained, his expression darkening. "It's more like... detoxing from an addiction. Back then, I craved it. It tasted... so good. The rush of hunting humans... it was like a heroin high. I didn't see people as people. They were just sustenance."

"And now?"

"Now, it's like waking up from a coma. When you fed me real food for the first time, things started clearing in my head."

Dr. Mercer studied him carefully. Charlie seemed lucid, even regretful. "Do you think you could try eating on your own? You know, with your mouth?"

Charlie chuckled softly. "I'd like that. Thank you... uh—"

"Dr. Elias Mercer," he offered.

"Thank you, Dr. Mercer."

Dr. Mercer nodded, feeling another flicker of hope. He headed to the kitchen, making a simple ham sandwich. As he returned to Charlie's room, his optimism shattered.

The bed was empty. The chains lay discarded on the floor, severed. The feeding tube dangled uselessly from the edge.

His heart thundered in his chest. When he turned to leave, the door slammed shut behind him.

Charlie stood there, blocking his escape. His eyes gleamed with something far darker than hunger.

"What are you doing?" Dr. Mercer asked, his voice barely above a whisper.

Charlie's smile was lethal. "I lied."

"About what?"

"I still crave flesh," Charlie said. "I always will. But now, thanks to you, I can fake being human. I can make them trust me, pity me, right up until the moment I strike. And even better —" He leaned closer, his breath hot and rancid. "I can Purify others. Together, we'll hunt in packs."

"But you remembered your life before," Dr. Mercer stammered. "You said—"

"That man is dead." Charlie's grin widened, his teeth unnaturally sharp. "This world is kill or be killed. And I prefer to kill."

Dr. Mercer lunged, slamming Charlie against the door. But Charlie's strength was monstrous. He hurled the doctor across the room, knocking the wind from his lungs.

As Dr. Mercer scrambled backward, pain seared through his leg. He looked down to see Charlie tearing into his calf, blood spraying as teeth sliced through flesh.

Dr. Mercer screamed, kicking at Charlie's face. It didn't even faze him.

Charlie met his eyes, blood dripping from his mouth as he

chewed. "Thanks for the second chance, Doc," he said, grinning.

The last thing Dr. Mercer felt before darkness consumed him was the agonizing sensation of being devoured alive.

1

INSULIN

PRIYA

"Maybe if we head back south on I-25, we can find some in the pharmacies along the way," Honor says as she puts away her son, Gratian's, glucose meter.

"How much do we have left?" her husband, Lux, asks, taking a sip of water from his canteen.

"We have about half a vial left, but we aren't having any luck here in Wyoming."

"I know. I've been here with you," Lux shoots back, his brown eyes glaring daggers at his wife.

"Don't snap at me. I'm only looking after our son!" retorts Honor.

"Quick bickering, you two," Priya interrupts, the lone survivor they'd picked up along the way. "We're all on the same side."

"I know. It's just frustrating," Honor says. "In all the movies and shows about zombie apocalypses, none of them showed how diabetics would fare—or people with cancer, or cancer survivors like myself."

"I know," Priya answers, her dulcet Indian accent cradling

her concern for her friend. Even though they haven't known each other long, they've found comfort in their apocalyptic friendship.

The way the husband and wife speak to each other sometimes sets Priya's teeth to grinding. "I know you're only looking after your son. But all we have is each other. We need to remember that, even when we feel most helpless."

Honor lets out a noncommittal sound, rolling her eyes as her dark fro sways gently in the breeze. She wipes the sweat from her brow and says, "I was thinking"—sidestepping Priya's comment—"since we came up 287, we could head down I-25 and hit the pharmacies along the way. We can make our way to where my oncologist used to be. They're bound to have insulin there, and it's far enough out of the main town that it might still be untouched."

"You mean Front Range Cancer Specialists?" asks Lux.

"Yes, they surely have plenty of insulin there. They had their own pharmacy."

"And there's a Walmart along the way," adds Michael, Lux's friend. "We can stock up on food."

"Good call," Lux says, leaning against one of the deteriorating gas pumps. "We should start heading that way now. There are Ronas moving around way down that way," he adds, pointing in the northern direction.

An echoing blast of a large gun cracks through the air, the sound reverberating off the abandoned gas station's concrete walls.

Honor's head snaps toward the distant gunfire, her hand instinctively shielding her eyes from the dying sun. "Who's shooting out there?"

Michael steps forward, scanning the horizon. "We shouldn't stand here long enough to find out. Gunfire means Rotters are coming."

Honor's voice wavers with worry. "What if someone's in trouble?"

"Honor," Priya says, her tone firm but sympathetic, "you've got the biggest heart, but we can't save everyone. You know that."

Before Honor can respond, a scream tears through the silence, high-pitched and desperate. The sound jolts the group like a lightning strike.

Michael stiffens, his hand moving instinctively toward his weapon. Lux curses under his breath and rushes toward the hill's edge, signaling wildly to the others. "Eyes up!"

From the shadow of an overpass, a figure bursts into view—a flash of red hair catching the sun, fiery and impossible to miss. The woman is running full tilt, a shotgun bouncing across her back. Behind her, a pack of Rotters hurtles forward, their emaciated bodies moving with terrifying speed.

"Four of them!" Lux shouts, pulling his rifle from his shoulder. "Move now!"

Honor grips the handles of her son's wheelchair tightly, pushing him back toward cover. Maria, another survivor they accumulated—along with her husband and son—is already drawing her bow, her fingers steady as she nocks an arrow and takes aim.

The red-haired woman stumbles, falling to one knee, but somehow pushes herself upright, scrambling up the incline. One of the Rotters is nearly on her, its decaying hands grasping wildly.

"Not today," Maria mutters under her breath. Her arrow sails true, sinking into the Rotter's forehead. It drops mid-stride, crumpling into the dirt.

Lux fires a single, precise shot. The second Rotter collapses, tumbling over the embankment and out of sight.

The woman screams again, her voice ragged and raw, as she crests the hill. A Rotter lunges from the shadows—but a thunderous blast cuts through the air. Antonio, one of the survivors they picked up along the way, fires his .45, tearing through the creature's chest. It hits the ground hard, twitching violently.

The final Rotter hesitates, turning its head with an almost unnatural jerk, its attention flicking between the fresh bodies and the group. It hisses, low and guttural, before charging.

Michael steps forward, swinging his shovel-turned-spike with brutal efficiency. The sickening crunch of impact echoes as the creature collapses, its momentum halted by sheer force.

Panting, the red-haired woman stumbles to her knees, shaking uncontrollably. Her hands are raw and bloodied, clutching the strap of her shotgun like a lifeline.

Lux approaches cautiously, his rifle still trained on the woman. "Are you okay? Have you been bitten?" His voice is hard—clipped, but not unkind.

She shakes her head, gasping. "No... I was asleep under the overpass... woke up to them right there. Shot one... ran... fell... just kept running..." Her words come in fragmented bursts, punctuated by shaky breaths.

Honor kneels beside her, gently placing a hand on her shoulder. "You're safe now," she says softly, though her own voice trembles.

The woman's fiery hair clings to her sweat-slicked skin, framing a face etched with exhaustion and terror. She glances up, her green eyes wide and haunted. "Safe?" she repeats, as if the word is foreign. "Nowhere's safe."

A tense silence settles over the group, broken only by the distant groans of more Rotters in the fading light.

"Well, I'm glad you're alright," Honor says. "What's your name?"

"Krishna Pope. And you are?"

"I'm Honor. This is my son, Gratian, and my husband, Lux. This is Michael, and this is Priya. There are more of us back there."

"Nice to meet you all," Krishna says, nodding. "Where are you headed?"

"Back to Fort Collins. My son has diabetes, and we need more insulin."

"Oh wow, how awful for you," Krishna says to Gratian.

"It's okay. I'm used to it."

"Well, you're a very brave young man. To have it in the first place and then to have it in this sh—uh, crap. Gotta be hard to keep up on it."

"We do what we gotta do," Lux answers, somewhat coldly.

"Where are you headed?" Priya asks, as Honor shoots Lux a scornful look.

"Not really sure, as a matter of fact. I just wander, try to find food, and kill the Ronas. Rid this world of those awful things."

"You're welcome to join us if you want," Priya offers, skirting the sideways look Lux is giving her. "It's safer to have numbers, take shifts sleeping."

Her features are delicate yet sharp, her thin lips and pointed nose giving her a slightly mouse-like appearance. Her eyes, a soft meadow green, are wide and alert, scanning the group warily. "Thanks, that would be great."

"We need to move," Michael says grimly, reloading his weapon. "Those things are heading our way.

Lux nods and whistles for the remaining survivors to move out.

Priya slings on the backpack she'd packed moments prior.

They'd been holed up at the gas station camp for a few days, but it was time to move on. They need to find more insulin and food. The snares they'd set had caught a few rabbits, but with the group's size, it won't sustain them for long. Moving closer to the mountains promises bigger game and better opportunities.

As they set off down the abandoned highway, Krishna turns

to Priya, her voice breaking the heavy silence. "So, who is everyone?"

Priya glances at the others walking ahead. The road stretches out before them, eerily quiet, scattered with cars long since stripped of purpose. The empty shells of vehicles seem to carry a weight heavier than the stale gasoline lingering in the air.

"That's Maria," Priya says, gesturing with her chin toward the woman walking beside a Hispanic man and a young boy. "Her husband, Juan, and their son, Jesus."

Krishna studies the small family. Maria has her arm around Juan and Jesus carries their supplies with the quiet determination of someone who's been through too much for being so young.

"They're a sweet family," Priya adds. "We found them living in an abandoned house on the way to Wyoming."

Krishna nods as Jesus looks back at her and winks.

"And them?" she asks, ignoring the teenager.

Priya sets her jaw. "That's Jerod and Heidi," she answers shortly.

"Ooh, do I sense some tension?"

Priya adjusts her backpack and hooks her thumbs under the straps. "She's just... how should I put this... always mad and negative about absolutely everything. I can only handle her in doses."

"Ah, good to know, good to know. What about her?" she asks, pointing at Amy.

"Oh she's an angel," Priya answers, watching as Michael and Amy walk shoulder to shoulder.

"Are they a thing?"

"They like each other, but nothing has come of it yet. I was attracted to her at first when she joined the group, but then he swooped in and..."

"Cock-blocked you?!" Krishna asks with a smile. "That bastard!"

Priya chuckles. "No, Michael is as sweet as they come too. They're good together."

"And the two behind us?" Krishna asks, her gazed pinned forward so as not to look like they're gossiping.

"Oh, just a few stragglers we picked up along the way," Priya answers, watching ahead as Lux and Honor bicker about something else now. "Antonio is a little Italian man with a big attitude, and Janice—who's as white privileged as they come."

Krishna steals a glance over her shoulder. "How so?"

"She's just not built for an apocalypse. Was rich in her former life—can't stand being dirty, eating out of cans, sleeping on the dirt, or running from things that eat you."

"Lovely," Krishna replies. "And why is the little one in a chair?"

"Something he was born with. I couldn't tell you the name, but I know it starts with a 'c.'"

Krishna's eyes glimmer toward Gratian. "He seems like a bright shining light."

"He truly is."

Their chatter fades into the melancholia of the journey, everyone engaging in conversation while also staying cautious of what may be lurking in the shadows.

Priya watches as Lux and Honor's bickering simmers to a boil, and Lux breaks off from the group to walk ahead, alone. She lets her gaze drift to the mountains in the distance, sad for her friend.

"I just—I have to go make sure she's okay," Priya says to Krishna.

Krishna nods, and Priya jogs to catch up with Honor.

"Hey, are you alright?" she asks as soon as she's walking alongside her.

Honor's brown eyes find hers, a sheen of unshed tears glistening in them. "Fuck him," she mutters under her breath.

Gratian has fallen asleep, his head lolling to the side as Honor pushes him onward.

"You guys have got to start getting along," Priya says gently, putting her arm around Honor.

Honor leans into the sideways hug. "You had a wife, and you were unbelievably happy. I am a wife and am unbelievably sad. This dates way before CoRona. He was never there for me —through Gratian almost dying, or my cancer, or any of it. God, I just wish..." Her voice breaks, and she exhales through the sob.

"Wish what?"

Honor wipes the tear that slips, unbeckoned. "No. It's too awful to say."

"Honor, I'm your best friend. You can tell me anything."

"I just wish that Nora was here, and Lux was gone."

The way Priya's heart breaks for Honor.

"You're just upset. You don't mean that."

She can't mean that.

Can she?

Honor lifts her head and pierces Priya with her stern gaze. "But I do."

Over the past three months, Priya had barely seen them hold hands or kiss the way a loving married couple should. Of course, they'd been through some things—everyone had. But those should be the things that bring people closer together, not push them farther apart.

Having not known either of them for very long, it was hard for Priya to pinpoint exactly why Honor and Lux fought the way they did.

Part of it might be that Honor was Black and Lux was white. While that wouldn't always seem like a primary factor in marital struggles, Priya couldn't help but sense that Honor felt misunderstood by Lux. It was as if Lux took pride in being with a strong Black woman, but didn't fully grasp or appreciate what that truly meant for her.

The sting of tears pricks Priya's eyes as her thoughts shift to her late wife, Nora. When Nora died, a part of Priya died too. She often wondered if she would ever be able to love again.

That's why her heart breaks for Honor. To see someone weighed down by a relationship that doesn't lift her up—unable to leave because of the grim circumstances of the apocalypse—fills Priya with sorrow. She finds herself silently wishing that one day, Honor can break free and find a love as pure and soul-enriching as the one Priya had found with Nora.

2

KHAKI KISS
PRIYA

Late spring wind punctuates the trek between Wyoming and Colorado with its icy breath. Crisp, golden waves of grain speckle the horizon with a khaki kiss, remnants of winter clinging to the edges of spring in its eternal longing for dead things.

An exit sign, riddled with bullet holes, sways lazily in the breeze. Beyond it, the faint sounds of a struggle echo, carried through the trees off to the right.

"Behind you, Shamus!" a woman's voice shouts, sharp and urgent.

The cry isn't far off, but it's muffled by the thick brush.

A gunshot cracks through the air, followed by a scream.

Then, silence.

Lux steps toward the source of the voices, pushing through the brush with his machete poised and ready.

Krishna pulls her gun from her back, steadying it as her eyes scan the woods.

Honor wheels Gratian to the left, her sharp gaze locking on the overgrown path leading to the exit ramp.

Michael sticks close behind Amy, while Priya walks behind them, her hand brushing the knife strapped to her thigh.

Four people are stranded in a clearing surrounded by a plethora of Ronas, in the middle of what used to be a park-and-ride.

A curvaceous Black woman with long braids cascading down her back swings her swords at them, decapitating one and slashing the torso off another. A tall, thug-looking man fires at others, while another—a muscular, shorter man—stabs at any that get close. A nerdy-looking fellow attacks with a Viking-style spear.

Lux and Michael rush up to the group and begin hacking away at the Ronas with their machetes, as Krishna stays close to Priya and aims her shotgun at one in the distance. Priya pulls her own .45 from the back of her pants and does the same at another beside it.

After the last Rona is dead, nothing left but pieces of rotting flesh on the ground, Priya makes her way down the hill to the middle of the parking lot.

Immediately, she is taken aback by how beautiful the woman is.

"You guys okay?" Lux asks as Priya approaches.

The woman is wiping the brown blood and guts off her sword. "Yes. Thanks for the assist."

"Not a problem at all. Name's Lux. This is Michael, that's Priya, and this is Krishna."

"Hi, I'm Sariah," the beautiful woman says, stepping closer.

Priya takes in the jewels adorning her braids, her melted turquoise eyes rimmed with daffodil, and the way her tight brown pants hug her thick thighs. Sariah's caramel skin glistens in the sun, and her large breasts barely remain contained in her leather top and vest.

"This is Shamus," she adds, motioning to the large man standing beside her. He looks like he belongs in a motorcycle gang, with short, curly gray hair covering his head and face. "Jesse and Pacious."

Jesse is strikingly handsome, with a muscular frame and clear blue eyes reminiscent of a cloudless summer day, while Pacious is thinner, his black hair and square glasses giving him a more bookish air.

Handshakes are exchanged as Lux secures his machete across his back. "Where are you guys heading?" he asks.

"Just the same as all of you," Pacious answers. "Trying to find somewhere safe."

"Well," Priya offers, averting Lux's surely disapproving gaze, "you're welcome to tag along with us. We need to find insulin and a safe place to sleep tonight. We're heading for an old cancer center off Harmony Road in Fort Collins."

Shamus's skeptical expression deepens, his stance heavy with doubt.

Sariah catches Priya's eye and smiles slightly. "Sure, we can tag along," she says, before Shamus can voice his objections.

"I don't know about all that," Shamus grumbles.

"Do what you want," Lux replies indifferently. "I'm heading back to my wife and kid. We've got maybe two hours of daylight left and plenty of ground to cover."

With that, Lux turns and strides back toward the rest of the group. Priya watches as Sariah, Shamus, Jesse, and Pacious huddle together for a quick discussion. Michael falls in step behind Lux, while Krishna lingers, waiting for Priya.

Sariah's voice calls out, firm and decisive. "Alright, we'll join you."

"Perfect," Priya replies, already turning to follow the others.

3

FAR FROM OKAY

PRIYA

The sun sinks lower on the horizon, stretching the shadows long and thin across the cracked pavement. Darkness means danger. Ronas thrive in the night, and with every passing minute, Priya grows more anxious.

After passing only two more exits, a dilapidated hotel looms off the next ramp. Its broken neon sign flickers faintly, casting eerie shadows over the parking lot.

Priya spots it first. "Hey, everyone," she says, raising her voice. "Maybe we should head to that hotel for the night."

Sariah nods in agreement, giving her a small smile. "Makes sense to me."

Honor, slightly out of breath from pushing Gratian up a small incline, chimes in. "I agree. I need to check his sugar levels and get him somewhere safe before dark."

"On it," Michael says, taking the lead as the group moves off the highway and toward the exit ramp.

As they approach the hotel, Priya notices a few Ronas wandering in the distance. Thankfully, the area isn't swarming.

Yet.

When they reach the parking lot, the Ronas begin to notice them. Their lumbering forms change direction, shambling toward the group.

"Get ready," Lux orders, pulling his machete free.

The thing is with Rotters, you never know how fast they're going to be. Fresher Ronas move faster; the ones dead a long time are slow and clumsy. But it's like Russian roulette—you never know when a runner will jump up out of nowhere.

A rotting woman emerges suddenly from behind a rusted minivan, nearly reaching Pacious before he reacts. He thrusts his spear into her eye, and her decayed brain spills out as she collapses to the ground.

Closer to the entrance, a male Rona charges from the side of the building. Sariah steps forward, calm and precise, and fires her .357. The bullet finds its mark, silencing the creature instantly.

As the group moves toward the double doors, a sudden commotion erupts. A Rona bursts out from beneath a pile of rotting wood and lunges at Honor.

"Gratian!" Honor cries, shoving the wheelchair forward with such force that her son goes flying out of harm's way.

"Honor!" Priya shouts, darting toward Gratian.

Lux and Michael race to Honor's aid, Lux's machete cleaving through the Rona's neck. Its head topples to the side as Michael kicks the lifeless body off Honor, the crunch of shattered glass echoing as he steps on a vial that has spilled from her satchel.

Honor sits up shakily, wiping blood and vomit from her mouth.

"Mama!" Gratian cries, his small hands reaching toward her.

Priya wheels him over, his face scrunched in worry.

"I'm okay, baby," Honor murmurs, her voice trembling. "I just... I need a shower."

"Let's hope this place has water," Lux mutters, helping her to her feet.

Priya reaches the front door and pulls at the handle. It doesn't budge. "Fuck," she hisses, stepping back.

Sariah joins her, examining the door. "Boarded up from the inside. Someone must've tried to turn this into a safe house."

"There's an open window up top," Priya says, scanning the building. "We'll need to climb up and get inside."

"I'll do it," Shamus offers, stepping forward with a cocky grin.

"Of course you will," Sariah retorts, rolling her eyes. "Breaking in is your specialty."

"Don't start," Shamus shoots back, smirking. "I only rob corporations."

"Corporations are still people," Sariah quips, folding her arms.

Shamus ignores her, jogging around the building to find a way up.

Minutes tick by, the silence oppressive, broken only by the occasional rustle of leaves or distant moan of a Rona. Priya shifts nervously, her eyes darting toward the horizon as darkness creeps closer.

Finally, the sound of splintering wood and rattling chains shatters the quiet. A sledgehammer bursts through the doorframe, followed by Shamus's triumphant face.

"Got it," he says, pushing aside the broken pieces to unlock the glass doors. "Place is a mess, but it'll do. Looks like someone lived here for a while."

Lux steps forward, clearing the remaining debris. "Let's get inside and secure the place before we attract more attention."

One by one, the group files into the dimly lit lobby, the faint scent of decay mingling with dust. Priya casts a final glance outside, her grip tightening on her weapon as the last sliver of sunlight disappears.

They move through a hotel that was once grand and inviting, now deteriorating and ominous. Whoever had made a home of this place seems to be long gone—or so it seems—as the building sits dark, damp, and full of silence.

"We should seal this back up," Jerod says, Heidi glowering behind him.

"Yes, good call," Antonio answers, and he and Jerod start boarding the front door shut.

"I'll start a fire," Juan says, making his way to the grand sitting area of the hotel, where a large stone fireplace is set into the far wall. There are remnants of an old fire, burnt logs within it, surrounded by ripped couches and lounge chairs.

"I need to find a shower," Honor states, wheeling Gratian toward the bar in the back, Priya by her side. "But first I need you to check your blood sugar, yeah?"

"Okay, Mama," Gratian replies, as Honor pulls the pokey pack—the old lunch pail they use to keep his glucose monitor, juice, snacks, and other things for lows—from the back of the chair and hands it to him.

Gratian goes through the motions seamlessly, not even flinching as he pushes down on the lancet to draw blood. He digs in the canister for a fresh strip, adding the blood to it.

"Three-fifty," he reads.

"Oh god," Honor gasps. "Okay, we need to give you some insulin. Why are you so high?"

"Jerod gave me a piece of his candy bar," Gratian answers truthfully.

Honor shoots Jerod a look of death, though he's busy hammering the door back together and doesn't see it.

She sits on one of the bar stools and pulls her satchel off her shoulder, opening it to dig around for the insulin.

Priya takes the stool next to her and smiles at Gratian.

Honor's digging becomes more frantic until she finally

upends the bag, pouring the contents onto the bar. Sifting wilding through the mess, there are no vials of insulin among the detritus.

"It's not in here! It was in here!"

Lux, having seen her frenzied attempts at searching, comes over and places a hand on her back. "Babe, what's up?"

"The insulin! It's not in here!"

"Shit," Lux breathes.

Honor stops her overwrought attempts at making insulin appear and looks at him. "What?"

"When you were attacked out there, I saw the satchel fall and heard a crunch as Michael came up to help. I didn't think anything of it, but now that you mention it—I think it was the vial of insulin."

"That was the last vial!" Honor screams, the echo drawing the attention of everyone in the building. "What are we gonna do!"

Priya watches as Honor's face shifts from hectic worry to utter devastation.

"Baby, it'll be okay. Okay?" Lux soothes her. "How high is his blood sugar?"

"Three-fifty," Honor cries.

"Okay." Lux puts his hands on her shoulders, the sleeves of his rolled-up flannel pushed up to his forearms. "He's been this high before, and we've gotten through it. We'll just have to watch what he eats until we can get a move on tomorrow, okay?"

He helps her sit back down in the chair as Gratian and Priya keep quiet, watching the two parents figure life out.

"Okay," Honor answers on an exhale.

Priya stands and rubs Gratian's back. Sometimes his parents forget that he's the one who has it—they get so wrapped up in being caretakers.

"You okay?" she bends over and whispers in his ear.
"I think so," he answers in a small, quiet voice.
But the uncertainty in his tone sends a chill through her.
Somehow, Priya knows—things are far from okay.

4

DANGER MOUNTS

PRIYA

Priya stares at the fire, watching the fiery tongues lick at the night as though thirsty for darkness. She steals glances at Sariah as often as she dares, a glamorous ray of hope in a broken world. Sariah sits across from her, cleaning her nails with a knife.

Studying the mysterious woman across from her, Priya watches how she interacts with her comrades as though they've known each other forever. The way Jesse leans in to tell her something—and the smile he pulls from her face—makes Priya jealous. How she wishes she had the nerve to go sit by Sariah and ask the beauty her story.

But the nerves escape like shadows fleeing from light.

Jesse and the other two rise from the couches, leaving an empty seat. Priya almost—*almost*—gets up and goes to sit by her, but Honor appears, stealing all of Priya's nerve and replacing it with concern for her forlorn friend.

Honor wears a towel on her head and fresh clothes she must've scrounged from a long-forgotten guest of the hotel. Her face is still painted with agonizing worry as she sits next to Priya, parking Gratian beside her.

"Where's Lux?" Honor asks Priya.

"He, Jer, and Juan went off to find any kind of sustainable food they could," Maria answers, sitting on a couch with her son, Jesus.

"I see," Honor says. "And the newcomers?"

"I think they went to do the same thing, but for supplies," Priya replies. "How was your shower?"

"Cold," Honor answers with a shiver. "But I feel much better —as far as being covered in rotting guts goes. How's your blood sugar?" she asks Gratian.

"I haven't checked it since last time," Gratian admits. "I'm running low on strips too."

"Great," Honor huffs on an exhale. "We need to get to the cancer center like yesterday."

"We will, love," Priya answers softly. "We can leave at first light. You know me, I'm usually up at the crack of dawn."

"Yeah, it's annoying," Heidi mutters, settling into the seat opposite Priya and beside Sariah.

"You're annoying," Priya shoots back, her voice sharp with bubbling frustration. She's had enough of Heidi's negativity. "You know what, Heidi? We're all stuck in this apocalypse together, and yeah, it sucks. But your whiny, bitchy, holier-than-thou attitude? It can kick rocks. And so can you if you don't cut it out."

Heidi's face flushes an angry red. "Well, you—"

"ENOUGH!" Honor's voice cuts through the tension like a blade, her stern, motherly tone demanding attention. "I don't need you two bickering right now, okay? I've got enough on my plate with Gratian."

"You're right," Priya says, her anger fading into regret as she exhales. She shouldn't have let Heidi get under her skin. "Let's talk about something else. Krishna, what about you? Where are you from, and where were you when the CoRona hit?"

Krishna, who's been sitting quietly on the edge of the group, looks up at Priya. The firelight dances across her face, igniting her bright red hair in a fiery glow.

"I was in Casper with my fiancé," she begins, her voice low and solemn. "I worked as a bartender and went to pharmacology school. He was a mechanic. We were supposed to get married this summer. But one day, he went to work and never came home. When I went to look for him, all I found was blood at his workstation."

Her words hang in the air, heavy with grief.

"I tried to make it to my parents' place, but their town was overrun with Ronas. So, I figured I'd head to Colorado to see if I could find anyone—maybe some kind of compound where people were surviving. That's when I found you guys."

She finishes with a faint, bitter smile—her tone far from enthusiastic, but full of quiet determination.

"I'm so sorry about your fiancé," Priya says.

"What about you?" Sariah slides her eyes to Priya, and the glance sends her stomach flying into her throat. "What's your story?"

"Me?" Priya questions, wondering if she's honestly curious about her or just the group in general.

"Yeah, tell me about you. Where you're from, how you ended up here. You know—your story."

Priya smiles and pulls her legs up under her so she's sitting cross-legged.

"Well, I'm from India originally. I came here on a work visa when I met and married the love of my life, Nora. She's gone now."

"Oh, I'm sorry to hear that," Sariah responds, her tone soft. "What were you doing here for work? Or what brought you here?"

"I was a lawyer. I was practicing criminal law, and my wife was a district attorney. We met on a big case and fell in love. We were happy—until the outbreak." Priya stops here, the memory still fresh, raw, and painful. The way Nora smiled, how she always smelled like Coach Poppy, the way her eyes lit up when she was being mischievous.

"Oh, Priya, I'm so sorry," Sariah says, and Priya can see in her eyes that she's sincere.

"Thank you," Priya replies, shifting in her seat and wiping away the tear that falls. "We've all lost someone in this, haven't we?"

"Yeah, I lost all my kids," Heidi says in a snooty undertone, crossing her arms.

"Oh my god," Krishna gasps, her eyes wide with shock. "How terrible!"

Priya rolls her eyes. "Don't let her fool you into thinking all her kids are dead. She lost three of them before CoRona hit and has no idea if they're alive or not. The other two are in Greeley with their dad. None of them are dead, despite what she wants you to believe."

"Priya!" Honor scolds, her tone sharp.

"What? It's true!" Priya replies, defensive. "She does this all the time—making it seem like her story is worse than it really is so people feel sorry for her."

"That is not true!" Heidi snaps, glaring daggers at Priya.

"Then where *are* your kids, Heidi?" Krishna asks calmly, her curiosity genuine.

Heidi exhales loudly, her glare still fixed on Priya before she turns to Krishna. "The older two went to live with their mom in Texas before CoRona hit. Jer and my youngest went to visit them. The last time I spoke to her, they were planning to make their way here to meet me. We agreed to meet at the event center—there's supposed to be a compound there. My other two are with their dad in Greeley, and as far as I know, they're heading to the same place."

"Compound at the event center?" Krishna asks, her brows furrowing. "Where'd you hear that?"

Heidi shoots one last withering glare at Priya before answering. "Jer and I lived in Laramie, along with my mom and stepdad. My stepdad had one of those CB radios he'd always listen to. When things started getting bad, Jer and I went to their place since it was out in the boonies—we figured the Ronas wouldn't get there as easily." She pauses, her tone softening as she recalls. "One night, while listening to the radio, we heard talk about a group setting up a compound at the event center. It's a closed-in ranch area, so it made sense. That's where we were heading when we ran into Honor, Lux, and Priya."

Heidi's voice hardens again as she glances back at Priya. "And that's the truth, whether she likes it or not."

"They were in a bad way," Priya adds. "The Ronas had already eaten her mom and stepdad and were about to eat her too, if we hadn't saved her." She meant for her tone to be harsh, to make the unspoken point that Heidi should be grateful.

"And you had five children, and now none of them are with you?" Krishna asks.

Priya is starting to like her—she seems to be the no-bullshit kind of person.

"He had two from his first marriage, I had two from mine, then we had one together."

"And none of them wanted to be with you?"

Priya would have spit out a drink she'd been drinking at that moment.

"His two made their own choices to live with their mom," Heidi snipes back. "My two just happened to be with their dad when all this shit hit the fan."

Priya makes a noncommittal sound, clearly indicating she doesn't believe that for a second.

Heidi is about to shoot a retort her way when Lux, Juan, and Jer return to the lobby from their foraging.

"What'd you find, babe?" Honor asks, craning her neck in

his direction as they come meandering in, carrying heavy backpacks filled to the brim.

"Vending machines that hadn't been touched yet by whoever was here before us," Lux answers, dropping the backpack he was carrying to the floor next to Honor and kneeling beside her.

"And lots of canned goods from one of the dry storages that hadn't been found yet either," Jerod adds, slinging his bag down next to Lux's.

"Yeah, and lots of bottled water and sodas too," Juan says, his Spanish accent amplifying his A's.

"Nice work," Krishna responds.

"Any sight of my boys?" Sariah asks.

"Nah. I didn't even know they were foraging around," Lux replies. "Where are Michael and Amy?"

"They went off 'exploring,'" Honor answers, using air quotes around the word.

"Ah, off to find an empty bedroom to finally get it on, eh?" Jer says with a chuckle.

"Do we have anything to eat besides antelope, rabbit, or refried beans?" Janice interrupts, having been quiet for most of the night—except to ask for better food.

How Janice is still surviving the apocalypse, having to eat what's available and sleep outside most of the time, is beyond Priya.

"There's some green beans and things in here we can heat up," Lux says, inclining his head toward the backpack. "I think we ate the rest of that antelope earlier."

"Yeah, that's gone," Juan replies.

"Once we get to a place we can stay for a bit, we can go out hunting again," Jer adds.

"Well, I guess that's better than refried beans. *Again*," Janice mutters.

Lux rolls his eyes, stands, tosses her the bag, and then takes a seat in one of the empty chairs. "Help yourself."

"Thanks," Janice answers methodically, annoyance riding the undertone of her voice.

She probably wants someone else to cook the meal for her too.

"There's a can opener in the front pouch," Honor states.

"Thanks," Janice says again, opening the bag and rummaging through it.

"Are you hungry, baby?" Honor asks Gratian.

"A little," he answers, laying his head on her shoulder. "But I don't wanna eat anything. My sugar will skyrocket."

"You still need to eat," Lux responds.

"If he can skip a meal, I'd rather he did, babe. We don't wanna risk DKA."

"What's DKA?" Sariah asks, before Lux can shoot an angry retort at his wife.

"It's when a diabetic's blood sugar gets really high and they don't have any insulin to bring their levels down," Krishna answers. "The body starts attacking the fat cells much too fast, releasing ketones—which cause the blood to become acidic. It's life-threatening."

"Oh my god," Sariah gasps. "How scary."

"It is," Honor says.

"Yes, but it takes days of being high to get to that point." Lux deadpans.

Honor rolls her eyes. "I am so tired of you playing this off like his disease isn't a serious, life-threatening thing!"

"Oh, Jesus fucking Christ, Honor, I'm just saying—" Lux snaps, his voice rising in pitch.

"STOP IT!" Gratian shouts, covering his ears and hiding his face behind Honor's shoulder. "Stop fighting, you two. Just stop!"

"Okay, love. I'm sorry, honey," Honor says, her voice leveling to a more soothing tone.

Priya is starting to get sick of their bickering as well, so she doesn't blame Gratian for his outburst at all.

"Just make one of those cans of green beans for him—they don't have many carbs at all," Lux offers, his voice retreating back into normal conversational tones.

Honor shoots him one last look of disapproval before Janice slides the backpack her way.

"Is there a pot or anything to cook these in?" she asks, cranking the can opener around the lid.

"Juan has a pot in his bag," Maria offers.

"Yeah, here," Juan says, standing and retrieving his bag. He digs around and pulls out a small pot, handing it to Janice.

"Thank you," Janice says.

Juan nods.

Michael and Amy enter the room at that moment, holding hands and giggling, Amy's hair a little disheveled.

"Ah, so there you two are, finally," Lux says as they reach the group. "Have fun exploring?"

Michael whips Lux in the back of the head before plopping down in one of the empty seats, pulling Amy into his lap. "We did, thank you," he says with a devilish smirk.

Janice, having successfully opened the can of beans, pours it into the pot and sets the grate over the fire that's burning off to the side.

"What's for dinner?" Michael asks playfully.

"Not sure what you're having, but I'm having green beans," Janice grouses.

"What else is in there?" Amy asks.

"Have a look," Janice says, passing Amy the bag.

Amy bends down to retrieve it, but a loud commotion stops her cold. The sound of boots pounding against carpet, followed by the crash of double doors slamming open, draws everyone's attention to the far wall.

Pacious, Shamus, and Antonio burst into the large hotel lobby, stumbling over each other as though being chased. Pacious spins and slams the double doors shut, shoving his back against them and bracing his feet as if keeping someone out.

Lux and Jer rise from their seats, Lux pulling his shotgun from the ground. Michael steps protectively in front of Amy, shielding her with his body.

"What is it?" Lux demands, cocking his gun. "What did you find?"

Pacious, panting heavily, shakes his head. "The people who lived here before us," he says, his voice trembling. "And it ain't good."

"What could possibly be worse than the Ronas eating them?" Lux asks, a faint edge of curiosity threading his voice.

"Something else hunting them," Shamus replies grimly.

Jer tightens his grip on his baseball bat. "What?"

"What gives you that impression?" Lux presses.

"I don't think we should stay here and chat about it," Pacious cuts in, still bracing the door.

"Is something chasing you?" Michael asks sharply.

"No," Pacious replies, glancing at the door warily. "But something was down there recently, and I don't want to be here when it comes back."

He peels himself away from the door, his eyes scanning the room, and starts walking toward the fire. Shamus and Antonio fall in behind him.

Lux steps forward and grabs Pacious by the arm, stopping him in his tracks. "What happened down there?" he demands.

Pacious glares at the hand on his arm, his face darkening. "It'd be in your best interest to let go of me," he growls.

"You need to explain why you want us to leave in the middle of the night," Lux says, unrelenting.

"I don't need to explain a damn thing to you," Pacious snaps, his anger rising.

"Babe, that's enough," Honor interjects, quickly moving between them and breaking Lux's hold on Pacious. She turns to him, her tone soft yet firm. "Pacious, please. I have my son to think about."

Pacious's gaze flicks to Gratian, who watches silently from a corner. His expression softens slightly, and he nods. "Alright, ma'am."

The group gathers by the fire, Antonio staying behind to bar the doors securely shut. Pacious perches on the arm of a chair, his face still drawn tight.

"We went searching the hotel for supplies," Pacious begins. "Started at the top, checking rooms and cabinets. That's when we noticed it—a trail of blood. It started in one of the rooms, a big pool of it, and then it moved. Room to room. We followed it to an elevator shaft and checked each floor to see where it led."

"And?" Lux prompts, his impatience evident.

"When we got to the basement, things got bad," Pacious says, his voice dropping.

Lux scoffs. "So far, it just sounds like normal Ronas chasing people. Maybe they got in somewhere, or maybe a group of them—"

"It doesn't make sense," Antonio cuts him off. "How did it start at the top floor and end in the basement? And it's not just that."

Pacious picks up where Antonio leaves off. "The blood trail kept going, but at every spot where it pooled, there was... a piece of someone. An arm here, a leg there."

Lux shakes his head, his tone turning sharp. "That's just Ronas eating people."

"No," Pacious insists, his voice firm. "You've seen Ronas.

They devour everything. They don't leave behind cleanly cut-off limbs."

The group falls silent, the weight of his words sinking in.

"It gets worse," Antonio adds. "We found a barricaded room. People had been hiding in there. But they were still there—pieces of them missing. And in the middle of the room…" He pauses, visibly shaken. "There was a man tied to a chair. The top of his head had been sawed off. His brain was gone."

"What the fuck," Michael mutters, his voice low.

"So you're saying—" Lux starts.

"I'm saying," Pacious interrupts, his tone grave, "that either these Rona things are getting smarter, or we've got a much bigger problem."

Chills run down Priya's spine as the fire crackles in the heavy silence.

"What in the hell does that mean?" Heidi asks, her voice trembling.

"It means," Pacious says, staring into the flames, "there's something out there. Something worse. And it's hunting."

5

A GRAVE MISTAKE

PRIYA

A gust slips through a gap in the window frame, brushing Priya's forehead like a cold kiss as she struggles to fluff the lumpy pillow in the decaying hotel room she'd chosen for the night. Lux had made the call to stay rather than risk the dangers of the streets after dark. The group would take turns keeping watch.

It was around midnight—or so the only functioning clock in the dilapidated motel claimed—when Priya left Jer, Lux, Antonio, and Juan in the lobby and wandered down the first-floor hallway in search of an empty room.

Initially, it seemed Pacious, Jesse, Shamus, and Sariah were set on leaving after the grim discovery. But after combing through the hotel, it appeared that whoever had committed those heinous acts was long gone.

Or at least, that's what they wanted to believe.

The thought weighs heavily on Priya's mind as she tosses and turns, struggling to banish the gruesome images long enough to sleep.

Who could've done that to those people?

As much as she doesn't want to stay in this cursed place, the fear of what might be lurking in the dark outside is far more pressing. Since the CoRona mutation, the creatures that come out at night—the younger dead—are fast, lethal, and utterly relentless. The older ones, the "long-dead Ronas," or Rotters, move slowly, their decaying brains making them less of a threat.

But nothing she'd encountered before compared to what they'd found in the basement.

She had subtly urged Sariah to stay, hoping her light flirtation helped sway the decision. Whatever convinced the newcomers to stick it out until morning, Priya was grateful. She couldn't shake the image of Sariah's face, her soft laugh, the way her eyes held something steady in the chaos. Tomorrow's trek to the cancer center might finally give her the chance to know her better.

Thoughts of Sariah fill Priya's mind, slowly lulling her into uneasy sleep—until the sharp, choking pressure on her throat jerks her awake.

Jer looms above her, his face twisted with rage, spittle flying as he screams, *"What did you fucking do you bitch!?"*

His words slice through the stillness, leaving Priya frozen, her pulse pounding in her ears.

She struggles to understand what the hell is going on, but she can't breathe. The feeling of her throat being crushed—like it's being shoved down the back of her head—is by far the worst sensation she's ever experienced.

What I did?

What did I do?

Everything is foggy. All she knows is that her windpipe feels like it's about to snap under the pressure of his hands, squeezing the life out of her.

"How fucking dare you, you prissy, Indian bitch!" he screams, shaking her—trying to kill her.

Just before she loses consciousness, she sees Honor, Lux, and Krishna burst into the room.

The world goes black around the edges, then tunnels away.

The sound of soft chatter pulls Priya from sleep. Her eyes flutter open—and panic surges as the memory comes flooding back: Jer's furious, twisted face, the rancid stench of his breath, his hands crushing her throat.

She jolts upright, gasping for air.

But Jer isn't there.

Instead, Honor sits on the edge of the bed, her expression calm but shadowed with something unspoken.

"What happened?" Priya croaks, her throat raw, each word scraping like sandpaper.

"Heidi was murdered," Honor says. Her tone is measured, her face a mask of stoicism. But her eyes betray her—muted and heavy with sorrow.

Priya's heart plummets. She tries to sit up. "What?!"

Honor gently presses her back down. "Don't strain yourself, love. Just lie back."

"What the fuck happened?" Priya demands, her voice hoarse but insistent.

"I don't know," Honor replies, her voice steady but laced with unease. "Jer says he went to check on Heidi and found her bed empty. There was blood everywhere, and the window was smashed open. When he looked outside, she was on the ground with her throat cut."

She pauses. "Nothing was eaten off her, though, so he immediately assumed it was you. Flew into a rage, screaming, woke everyone up, and that's when I found him choking you."

Priya stares at her. "What the hell?" she whispers, her voice still raspy. "It definitely wasn't me."

"I know it wasn't you. But... you have to admit—it looks bad."

Priya groans, leaning back against the bedframe. "I didn't like the bitch. I'll be the first to admit that. There were plenty of times I wanted to slap the hell out of her, but I wouldn't slit her throat. I've never wanted anyone dead."

"I believe you," Honor says gently. "But Jer won't. And now... I'm not sure what we're going to do about him. He's convinced it was you."

"If I didn't do it, then who the hell did?" Priya mutters, her mind racing. Images of Pacious and Jesse flash through her thoughts—they're the only ones that make any sense.

"I don't know," Honor replies with a frown. "But Lux wants to leave. Now. And he wants to leave Jer behind."

"Now? What time is it?"

"Quarter to four. The sun'll be up in about two hours."

"That's not terrible," Priya concedes, but the thought of leaving someone behind gnaws at her. Even if Jer had tried to kill her, leaving him to die didn't sit right. "Where is he?"

"Michael and Lux knocked him out to stop him from strangling you. They hog-tied him and are keeping him in the lobby so he can't get to you. But I don't think there's any convincing him you didn't do it."

Priya exhales. Her voice softens. "I get that. Even if Heidi was insufferable, she was his wife. He's grieving. I just wish there was another way. Leaving him behind feels wrong."

"Either way, he knows where we're headed," Honor points out. "If we don't kill him, he'll come after us—and you."

"No!" Priya snaps. "You can't kill him. He doesn't deserve that. Maybe I can talk to him—make him understand I didn't do it."

"I don't think he's in any state to listen right now. But if *you* didn't do it, then who did?"

"I think it was those newcomers—Pacious and Jesse," Priya says firmly.

"Or," Honor counters grimly, "maybe the slasher from the basement is still lurking around."

Priya shudders at the thought. "If that's the case, we need to leave now. Where's Gratian?"

"He's with Krishna and Maria, in Maria's room. Juan's watching over them."

"We should've listened to Pacious when he found those people," Priya mutters bitterly. "We never should've stayed."

A light knock at the door draws their attention as Lux steps in. "Hey," he says urgently. "We need to move. Now. The busted window's just begging the Ronas to swarm us—not to mention, whatever killed Heidi is probably still around. And with that fresh corpse out there, it's only a matter of time before something takes the bait."

"And what if that's just it?" Priya asks. "What if whatever—or *whoever*—killed her is among us, and we're taking them with us to the cancer center?"

Maria slips in under Lux's arm, her expression grave. "Honor, I don't know what's wrong with Gratian, but he's talking all sorts of nonsense—like he has no idea where he is."

"Shit," Honor spits out, bolting from the bed and rushing toward the door. "His blood sugar. He's delirious."

"All the more reason to get a move on," Lux states, scratching his salt-and-pepper goatee.

Priya rises slowly, clutching her sore neck. "Is he going to be okay?"

"He is," Lux replies as Honor races past him and disappears down the hallway, her heavy footfalls muffled by the carpet. "We just need to get him that insulin. And soon. Let's round everyone up and get the fuck out of here."

"What about Jer?" Priya asks as she follows Lux down the dim corridor toward the lobby where her attacker awaits.

"I want to kill him, but others are opposed to that," Lux admits.

"I don't think we should either," Priya says, her voice sharper than she intended. "He just lost his wife. You'd be a little upset too, had it been Honor."

Lux shoots her a look—half smirk, half shadow—and she can't tell if it's playful, malicious, or both.

At this point, *anyone* could be the murderer.

When they arrive at the lobby, Jer is in the middle of the room, tied to a chair, his face bloody and bruised.

Michael stands over him, breathing heavily, fists clenched —like he just punched him right before they walked in.

"Ready to go?" Lux asks.

"Yeah, I'm ready. What are we doing with this piece of shit?"

"Leave him. Let whoever killed her have him too," Lux says, grabbing his bag from the floor near the fire and slinging it over his shoulder.

Michael turns to do the same.

"Where are the newbies?" Priya asks, wondering if Sariah knows about any of this.

"In their respective rooms, I'd imagine," Lux replies. "They can stay here too, for all I care."

"Yeah, it may have been one of them that did it," Michael adds, securing his bag in place across his shoulders.

"It wasn't them—it was that brown cunt right there." Jerod groans, glaring at Priya.

Michael's fist connects with his face before the last word fully lands, the crack of bone echoing through the lobby.

"I said to keep your trap shut!" Michael spits venomously, shaking the sting from his knuckles.

Jer's head lolls to the side, blood dribbling down his chin as he sneers at Priya. "I hope you die miserably for what you did, you wretched, filthy foreigner."

Priya meets his hatred with a calm, unnerving smile as Honor wheels Gratian into the lobby. The boy's face is pale, his eyes glassy and unfocused in the dying firelight.

"Is he okay?" Priya asks.

"He'll be okay," Honor replies. "He just needs water to pee and flush the ketones out. Lux, give me some water."

Lux quickly unzips his bag and pulls out a plastic bottle from their vending machine haul, handing it over.

Honor unscrews the cap and presses it into Gratian's hands. "Drink this, baby. As much as you can."

Gratian clumsily brings the bottle to his lips, spilling more than he swallows.

"Alright, ready?" Lux asks, scanning the dark windows.

"What about Sariah?" Priya asks as the group moves toward the boarded front doors.

"She knows where we'll be Priya," Lux says flatly. "If she wants you back, she'll find you."

Priya can't risk it.

Before she knows what she's doing, her feet are already moving away from the group, back toward the hallway she'd come from.

"I'll catch up!" she yells over her shoulder as she runs.

"Priya!" Honor voice cuts through the dark, laced with panic.

But she doesn't stop.

She won't lose another.

6

NOT ANOTHER ONE

PRIYA

Glancing at Jer, still tied to the chair as she sprints past him, Priya can't help but notice the sinister gleam in his eyes. Blood drips down his face, coating his teeth as he smiles wickedly at her.

Maybe he killed his own wife.

The hallway is dark and oppressive.

What the hell is she thinking?

With her .45 drawn, she tries a few doors. The rooms on the right are pitch-black, the void swallowing anything beyond the threshold.

The first two are empty.

If you were Sariah, which room would you have picked?

Which room was Heidi murdered in? Did they move the body, or is it still lying there, exactly where Jer found it?

She shudders. She won't go in there.

Where the hell could Sariah be?

Why hadn't the others woken when Heidi was killed? The rest of the camp had.

Another room. No Sariah.

The rooms on the left—at least the ones with open curtains —are illuminated in a soft, gauzy glow of moonlight. The first three are empty, but in the fourth, the shape of legs lies beneath the covers.

Priya's pulse pounds. It's so dark she can barely see beyond the foot of the bed. The bathroom is directly to the right, casting deeper shadows. She creeps forward, holding her breath.

The door slams shut behind her.

She whirls around, heart hammering—but it's just the automatic hinge. Heavy. Final. Like most hotels.

Exhaling, she turns back toward the bed.

The figure hasn't stirred.

Scanning the room, her eyes land on Sariah's bag. Relief surges through her, and she hurries forward, grabbing the figure's legs and shaking them.

Moonlight spills across Sariah's face.

She's pale—too pale.

No. No, no, no.

Priya's stomach plummets.

She presses a hand under Sariah's nose.

No breath.

A mournful chill laps at her skin. Did she die before Priya even got the chance to know her?

Then, Sariah gasps, bolting upright at the sight of a shadowy figure looming over her.

"Shh, it's me," Priya whispers, rushing to her side. "It's just me."

Sariah's wild eyes focus. "Priya? What's going on?"

"Oh, thank God." Priya exhales shakily, hugging her." I thought you were dead too," she whispers into her neck. Her braids smell of campfire and pine.

"Too?" Sariah gently pushes her back. "Priya, what happened?"

"Heidi's dead. Jer thinks it was me. We have to leave—now. The window was busted in her room. They think the Ronas will get in—maybe already have."

"What?" Sariah asks, shaking off sleep as Priya tugs her arm.

"Come on! They're already outside. We have to catch up."

Sariah pulls on her boots. "Where's Pash, Shame, and Jesse?"

"I don't know. They haven't come out yet."

"I need to get them."

Priya shakes her head. "There's no time."

"They're my brothers, Priya. They wouldn't leave me."

Priya exhales. "Fine. Just hurry."

Sariah slings on her backpack and disappears into the dark.

Silence.

Priya tries not to focus on how dark the dark really is.

A rustling sound—near the exit.

She stiffens.

It stops.

Her pulse pounds.

Then—a bang from one of the rooms.

She jumps, gasping. "Sariah?" she calls, her voice shaky.

Something slams into her from behind.

Her breath vanishes. She crashes against the wall, vision blurring. Scrambling, she reaches for her gun—but a hard blow cracks against her skull.

Scattered stars explode behind her eyes.

Crawling away, she fumbles for her waistband.

A kick lands in her stomach. She retches, pain blinding her. Kicking wildly, she connects—hard. A cry of agony.

Jerod.

Ronas don't fight like this.

Kicking again and again, she finally hits her mark. He groans, doubling over.

She staggers to her feet and runs—toward the dark, toward where Sariah vanished.

She wants to scream for help. But that would give him her location.

Her hand grazes a glass case.

A fire ax.

She smashes the glass with her elbow, grabbing the handle just as the sound of heavy footsteps closes in. Spinning, she swings blindly.

The blade connects.

A scream rips through the air. The ax is stuck in something solid. She yanks, but it won't come free.

Shit.

She turns to run—and slams into someone.

"Priya?" Sariah's voice cuts through the dark.

"Run!" Priya gasps.

They sprint toward the exit. Jer's chair is smashed to bits in the lobby.

The doors burst open, spilling them into the night.

Priya runs until she hits the road, lungs burning, legs shaking. Sariah, Shamus, Pacious, and Jesse are right behind her.

"What the hell was chasing you?" Sariah pants.

Priya gulps for air. "Him!"

Jerod stumbles through the doors, the ax still lodged in his arm.

"Oh, that fool?" Pacious mutters, pulling the spear from his back. "I got this."

"I got it," Jesse says, leveling his crossbow.

The first arrow buries itself in Jerod's leg. He stops, glaring.

The second hits his shoulder.

"What's up with your shot, Jes?" Pacious teases.

Jesse exhales, steadies, and fires again.

This one sinks deep into Jerod's chest.

He drops to his knees.

Then, the ground.

"Got 'im," Jesse mutters.

Priya doesn't wait. "Let's go."

She takes off down the road, the others following close behind, heading toward the highway.

7

FRACTURES IN THE FOLD
PRIYA

"Where are they?" Priya asks after they've been traveling along the highway for over an hour. "I thought for sure we would've caught up with them by now."

The sun is beginning to make its debut, painting the sky in eerie shades of orange and pink. Rotters lumber far off in the distance, but judging by how slowly they move, she concludes they're in no danger—at least not yet.

But where the hell are Honor, Lux, and Gratian?

"We'll find them," Pacious says, switching his bag from one shoulder to the other. "We know where they're headed, so even if we don't pass them on the road, we'll catch up eventually."

"How much farther is it?" Priya asks.

"We're coming up on the Prospect exit. We've got to make it to Harmony Road," Shamus answers, his gray, curly hair blowing slightly in the wind, "and then west past Ziegler, I believe. I'd say a few hours yet."

Priya kicks at a rock in the road, a little perturbed Honor didn't wait for her.

"So what do you think actually happened to that chick?" Jesse asks, his blue eyes scanning Priya mischievously.

"It wasn't me!" she retorts, tired of the constant insinuations. "I think it was one of you."

"I didn't do it," Jesse says quickly—making him seem all the more guilty.

"Me neither," Pacious adds. "Maybe it was Lux. He seems like he's itching to kill someone."

"I don't think it was him," Priya replies. "He seems like a total hard-ass, but really he's just a giant pussy."

Sariah laughs.

"What? It's true."

"What makes you say that?" Sariah asks, shooting her a sly smile.

"Just the way he acts sometimes. Like, he puts on this whole demeanor—tall, sort of built, tattoos, all that. But when it comes down to business, Honor's the real badass in that family."

"Sounds like you're sweet on her," Sariah says.

"No, not sweet on her. I respect her. She's been through so much shit and she's still kicking. I admire her. And think if the world were different, she'd find someone who truly respects her and treats her the way she deserves. Someone who doesn't take her for granted and is her equal."

"What makes her such a badass?" Jesse asks.

"Gratian almost died at birth, but she fought harder than anyone—even when everyone, including Lux, had given up. After she and Lux married, she was pregnant with their second child when she was diagnosed with leukemia. Her body was ninety-seven percent leukemic cells, so she had to abort the baby at eleven weeks and start chemo immediately. The treatment lasted two and a half years, and she endured it mostly alone, since Lux had to work to support them. Not long after, Gratian was diagnosed with diabetes, so she fought cancer while caring for a diabetic child. The stories she tells about her treatment and survival... she's been through more than anyone I know—even this apocalypse."

Jesse tilts his head, intrigued. "Is that why we're heading to the cancer center?"

"I guess. It's where she did a lot of her chemo treatments, and she figures there's insulin stashed there—somewhere raiders wouldn't have thought to hit yet."

"It's too bad she's married to that idiot," Jesse says. "She's hot as fuck. I'd wife her up in a heartbeat."

"You're a sucker for those long-legged, dark-skin, warrior types, aren't you?" Sariah chuckles, laughing like she's remembering something the two of them once shared.

"No!" he says defensively, though his tone hints that she's nailed it.

"Tried to holla at me—till he found out I bat for the other team," she teases, giggling as she kicks a rock his way.

The information nestles sweetly into Priya's bones.

She kind of had a feeling, but she's glad to know her gut was right.

"It's alright love. I still think you're hot, I just wouldn't fuck ya."

"Missing out," Jesse says, grinning. The gap in his front teeth punctuates his dimples. "It'd be the best dick you ever had."

"The only dick too." Sariah laughs.

"Hey," Shamus cuts in, shifting the tone. "Who do you think did that to the Heidi bitch? If it wasn't her, and it wasn't us, then who was it?"

"I think it was whoever was doing that shit in the basement," Sariah replies.

"Yes, but if that's the case, why didn't we all get murdered in our sleep?" Pacious asks. "It's very curious that the one person who had beef with Priya is the one who ended up dead."

"We didn't have beef!" Priya nearly yells. It's getting harder to keep the annoyance out of her voice. "She was annoying and negative and had a holier-than-thou attitude, but that's not something I would kill anyone over! I wouldn't kill anyone, really. Unless they messed with Gratian. Or my family."

"Don't let them get you going, Priya," Sariah soothes, rubbing her shoulder. "They live for pissing people off."

"How did you all meet each other, anyway?" Priya asks.

A sharp whistle from behind interrupts them. They stop and turn in the direction it came from.

Coming down the exit ramp off the Prospect exit is Lux.

Priya's heart and muscles relax as relief washes over her. She runs in their direction as Honor comes into view, pushing Gratian.

As Priya gets closer, she realizes there are more people with them now—and Honor looks pissed.

She hugs Honor and Gratian, who looks awful. He's pale and sweating, and as Priya lets go of him, he leans to the side and vomits.

"What happened to you guys?" Priya asks.

"Fucking Lux wanted to go check a supply store by the jail, and we just had to go now," Honor spits viciously. Lux sends her a glare that could cut steel as she rubs Gratian's back. "We've got to hurry—he needs insulin now."

They pick up their pace, speed-walking in the direction of Harmony Road.

"Who are the new people?" Priya asks under her breath as they move ahead of the group.

"We were walking at a normal pace, waiting for you. But after you didn't show up for a while, we got to the Prospect exit, and Lux remembered there was a Sutherlands down the road by the jail. So he made us turn and said it wouldn't be a big deal. As we were raiding the store for supplies, those three showed up, trying to get us to go to the jail—where supposedly there's a compound. Lux was about to agree since they said they have medicine there, and I protested because I needed to get back to you, and we had a plan to go to the cancer center. I'm sure we can make a home there for a while, at least. After a lot of fighting, I just left with Gratian, and he followed—talking those idiots into coming with us."

"Who the fuck are they?" Priya asks.

"Tesslyn, Baxter, and Jessica, I guess."

Priya steals a glance behind her again.

One tall Black woman with long black dreads—like Sariah's, except without the jewels. One short white woman with long blonde hair. And one tall white bald man with a red handlebar mustache.

"Why are they coming with us now, then?"

"I have no idea," Honor answers, the exasperation in her voice audible. "I'm so mad at Lux right now I could strangle him. But I need to get Gratian to the cancer center and take care of him. I'll deal with Lux's stupid shit later."

"I'm sorry he's such a dumbass," Priya says.

"What about you guys? What happened back there, and why were you so late?"

"Oh my god," Priya mutters, not wanting to relive the terror of the night.

She quickly paraphrases the events, shuddering at the memory.

"Did he die?" Honor asks when Priya finishes.

Thinking back on the whole scenario, Priya really doesn't know. "I'm not sure. He was hit three times—once in the leg, once in the arm, and then square in the chest. He did fall to the ground, but we didn't check to see if he was dead."

"Well that's just great, Priya," Honor says, her annoyance at Lux bleeding into the situation at hand.

"He lost a lot of blood, Honor," she replies tersely, offended. How dare Honor make her feel bad for defending herself. "He was bleeding pretty badly from the ax wound in his arm, and then an arrow to the heart. I'm pretty sure he's dead."

"And if he's not, then he'll come looking for us. That's the great part."

Honor does have a point.

After all, Priya isn't sure Jerod actually died.

And Honor's right—if he's alive and wounded, he'll be pissed off and out for retaliation.

8

BITTEN

PRIYA

The cancer center finally looms in the distance as they crest the last hill. The midday sun hangs high, its light fractured by drifting clouds. A dark, luminous cluster gathers above the mountains, hinting at a late spring storm—rain, or possibly snow, if the temperature dips low enough.

In mid-April, the shifting weather can bring either. This afternoon hovers around fifty degrees, but if the sun slips behind the clouds, cooling the air, those dark masses rolling in might deliver snow instead of rain.

Words have been sparse along the journey—part of it owing to the harsh things Honor said, but most of it belongs to her worry.

It doesn't help that the strangers among them are quiet too.

From what Priya has overheard, the tall Black woman with dreads is Jessica, originally from the Bronx; Tesslyn is the white firecracker from the South and has the accent to prove it, using *y'all* in nearly every sentence; and Baxter is from a little town called Lyons, Colorado, but was up in Fort Collins for construction work when CoRona hit. Judging by some of the stories he's been telling, he's done prison time. For what, Priya isn't sure—and part of her really doesn't want to be.

As they approach the cancer center, it's apparent someone's been living there—or at some point, someone made it a compound. The windows are boarded up and reinforced with additional planks. The front door is barricaded shut and impossible to get through from the outside.

Whoever was, or is still, in there doesn't want anything else getting in.

"I'll check around the building," says Lux.

"I'll come with," Michael adds.

"Please hurry," Honor pleads, stopping to kneel in front of Gratian to check on him.

His face has gone completely pale, and beads of sweat line his forehead, dripping down his face. His eyes are black beads, and he's limp and lethargic in his chair.

"Baby, are you okay? Talk to me."

Gratian's stare is blank, his eyes pinned somewhere beyond his mother.

Honor hurries to the back of the wheelchair to retrieve the pokey pack and pulls out a different glucose monitor—the one that checks for ketones.

Fumbling, panicked, with the wrapper the strips are in, Honor shakily pulls one out—and it falls to ground.

"Here," Priya offers. "Let me help."

"Thank you," Honor says, her voice trembling as well. "Just put that strip in this, and then prick his finger with this." She pulls out the lancet and hands it to Priya.

Priya nods and places the strip into the meter. Kneeling in front of Gratian, she takes his tiny hand in hers, presses the lancet to one of his soft little fingers, and pushes down—the click letting her know the needle has made contact. Gratian doesn't flinch as she removes the lancet and touches the strip to the blood pooling from the pinprick.

The meter beeps in response, and Priya pulls it away, watching the countdown:

5, 4, 3, 2, 1...

"What is it?" Honor asks.

"6.1," Priya reads.

"Oh my God," Honor gasps.

"What does that mean?" Sariah asks, looking over their shoulders.

"It means he's now in DKA," Honor breathes, nearly choking on the tears streaming down her face.

"What's DKA?" the newcomer, Jessica, asks.

"Diabetic ketoacidosis," Priya answers, recalling the words Honor had once told her. "It basically means his blood is too acidic and making him really sick."

"What do you do for that?" Jessica presses.

"He needs insulin," Honor snaps, dropping to the ground beside Gratian. "He needs it now. If he doesn't get it soon, he could fall into a coma. Priya, please check his blood sugar."

Priya grabs the pokey pack from the back again, swapping out the ketone meter for the regular one. Pulling the last test strip from the canister, she places it in the meter, then takes the smaller lancet and moves back in front of Gratian.

"I'm sorry I have to poke you twice, sweetie," she says softly.

Taking a different finger, she presses down on the lancet and pricks his other pointer finger—this one not making as big a hole since the regular meter doesn't need as much blood as the ketone meter.

She brings the strip to the droplet of blood, and this one flashes the reading on the screen right away.

"It says, 'Above 600, consult your physician.'"

"Shit," Honor says, getting up and running to the front door.

She begins frantically pulling on the doors and kicking them, screaming and trying to tear the boards off.

Priya knows she needs to do this—to scream and yell and blow off steam—but all this noise is going to attract the Ronas, and that's something they don't need right now.

Running up to her, she pulls her close and grasps her tightly, letting her scream and thrash and yell into her shoulder.

"Shhh," Priya soothes, stroking her hair. "We're here now. We just need to get in. The boys will find a way. Gratian will be okay."

Honor doesn't stop sobbing, but the thrashing ceases.

"Hey," Priya says, pulling Honor away to look at her. "You've been through this before, haven't you?"

Honor nods, her eyes bright red with tears.

"Alright. What were his numbers then?"

"His ketones have never been this high, but his blood sugar has. Last time his ketones were above 5.0, we took him to the ER"

"Okay, but he made it, right? You got him through it?"

Honor nods again, her breathing becoming less rapid. "Yes, but this isn't an ER, and there are no physicians here."

"Right. But what did they do to get his ketones and blood sugar down?"

"An IV insulin drip."

"Alright, well, we don't have anyone who can do an IV, but we can give him insulin all the same, right?"

"I can set up an IV, y'all," Tesslyn says, her drawl stretching out her vowels. "I'm a nurse. Or was, in my past life. I know how to set one up."

"See? There you go. Now we just need to get in. Okay?"

Honor nods and backs away from the doors.

The distant and familiar sound of feet scraping along pavement has Priya glancing over her shoulder.

Rotters are slow and drag their feet as they walk. Their gait is ungraceful, to say the least—the way they meander aimlessly, usually soundless unless shuffling across pavement.

Priya and Honor both turn to see an entire group of them lumbering toward them from the far end of the parking lot.

Honor's screams had lured them here.

"Shit," Priya curses.

"Alright, ya'll, we got company," Tesslyn announces, though everyone already heard the familiar scraping.

"There's too many of them," Antonio says, pulling the shotgun to his shoulder.

"We gotta try," Tesslyn replies. "We can't run, and I ain't fixin' to die today."

"Get your weapons ready," Juan orders, slamming a bullet into the chamber. "We have to try—like she said."

Pacious slides his spear to the front as Jesse readies his bow. Sariah twirls her pair of knife-like machetes in front of her. Maria, Jesus, and Antonio all draw their guns.

"Those of us who are better shots—start taking them out," Shamus instructs.

Shots ring in Priya's eardrums—her own included—as she switches off the safety on her .45. She picks out one of the Rotters in the middle of the horde and aims at its head. Taking a deep breath, she closes one eye and pulls the trigger, watching the rotting woman collapse to the ground, brown blood and brains scattering behind her. She drops another one.

The ringing in her ears makes it hard to hear anything else.

More Rotters fall as the group fires, but there are too many of them. Priya fells another, and sees one of Jesse's arrows pierce the skull of another.

They're making headway now—but there are still fifty or sixty Rotters, halfway through the parking lot, closing the distance fast.

Out of the corner of her eye, Priya sees Gratian slump in his chair—almost spilling out of it—while Honor remains laser-focused on the horde.

"Honor!" Priya yells over the gunfire, nodding toward Gratian. "Take him and run!"

Honor nods and hastily stows her gun in her waistband, wheeling Gratian away from the incoming Ronas.

Pacious dashes toward the mob, slashing with the sharp tip of his spear—slicing off the tops of heads and jabbing some through the eye. Jesse maneuvers quickly with his bow, knocking arrows into it as fast as he can.

Maria is shooting alongside Jesus and Juan when Sariah plunges into the mass of rotting bodies, following Pacious and Jesse. She's slicing and gashing, stabbing and gutting anything that comes near.

Michael is muderously hacking at Rotters with his shovel weapon while Amy shoots from behind him, following him along the side of the horde.

One of the Ronas reaches Janice. She tries to run, but he catches her by the hood of her crop-top hoodie. He grabs her arm and tears a large chunk out of it.

Her screams reverberate through the group as Amy and Maria race to save her.

Priya can't focus on that. She can only concentrate on the hoard of Ronas among them—about to devour them all.

"Guys, get in here!" Lux's voice shouts from behind.

Priya whistles, catching the group's attention over the chaos.

Maria, Juan, and Jesus dive inside, followed by Michael and Amy. The rest begin making their way to the door.

But Priya doesn't go.

She has to find Honor and Gratian.

"Priya, what the hell are you doing?" Lux yells as she runs past him.

"I've gotta find Honor and Gratian!"

"You get inside—I'll go find them. They're my family."

Priya nods and runs inside, slamming the door shut behind Lux.

9

SANCTUARY OR TOMB?

PRIYA

She holds the door shut, her heart pounding as she silently prays for Honor and Gratian's safety.

Minutes drag by like hours until a sudden pounding jolts her. She yanks the door open, and Honor rushes in, pushing Gratian ahead of her, with Lux close behind.

The Ronas on their heels nearly force their way in, but Priya slams the door shut just in time, crushing one's hand in the heavy metal. Fingers snap off and drop to the floor. Lux braces against the door while Michael secures the siege lock over the boards.

"Are you guys okay?" Priya asks, breathless.

"Just barely," Lux replies. "Lost my gun in the horde. There are more now—probably around a hundred."

"I need to find him insulin," Honor blurts, sprinting toward a set of glass doors bearing the center's name.

Priya grips Gratian's chair and takes in the scene around her —the wreckage of Honor's oncologist's building. The front lobby is in chaos: chairs overturned, trash scattered across the floor. She hurries after Honor through the heavy glass doors leading to the doctor's office, which Honor flings open effort-lessly in her panic.

Inside, the destruction is even worse. TVs dangle by their cords. Plants lie toppled. Shards of glass glitter on the floor.

In the middle of the waiting area, Janice sits slumped among the red chairs, pressing a blood-soaked shirt to her wound. Her expression is distant, as if she's already resigned herself to her fate.

Maria, Krishna, Tesslyn, and Amy huddle around her, murmuring soft reassurances as she weeps.

Priya's heart goes out to her.

Once you're bitten, there's nothing you can do.

Honor runs back into the lobby with a vial and syringe, quickly loading the syringe with what can only be insulin. She pushes Gratian's shirt up and sticks the needle into his arm, pressing down on the plunger to get the medicine into him.

"Alright, that should start working," she breathes, capping the needle with an orange top and stowing it in the satchel. "But we still need to get him on a drip. Tesslyn, can you come help me with that?"

Tesslyn squeezes Janice's hand and stands, brushing off her pants. "Of course," she says, following Honor through the door to the right of the check-in counter.

"I'll come too," Priya states, falling into step behind them.

"Me too," Lux adds.

Priya walks down the hallway behind Honor, Gratian, and Tesslyn. Patient rooms line both sides of the dark corridor, dried blood smeared along the walls and across the floor—like something right out of video game. Drawing her gun, as Lux pulls out his large hunting knife, and she glances toward Honor, who seems unfazed.

"Honor, are you seeing this?" she whispers, not wanting to disturb whatever might still be here.

"I did," Honor replies, craning her neck back, still pushing forward fast.

Tesslyn has her gun out too.

Honor wheels Gratian into one of the rooms and locks the wheelchair in place. She lifts him by the armpits and gently lays him on the bed.

"There's more insulin in the med room where I found the vial."

"I'll get it," Tesslyn offers.

"No, it'll take too long for you to find it. Lux, stay here with him while I go get it."

Lux nods and sits on the bed beside his son.

"I'll find the supplies to set up a drip," Tesslyn says.

"And I'll come with you, Honor," Priya adds.

As they move from Gratian's room toward the chemotherapy wing, the blood thickens—smeared in ominous streaks.

The rooms they pass are eerily empty, except for one on the right that appears to have been used recently. Scattered across the floor are discarded IV bags and tubing, large reclining chairs, and severed zip ties.

Farther ahead, following the trail of blood, Priya spots a pair of feet protruding from behind a wall near the treatment area. Honor sees them too and rushes forward. When she rounds the corner, a sharp gasp escapes her lips.

The first thing that pierces them is the smell. It's so overpowering that Priya nearly vomits on the spot. She yanks her shirt up over her nose and forces herself to look.

A man lies dead—nearly stripped of all flesh. His legs are bare bone, his chest hollowed out, his arms skeletal. His face is gone. His skull is split, the brain entirely devoured. The only reason he hadn't become a Rona is that his brain had been eaten.

"Oh my god," Honor mutters.

"Did you know him?" Priya asks.

With her own shirt pressed over her nose and mouth, Honors kneels beside the remains. "It's Dr. Mercer. My oncologist."

"I wonder how one got in here," Priya whispers, crouching beside her.

The scene is horrific, and yet she can't look away.

She places a hand on Honor's back, hoping it offers some comfort.

"He was a good man," Honor says thickly. "We discovered my cancer when I was pregnant, and he wanted to save both me and the baby. He sent me down to Denver so I could get the best care. He cared so much... gave me his personal number in case I needed him during chemo."

"I'm so sorry, love," Priya says softly.

Honor gazes at her doctor's remains for a few more seconds, then turns away.

"We need to make sure that whatever did this isn't still here," Priya says.

"Can you go get the others from the lobby? I'll find the insulin for Tesslyn," Honor replies.

"Sure." Priya nods, gripping her gun as she heads out.

When she reaches the lobby, she halts at the doorway. "Can anyone help me clear this place?" she calls out. "Honor's doctor is dead—eaten—and we need to make sure whatever did it isn't still in here."

"I'll come," Sariah says.

"Me too," Krishna adds.

"I'm in," Amy states.

"On it." Michael nods.

"Pash, Shame, and I will check the rest of the building while you guys clear this floor," Jesse offers.

"Sounds good," Priya agrees, turning back toward the doctor's office.

The main floor of Dr. Mercer's office resembles a typical infusion center. Large reclining chairs line the far wall, where windows once let in light but are now boarded up. It's clear the doctor spent significant time fortifying the place.

Patient rooms stretch out to the left and right, leading to the main infusion area. Beyond that—where they found Dr. Mercer—are more rooms and a nurse's station. At the back, a staircase leads to the second floor.

Priya moves cautiously, her gun raised, ears straining for any sound out of the ordinary.

When she reaches the second floor, she stops in shock.

The space has been transformed into a makeshift apartment. Against the boarded-up windows sits a large sectional couch and an entertainment center. A bed occupies one corner. To the right, a spacious kitchen with an island suggests a well-planned setup. A small hallway likely leads to restrooms, and in another corner stands a pool table.

This must've been his home away from home, Priya thinks.

Family photos of Dr. Mercer cover the walls. His desk sits against the far wall beside a boarded-up window, a large chalkboard filled with scribbled equations, and filing cabinets overflowing with papers.

Honor heads straight to the kitchen, yanking open the fridge and freezer—both fully stocked and still running.

"He must have a backup generator," she mutters. The pantry is packed, and a massive freezer nearby is filled as well.

After a final sweep confirming the area is secure, Priya heads downstairs.

Tesslyn hovers over Gratian, inserting an IV while Honor and Lux watch.

"The upstairs is clear," Priya announces. "No sign of Ronas anywhere. We might be able to stay here for a while—Dr. Mercer had a solid setup. A working generator, fully stocked supplies, and the place is completely sealed. He even turned his office into a living space—DVDs and everything. Once Gratian is stable, we can move him up there and get him comfortable."

"Until we run out of insulin," Honor says grimly.

"We'll deal with that when we get to it," Lux snaps.

"Can you, for once—"

"Guys, please," Priya interjects. "Let's focus on getting Gratian better. I'm going to check in with the others. And in case you didn't notice... Janice has been bitten."

Honor's eyes widen. "What?"

"We have to kill her," Lux says coldly.

"Babe!" Honor snaps.

"What? You want her to turn into one of those things and eat us all?"

"No, but we can at least wait until she's close to turning before we put her down like a rabid animal."

"Better sooner than later." Lux scoffs.

Priya rolls her eyes and walks away, leaving them to argue.

10

A TURN FOR THE WORSE

PRIYA

Shamus strides in first, rolling his shoulders like he's shaking off the tension of a fight. He unslings his rifle, checking the magazine before setting it against the wall with a soft clack. Pacious follows, flipping his knife effortlessly in his fingers before sheathing it at his hip. Jesse rubs the back of his neck, muttering something about needing a damn shower, while leaning one shoulder against the wall, arms crossing over his chest.

Sariah trails behind them, her movements fluid, predatory. She slides down onto the couch beside Priya, stretching out her legs like a satisfied cat. With a sly smirk, she bites her lip, eyes flicking toward Jesse before turning her attention back to Priya.

"What did you guys find?" Priya asks.

"All clear," Pacious reports. "Some vending machines and stuff in the upper levels, but mainly offices and such. The area across the hall is where they drew blood—lots of medical supplies in there. But all the windows are boarded up, all exits blocked, everything fortified and sound."

"There's a basement we weren't able to access," Jesse adds,

shoving a hand through his hair. "Needs a key. But nothing looks like it could get in or out without it."

"Well, I hope whatever got Dr. Mercer isn't down there," Priya answers as Krishna, Amy, and Michael return to the lobby.

Janice still sits in one of the lobby chairs, her face pale as a ghost. Maria is next to her, holding the towel against her arm, covering what must be one gruesome bite.

"What are we going to do about her?" Michael asks, his voice low enough that Janice doesn't hear.

"The most respectful thing we can do," Amy says, "is make her comfortable until she's gone—then pierce her brain."

"We need to get rid of the body back there too," Priya says, nodding toward the rooms where Lux, Gratian, and Honor are. "It already reeks. We don't need it getting worse."

"I'll have Lux help me take care of that," Michael says. "Might have to wait a while, though. That horde's still anxiously waiting for someone to come out."

"We can search the place for a key to the basement," Pacious offers, tossing a coin across his fingers. "Toss him in there 'til we can get outside."

"That works," Priya replies.

Shamus nods and slaps Pacious on the shoulder, knocking the coin to the floor.

"C'mon, let's go," he says as Pacious grunts and picks it up.

They disappear down the darkened hallway.

Krishna stands. "I'm going to see what I can do for Janice." She struts off toward the medical supply offices.

"Michael, do you mind helping me with something?" Amy asks, grabbing his hand and tugging him toward the door. Michael sends an innocent face their way and stalks off behind her.

"I think I'm going upstairs to try and figure out sleeping arrangements for us," Priya announces to the remaining group.

"There's a couch up there that probably folds out, and the bed —plus the patient beds—but I still don't think that's enough for all of us."

"I love that you're so concerned for everyone," Sariah says, grabbing hold of Priya's hand, and pulling her closer to whisper in her ear. "I'll take a bed next to yours." The soft breath of her voice on Priya's neck sends flutters erupting in the pit of her stomach.

Sariah walks toward the door, and Priya follows.

A FEW HOURS LATER, as Priya is making dinner in the kitchen, Sariah sits on the counter, handing her ingredients as she asks for them.

"And what about you?" Sariah questions, handing her the garlic. "When did you know you liked only females?"

Priya is trying her best to make spaghetti sauce, using the ingredients she has access to—left behind by the good doctor. She takes the garlic salt and adds it to the red liquid heating on the stove.

"I mean, I've always known. In school, I always had crushes on girls, while all my friends had crushes on boys. I didn't tell anyone, though, until I was a teen—when I got my first crush who liked me back."

"And how did everyone take it?"

"Oh my god," Priya breathes, remembering the way her parents reacted when she came out. "It was terrible. My father had already arranged a marriage for me with a boy from our community. My mother fainted. Then she didn't talk to me for weeks. And when she finally did... it was like she was talking to a stranger. She thought I'd grow out of it. That it was just a phase."

"I'm so sorry you had to go through that."

"Thanks. It is what it is, you know? Even when they were alive, we weren't close after that. They didn't come to the States for my wedding. I think their beliefs—what they were raised with—just couldn't stretch that far. Some families back home are still very traditional, especially when it comes to marriage. And two women? That broke a lot of rules in their eyes."

The way Sariah's eyes slide to Priya's and hold them makes her stomach lurch up into her throat.

Butterflies.

She hasn't felt that soft flutter since Nora.

"What about you?" Priya asks, still stirring the sauce.

"Same as you," Sariah says, sticking her finger in the spoon Priya just pulled from the sauce.

Priya smacks her hand away, but Sariah still gets a good dollop on her finger and licks it off seductively.

"I always knew I liked women," she continues. "I didn't realize how much I preferred women until I tried being with men. They were fine, but it just wasn't the same." She licks the rest of the sauce from her finger. "This is good."

Priya squints. "Is it? I don't have much to work with."

"No, it's good. Tangy. Needs more salt."

Sariah opens the cabinet in front of her in search of the spice.

"When did you come out?" Priya asks as she tries another cabinet.

"College," she answers, kneeling to spin the lazy Susan. "It was scary and uncomfortable, but my mom and sisters were accepting and amazing. My dad left when I was a baby, so I don't know how he would've taken it. But fuck that guy," she quips, finding salt and handing it to Priya.

Priya takes it and sprinkles it in. "And you were married before, or no?"

"No, never married," she replies, leaning on her elbow. "Close. I lived with my girlfriend when CoRona hit. She died. It was awful. I just—" Sariah looks away, and Priya can see it's still very fresh and painful.

"I'm so sorry," Priya says, putting a lid on the sauce. "You don't have to talk about it. We don't have to go there."

Sariah sets her jaw before returning her gaze to Priya.

Smiling, she clears her throat and pushes off from the counter. "So, we need a big pot to boil the noodles in, yes?"

"Yes," Priya answers, just as Honor barges in, flinging open cabinet doors with force.

"Hey," Priya says, setting the spoon in the ladle holder. "You okay?"

"No," Honor snaps, slamming another cabinet shut before yanking open the next.

"What's up? What are you looking for?"

"Booze," she grumbles, as Sariah silently hands her a pot.

"I saw some over there," Priya replies, pointing to a cabinet beside to the wine fridge.

Honor crosses the kitchen, locates an unopened bottle of rum, and wastes no time twisting off the cap. She takes a few heavy gulps.

"Hey—what happened?" Priya asks again, concerned.

"My husband is an asshole," Honor mutters, cringing at the burn of the rum.

"You want a chaser?" Sariah offers.

"Nah, I'm good." Honor takes another swig.

"What happened now?"

"He just doesn't fucking listen to any goddamned thing I say. Ever. It's like he purposefully tunes me out. It's always been like that, and it just keeps getting worse."

"What did he do this time?" Priya asks, filling the pot at the Deep Rock water dispenser. It gurgles softly.

Honor swigs again, then caps the rum and sets the bottle on the counter. "I asked him four times to find Gratian a blanket and pillow. Four. Fucking. Times. Because we're not going to be able to move him for a while. And when I go see what the fuck is taking him so long? He's out in the goddamned lobby flirting with Tesslyn . Needless to say, I was livid."

"Do you really think he was flirting?" Sariah asks.

Honor shoots her a death glare. "I know what flirting looks like, and he was fucking flirting."

"So what happened then?" Priya presses, trying to defuse the tension.

"I screamed at him to get the damn blankets. Then I went back to Gratian. He followed, yelling at me that I'm a psychopath and that he was *just talking*. I told him to keep his goddamned voice down 'cause Gratian was sleeping—but he wouldn't shut the fuck up. So I punched him."

"Oh no!" Priya gasps. She knows they have a tendency to argue—but this? It's never gotten physical before.

Until now.

"It was only a matter of time. Before the apocalypse, I constantly caught him messaging his exes on Facebook—always flirting, always lying. Even before we were married, I found messages. I printed them out, left them by the coffee pot with my ring, and told him to cut the shit or there wouldn't be a wedding.

"But he never stopped. After we were married, when he was working on the road, I found out he was sexting an ex. I nearly punched him then. Eight years of living in other women's shadows. Eight years hoping he'd finally put me first. And for what? I actually thought the apocalypse might change him. But no— he's still more interested in chatting up Miss Big Boobs than making sure his kid has a damn blanket.

"I'm done. I'm fucking done."

She grabs the rum again and takes three deep gulps.

"What are you going to do?" Sariah asks gently.

"I don't know." Honor sinks down onto one of the bar stools, defeated. "Can I even leave him? In this world?"

"Why not?" Sariah presses. "If you're miserable, just agree to go your separate ways."

"But with a child?" Priya asks, stirring the sauce again. "How would that even work out in this world?"

"I say just take him," Sariah offers. "You said you need to get to that diabetes center in Denver, right? Just leave. In the middle of the night. Go. We'll come with you."

Priya shoots her a disapproving look. "Don't do anything rash. Just wait for the anger to subside."

"And the rum," Sariah adds, as Honor tips the bottle back again.

Heavy footfalls echo from the stairwell as Pacious, Jesse, and Shamus emerge, heading their way.

"Hey," Jesse says, setting his weapon down and walking up to Priya. "Smells good. Spaghetti?"

"Yes," Priya answers. "So, what'd you find?"

"Well, we got the basement door open. And ho-ly shit." Jesse dips a finger into the sauce, licking it before Priya smacks his hand away.

"What?" she asks, putting the lid back on the pot.

"The doctor was up to some real weird shit down there."

"What do you mean?" Sariah asks.

"Beds with chains, bags of... something, rotten food—just a mess of creepy shit."

Sariah's brows shoot up. "Bags of something?"

"Yeah, like empty saline bags... except not saline," Shamus clarifies.

Sariah moves to one of the barstools. "What the hell was he doing?"

"No idea," Jesse says, his attention shifting to Honor, who's tipping back more rum. "What's up with her?"

"She and Lux got into a huge fight," Sariah explains. "She decked him."

Jesse laughs. "Fuck yeah."

Priya smacks his arm. "It's not funny."

"She's hot as fuck. I'm rooting for their demise."

Jesse abandons the stove and plops down beside Honor. She leans her head against his shoulder, and he casually takes the bottle from her, swigging it himself.

"Did you guys get rid of the body?" Sariah asks Shamus and Pacious, since Jesse is now occupied.

"Yeah. Locked him down there," Pacious confirms. "Not like he's coming back—his brain's been eaten."

"Gross," Priya mutters, motioning toward the sauce. "I'm trying to keep my appetite, thanks."

"You should be used to it by now, love," Pacious teases, reaching for the pot. Priya smacks his hand away before he can dip in.

As the water starts to boil, she dumps in the noodles. "And what's Janice doing?"

"Dying," Pacious says flatly. "Last I saw, she was still down there, holding her arm and crying."

Priya exhales. "It's a death sentence."

Then a sharp voice slices through the conversation.

"What the fuck?"

Lux crosses the room in two strides, grabs Jesse by the collar, and decks him square in the jaw. Jesse stumbles, crashing into Honor, who tumbles off the chair and hits the floor hard.

As Jesse regains his footing, he lunges at Lux, slamming him into the wall. Priya and Sariah rush to help Honor, while Pacious and Shamus move to intervene. But Jesse doesn't need help—he dodges Lux's next punch and counters with a brutal right hook to his nose.

Honor drunkenly staggers to her feet. "*Stop it!*" she screams.

The commotion draws attention from the living room, where people rise to watch. Michael rushes in, throwing a punch at Jesse in defense of Lux.

Lux, seizing the moment, sweeps Jesse's legs from under him and shoves him to the floor. He moves to straddle him, fist raised, but Jesse flips up like a damn ninja and slams his hand into Lux's throat.

Lux stumbles back, gagging and coughing. Jesse doesn't hesitate—he tackles Lux to the ground and starts pounding him until Pacious pulls him off. Michael helps Lux sit up, keeping him from getting up for another round.

"Enough!" Pacious snaps, holding Jesse back.

"He came at me!" Jesse shouts.

"I know. But let it be."

Lux coughs, his voice hoarse. "You were cuddling with my wife."

"I wasn't cuddling with him, you fuckbag," Honor slurs. "At least I wasn't flirting with him like you were with that bimbo." She jabs a finger at Tesslyn.

Tesslyn scoffs. "Don't fucking point at me, you witch."

Priya shuts it down before things escalate again. "Uh-uh. None of that. You two—downstairs. We don't need this right now."

Lux glares at Honor. "What do you call lying on his shoulder, huh?"

"Comfort, asshole!" Honor yells, staggering back to the island and grabbing the rum.

Lux steps closer, his eye already swelling purple. "Are you drunk?"

"No, I'm not drunk," she slurs, taking another swig.

He reaches for the bottle, but she pulls away. When he misses, he backhands her.

Hard.

A stunned silence fills the room.

Jesse sees red. Pacious barely holds him back—then finally lets go.

Jesse launches himself at Lux, tackling him to the ground,

fists raining down. Blow after blow until Lux's face is a bloody wreck.

Lux finally scrambles free and flees.

Jesse, Pacious, Shamus, and Sariah take off after him.

Priya grabs ice from the freezer, wraps it in a cloth, and hands it to Honor. "You okay?"

Honor's face is bright red, tears streaking down her cheeks. Cross-eyed from the rum, she looks up at Priya and smiles.

"I love your face," she mumbles. "You're my best friend. Just wanna say I love you."

Priya exhales. "I love you too. Now, let's get you somewhere to sleep this off."

"I'm fine," Honor protests weakly.

"No, you're not. You need sleep."

Honor suddenly grips Priya's arm. "Will you check on my baby? He should be good for the night, but please... just check."

"I will." Priya steadies her. "Come on. Let's get you settled in his room."

"Okay," Honor whispers.

Priya helps her out of the kitchen and down the stairs.

11

RUM & REGRET

PRIYA

After tucking Honor into a cot beside Gratian, Priya returns to the stove to finish making dinner.

Sariah still isn't back—nor are Pacious, Jesse, Lux, or Shamus. In the living room, Maria, Jesus, and Juan watch a movie while Jessica and Baxter sit nearby, engaged in quiet conversation. Krishna, Michael, and Amy play pool in the corner of the spacious apartment.

As Priya stirs the sauce, she wonders where Sariah could've gone. She tests a noodle, finds it soft and squishy, then drains the pot in the sink. After gathering utensils, she turns to address the group.

"Dinner's ready for whoever's hungry."

Helping herself to a plate, she sits at the island and digs in. Before long, the others follow suit. Just as they're settling in, Pacious, Jesse, and Shamus return.

"Where's Sariah?" Priya asks as Pacious loads his plate with noodles.

"No idea. Thought she was up here," he replies.

"And Lux?"

"Dunno," Pacious says again.

Priya frowns. "What do you mean? You guys went after him."

"Yeah, we followed him until he ran outside. Figured he was on his own then."

"And Sariah?"

Pacious sighs. "Look, I don't know. He ran—I chased him. I have no clue who else followed. He went through the lobby and out the front doors. I watched him go, then shut the doors. Only Shamus and Jesse were with me. We helped Antonio get Janice into a room, saw you bring Honor down. Jesse checked on Janice, Gratian woke up asking for water, so we got him some and stayed until he fell back asleep. Then we came back up."

Priya glances at the living room. Maria, Jesus, and Juan are still there. So are Baxter and Jessica.

But Tesslyn is missing.

A pang of jealousy grips her. Sariah is with Tesslyn.

Her appetite vanishes, and she pushes her food around her plate.

"You okay?" Pacious asks, mouth full of spaghetti.

"I'm fine," she lies.

Pacious snorts. "Yeah, right. We might be in an apocalypse, but I'm not new to women. Spill."

Priya hesitates, then mutters, "Do you see Tesslyn anywhere?"

He looks around. "Nope."

"No Tesslyn. No Sariah."

Pacious raises an eyebrow. "Oh, so you think they're screwing?"

"Where else would they be?"

"Fair point," he says, slurping a noodle. "Weren't you and Sariah into each other?"

"I thought so."

"Want me to look around?"

"You don't mind?"

"Nah," he says, shoveling in another bite. "By the way, this is good." Pushing his chair back with a scrape, he adds, "Be right back."

"Thanks."

Pacious winks before heading out, and Jesse slides into the seat beside her.

"Where do you think Lux went?" she asks, still toying with her noodles.

Jesse scoffs. "I don't give a fuck. He can get eaten by Ronas for all I care."

"But why would he run out there?"

Jesse shrugs. "Maybe he knew I'd beat his ass. I was working on it when he bolted."

"Still... he doesn't seem like the type to run to his death."

"Maybe he went to grab his gun," Shamus suggests, eating at the counter.

"He dropped a weapon outside?"

"Yeah. When he went out for Gratian and Honor, he lost it trying to get back in. Too many of them to retrieve it."

Priya groans. "Great. So he went back for something to kill you with."

Jesse smirks. "I'm not scared of him."

"Were there still a lot of Ronas out there?" she asks.

"They were scattered," Shamus says. "Not as many at the door."

"Well, that's something," Priya mutters.

Pacious returns and takes his seat.

"So?" she prompts.

He shakes his head. "Didn't find either of them. Sorry, love."

"Where the hell could they have gone?" she wonders.

"Ask Tesslyn's people," Jesse suggests.

Priya hesitates. "I don't want to look crazy if Sariah shows up and nothing happened. We haven't even kissed yet."

"Who cares? Just ask," Pacious says.

Priya exhales, then pushes back her chair. The legs scrape loudly against the floor as she stands.

In the living room, Baxter and Jessica lounge with their feet on the coffee table, watching a movie.

"Hey, how's it going?" Priya asks.

"Fine, thanks," Jessica replies.

"Where's Tesslyn? I haven't seen her."

Baxter frowns. "Not sure. After she got accused of flirting with Lux, she took off. She does that when she's upset—needs time to cool off."

"Do you think she's with Lux? He disappeared too."

Jessica stiffens. "What's it to you?"

Priya curses internally. Damn those guys for making her ask. "Nothing. Never mind." She turns and walks away.

Back at the island, she plops into her chair.

Pacious glances over. "So?"

"Oh, it went great. Thanks."

Jesse smirks. "What happened?"

"Jessica got all bitchy." She slides her plate to Pacious. "You want it?"

He grins. "Hell yeah."

As he digs in, Jesse takes his empty plate to the sink.

Soft footsteps echo behind Priya. She glances over her shoulder—Tesslyn walks in and heads for the couches. Priya watches, waiting for Sariah to follow.

She doesn't.

Priya exhales sharply, crossing her arms.

Tesslyn comes into the kitchen. "Mind if I grab some food?"

"Go for it," Shamus answers, rinsing his plate.

Jesse, blunt as ever, asks, "Seen Sariah? While you were off doing... whatever?"

Tesslyn looks over her shoulder as she spoons pasta onto her plate. "You talking to me?"

"Yeah."

"Nope." She adds sauce and grabs a fork.

"Where'd you run off to?" Shamus asks.

She glares at him. "What are you, my babysitter? I was clearing my head."

Shamus grunts as she brushes past him.

"She was probably off screwing Lux," Jesse mutters.

Priya exhales. "I hope so."

"For real?" Pacious asks, finishing his second plate.

Priya shrugs. "Better for Honor that way. Maybe it'll push her to leave him. He's a dick."

"Wow." Pacious shakes his head. "So you'd rather your best friend's guy cheat on her than your crush cheat on you?"

"Fucked up, right?" Priya mutters, grabbing the rum bottle. "But hey, it'd be a win-win. Honor deserves better."

Pacious chuckles. "Can't argue with that."

12

SLOW BURN, SHARP BITE
PRIYA

It's about an hour—and a bottle and a half of rum—later when Sariah finally walks in.

Meandering up to the drunken group at the kitchen island, she leans over Jesse and grabs the bottle from him.

"Where the hell were you?" he asks, holding the bottle firm, not releasing it right away.

"I was talking to Janice. She was really freaked out and panicking when I went to follow you guys to get Lux," she says calmly. Jesse finally lets go of the bottle.

"I didn't see you in there when I went looking for you," Pacious states evenly.

"Why'd you go looking for me?" she asks, glancing at Priya as she takes a long swig.

"We were worried about you," Priya answers quickly, cutting off any of the boys before they can speak the full truth.

Pacious gives her a wry smile. "Anyway, you weren't in there when I checked."

"I know. I went to fetch her something. Don't worry about it."

"What'd you fetch?" Shamus asks, holding out a hand for the bottle.

She hands it over. "She wanted drugs, okay? And I don't blame her. I got her nice and high—Tesslyn came and helped me hook up an IV and gave her some fentanyl. She's high as a kite now, and she'll stay that way 'til the end."

"That's actually a really good idea," Jesse says. "Good work."

"Still doesn't explain why you were gone so long," Pacious mutters, not letting it drop.

"Let it go," Jesse cuts in, defending her.

"Yeah," Sariah adds. "I told you where I was. I sat with her for a long time. Talked to her until she fell asleep. I'd hate to be in her place—knowing you're going to die. It sucks."

Priya believes her instantly. She doesn't know why, but she trusts her wholeheartedly.

Maybe it's the booze.

They sit around drinking and talking until both bottles of rum are gone.

The night blurs at the edges, softened by alcohol and laughter. The warmth of bodies pressed close, the easy camaraderie of new friendships—it all makes Priya's head spin. Sariah shifts beside her, their fingers weaving together, the heat of her palm seeping into Priya's skin. Every brush of contact is a slow burn.

When Jesse stumbles off to pass out on the couch, exhaustion pulls at Priya too.

"I need to pee," she mumbles, her words slurring. Her tongue feels thick, her thoughts sluggish with rum and fatigue.

But Sariah's gaze cuts through the haze—sharp, heated, impossible to misread. It coils low in Priya's belly, sparking beneath her skin. Maybe it's the booze, or maybe it's just the woman in front of her. But damn—Sariah is gorgeous.

Flushed and breathless, Priya teeters toward the restroom. She handles her business, washes her hands, and opens the door.

Sariah is there, leaning casually against the wall, watching her.

Priya's breath catches.

That look.

It's intimate.

Seductive.

Devastating.

Before she can think, Sariah steps forward in one smooth motion, pressing Priya back against the wall., her hands braced above Priya's head, caging her in.

"Is this okay?" Sariah murmurs, tilting Priya's chin up with a single finger.

Priya nods, her breath shuddering out just as Sariah claims her lips.

The kiss stuns her—electricity crackling through every nerve. Sariah tastes like rum and heat, like something dangerous and addictive. When her tongue slides against Priya's, she sees stars.

The luscious taste of her swollen lips makes Priya stutter, and she presses into them like leaning into the wind on a hot summer day.

Priya fists a hand in Sariah's hair, the other trailing down, unable to resist cupping the heavy weight of her breast. A moan vibrates between them. Sariah presses closer, their bodies flush, her hands skimming down to the buttons of Priya's flannel. With slow, deliberate movements, she unfastens them one by one, revealing lace beneath.

Sariah pauses, drinking in the sight before her.

Then, with no hesitation, she dips her head, lips dragging down Priya's neck and collarbone, until they find the swell of her breasts. She kisses, licks, bites. Priya gasps, her fingers fumbling with the laces of Sariah's corset—until Sariah reaches back, makes quick work of the ties, and lets the leather fall away.

Priya groans at the sight of her—curves framed in silk, dusky skin marked by faint scars, each one a story she aches to learn. She reaches around and unclasps the bra with practiced ease. The moment Sariah's breasts are free, Priya is on them—licking, sucking, teasing—until Sariah's moans turn desperate.

Hands and mouths tangle in a fevered rhythm as they stumble from the hallway into a small, dimly lit room. The cot is barely beneath them before Priya is falling onto it, Sariah stripping her down piece by piece, slow and savoring.

By the time Priya is bare beneath her, heat pools low in her belly, her thighs slick with need. Sariah trails kisses down her stomach, lower, lower—

Then her tongue finds Priya's clit.

A bolt of pleasure rocks through her. The swirling, the sucking, the sharp bite of teeth—Priya grips the itchy blanket, her body tightening like a bowstring. Then Sariah adds a finger.

Then two.

Then three.

The sensation is akin to heaven—a place where no monsters exist, where only a bright, sexy future awaits with the woman currently ruining her.

"I'm gonna come," Priya mumbles, grabbing hold of Sariah's hair, her nails scratching down her arms.

"Come for me," Sariah says between licks.

Priya shatters.

Her climax rips through her like a wave crashing against the shore, her cries swallowed by Sariah's mouth as she drinks her down. When the aftershocks subside, Priya pulls Sariah up, tasting herself on her lips as she flips them over.

Now it's her turn.

She makes quick work of Sariah's boots, socks, pants—until she's stretched out beneath her, utterly bare.

She's breathtaking.

Some scars hint she may have been in a fire once, but Priya doesn't ask. She just presses her mouth between Sariah's thighs, reveling in the way she arches, the way her hips chase every stroke of her tongue. She finds the spot that makes Sariah whimper and flicks her tongue just right. When she adds her fingers, curling them deep inside, Sariah comes undone.

"Oh my god," Sariah growls, arching her back as Priya moves faster—her tongue wiggling side to side before licking from taint to clit, lapping up the wetness she's coaxing from her.

Sariah's moans grow fierce. She plays with her tits, arching her back and lifting them into glorious mounds as she pinches a nipple.

Her release is catastrophic—a sudden rush bursts from her, catching Priya across the lips and cheeks, warm and wild. She doesn't hesitate, lapping up every bit, one hand fiercely massaging her through the orgasm.

Priya watches in awe as Sariah gasps, her body taut, pleasure wracking through her until her release spills over, wet and sweet against Priya's lips.

Sariah pulls herself up, a wicked grin spreading across her face. "Spread your legs for me," she demands.

Priya obeys. Sariah straddles her, their bodies aligning, slick heat meeting slick heat. The first slow grind makes Priya's head drop back.

Then Sariah moves faster.

"You like that?" she teases, making Priya beg for more.

Priya nods furiously as Sariah's thrusts grow wilder—grinding and gyrating until she sees stars.

"Fuck yes, baby, fuck me," Priya breathes as her head drops back, her own climax crashing over her—wet and sudden—coating their thighs in heat and ecstasy.

Their bodies rock together, harder, deeper, lost in it—

moaning, gasping, clawing at each other. The friction builds and builds, their pleasure feeding off one another until—

Priya shatters again, Sariah following right after, their bodies trembling as the waves crash over them.

When it's over, Sariah collapses on top of her, their breaths tangled, their skin still humming.

Priya doesn't know what this means.

But she knows she doesn't regret a single second.

13

THE HAND THAT FEEDS YOU
PRIYA

When she opens her eyes again, she's being spooned by Sariah, and her heart swells at the sight of her arm wrapped around her waist.

It's hard to tell what time it is, but she thinks it's morning—the softs sounds of someone rummaging in the kitchen drift through the cracked door, rousing her.

Lifting her head gently, she blinks the sleep from her eyes and slips out of bed, careful not to wake Sariah.

Priya pulls the door closed behind her and pads toward the kitchen, where she finds Krishna filling a pot with water for coffee.

"Morning," she says softly.

"Morning," Krishna replies.

"What time is it?" Priya asks, grabbing a cup for herself.

"A bit past six, I think. I couldn't sleep. Those patient beds down there are so uncomfortable."

"I'm sorry."

"Eh, it is what it is," she says as the coffee begins to percolate. "At least we're inside a secure building—and for that, I can sleep soundly."

"Touché," Priya says, lifting her empty cup in a small toast.

"Hey, have you guys seen Lux?" Honor's voice cuts in from behind them.

"Did he not come back in?" Priya asks as Honor leans against one of the chairs.

"Come back in?" Honor repeats, confusion and something else—fear, maybe—etched on her face.

"Yeah," Priya explains. "After the fight with Jesse and Pacious, he ran off. They chased him but stopped when he went outside."

"Outside?"

"Yeah. They think he went back out to get a weapon, but when they checked, he wasn't there."

"Shit!" Honor exclaims, her voice rising with panic as she bolts toward the staircase.

Priya looks at Krishna, who gives her a worried look, and they both take off after her.

When they reach the front door, it's wide open. Honor is already halfway under the awning of what used to be the drop-off area, scanning the street with frantic eyes.

The early morning air is still sharp, spring's infancy clinging stubbornly to the chill of winter. A few scattered trees show the first hints of budding leaves, but the dew remains frosty—like delicate icing on the blades of grass and sprigs of summer yet to come.

In the distance, Rotters meander aimlessly, not yet close enough to hear the crunch of broken glass under Honor's boots.

But they're still too close for comfort.

Honor stares at the ground where fresh blood smears the pavement, glinting among shards of broken glass. As Priya joins her, she realizes it's not the blackish-brown ichor of the dead—but the bright red blood of the living.

Honor follows the trail around the side of the building.

Near another structure, Ronas shuffle closer, drawn by movement.

Still, she presses forward, ignoring the dead who now surely see them.

Then she stops short at a cluster of bushes—and lets out a blood-curdling scream.

Priya bolts to her, slamming a palm over her mouth to silence her—but it's too late. The Ronas have heard. It won't be long until they're here.

"It's his hand!" Honor screams against Priya's palm, her voice muffled but unmistakable.

Krishna rushes up beside them, kicking the hand over to reveal a tattooed wrist and a black wedding band.

Definitely Lux's.

"We have to go," Priya whispers, tugging at Honor.

"No!" she cries, wrenching free and falling to her knees beside the severed hand.

The Rotters double in number, stumbling toward them in their clumsy, relentless gait. Priya locks eyes with Krishna, who shakes her head.

They've come out unarmed.

Only one fresh Rona among them could spell disaster.

"Honor, we have to go now!" Priya shouts, pulling at her harder. "Grab his hand if you want to bring it in, but we can't stay here! This doesn't mean he's gone, it just means—he lost his hand!"

The Ronas are almost upon them now, and in her grief, it seems Honor doesn't care that she's about to join Lux in death.

"Gratian needs one parent, Honor—c'mon," Priya pleads desperately, looking around for something—anything—sharp to protect them.

One of the Rotters stumbles over a rock and barrels straight for Honor.

The commotion catches the attention of fresh Ronas.

You can hear their snarled footsteps pounding on the pavement beyond the center.

Hundreds of them.

Honor looks up at Priya just as the rotting woman reaches her, grabbing for her leg.

Priya lunges, grabbing Honor's shoulder and heaving her up—just as the Rotter's teeth sink into empty air where her arm had been a second ago.

And then they see it.

The hill.

The Ronas have crested it, flooding down like ants—thousands of them.

Krishna bolts, and Priya takes off after her, dragging Honor along with her.

Frenzied footfalls thunder behind them as they race toward the doors. Priya slams them shut just in time, throwing the siege-style bar back into place.

But the danger doesn't stop.

The mob slams into the doors like a wave, and Honor is clutching Lux's severed hand, still dripping, as she collapses against the wall.

Krishna screams, searching the room for anything they can use to barricade the entrance.

The banging. The clawing. The growling.

Screams outside. Screams within.

The noise rouses the others.

Before the siege bar can splinter in two, Jesse, Pacious, Shamus, and Baxter sprint in. With a coordinated heave, they yank down a thick sheet of metal from overhead.

"Priya, watch out!" Sariah shouts.

Baxter slams the metal down.

It nearly takes off Priya's arms—almost cleaves her in half.

She drops hard, landing on her ass just as the wall of steel crashes into the floor, cracking the tile beneath it. Her breath comes in frantic gasps.

The boys shove their backs into the barrier, holding it steady against the chaos outside.

Snarls. Growls. Bangs. Screeches.

"How... how?" Priya wheezes.

Baxter, stretching out his neck, glares daggers at her.

Pacious picks up on the tension instantly, shifting his gaze to Baxter. "How *did* you know that was there?"

Baxter grunts, his breathing ragged. "Saw it when we first came in. Knew it was there."

"Thank God for that," Sariah says, seemingly unsuspicious —unlike Priya and the boys, who exchange wary glances.

Honor falls to the floor, cradling the bleeding appendage. It's been severed cleanly, layers of bone, muscle, and tissue capping the forearm, like a macabre work of art—delicate, grotesque, and awful all at once.

It still makes Priya want to vomit.

"I can't believe he's gone," Honor whispers, her eyes vacant, like dimming stars.

Krishna looks to Priya, who presses her lips together in silent sympathy.

"You don't know that, love," Priya says softly, getting up and crossing to sit beside Honor. She wraps an arm around her shoulders, careful not to touch the severed limb Honor holds against her chest. "It's just his hand. He may still be out there somewhere."

"Then I need to go look for him. What if he tried to get back in and couldn't?" she says, slamming her head against the cinderblock wall behind her.

"Why don't we wait a bit—'til they go away again?" Priya offers.

Honor's eyes are bloodshot and hollow, worn down by the morning's grief. She nods, laying her head on Priya's shoulder.

After a few minutes, the Ronas outside tire of their assault. The scraping and banging slow. Their retreat mimics the rhythm of Priya's heart, calming now that the danger has passed.

She stands and offers Honor her hand.

Honor takes it reluctantly, blood slicking their palms. Priya ignores the slippery warmth and helps her up, guiding her toward the office wing.

"I have to check on Gratian," Honor says as they enter the main lobby.

"You might wanna wash up first," Krishna suggests.

"I think that's best," Honor replies dully. "He's still recovering—no need to worry him just yet." She hesitates, then follows them down the hall. "What am I gonna tell him when he asks where his dad is?"

"We'll think of something, love," Priya murmurs.

"I'll grab a bag for that," Krishna says, nodding at the severed hand as she walks off ahead of them.

"Do you really think he might still be alive?" Honor asks quietly as they approach the bathroom.

"I think so, yes," Priya lies.

But how could the dead have only managed to rip off his hand and not devour the rest of him? If he *is* alive, he's bleeding out somewhere—alone, terrified, and probably close to death.

"Okay, here's a bag," Krishna says, returning and holding it out.

Honor drops the bloody hand into it, and Krishna rolls it up tightly.

"I'm gonna wash up," Honor says, slipping into the bathroom.

"I'm going to finish my coffee," Krishna replies.

"Me too," Priya echoes. "Come up after you check on him, okay?"

Honor nods and shuts the door behind her.

As Priya and Krishna climb the stairs, Krishna glances over. "Do you really think he could be alive out there?"

"I don't see how," Priya answers. "I mean, how could they just rip off his hand and not eat it? And if he was bitten, like Janice..."

"See, that's what I find strange," Krishna says, stopping halfway up the stairs. "Look." She unrolls the bag and pulls the goddamn thing out again. Priya, who had just started to regain her stomach, turns away.

"It looks like someone cut it off. Clean. Like the bodies at that hotel. This doesn't look chewed. You see what I mean?"

"You're right," Priya muses, frowning. "It *is* like what we found at that hotel."

"But what does that mean?" Krishna asks.

Priya pauses on the next step, turning back to face her. "That someone is following us... someone intelligent enough to cut pieces off people?"

"Right," Krishna says slowly. "But that doesn't make any sense."

"It doesn't," Priya agrees. "The Ronas don't do this."

"They don't. But who does?"

14

SEVERED TRUTHS
PRIYA

The scent of sizzling bacon thickens the air. In the corner, an old deep freezer hums, packed with meat long frozen—God only knows for how long. Hopefully, it won't make them sick. Still, Priya flips the breakfast strips, savoring the crackle, the grease spitting against the pan, the illusion of normalcy. It looks fine. Smells fine. Good enough to make her stomach grumble at the familiar comfort of a hot, greasy breakfast.

Krishna stirs a pot of gravy, the smell of sausage mingling with the bacon. No eggs, no fresh produce—just whatever they could scavenge.

Priya hadn't always eaten pork. It went against her Indian upbringing, her culture, her religion. But when she married Nora, a New Yorker by birth, she figured she was already living in sin in her parents' eyes. What was one more? One bite of crispy bacon had sealed the deal. She never looked back.

"Has anyone checked on Janice?" Tesslyn asks, pouring herself a cup of coffee.

"I haven't," Priya replies, glancing toward the others.

Sariah and Tesslyn had been the last to see her. After the

chaos downstairs, everyone had retreated back here. Sariah is still sprawled on the bed in the corner, fast asleep. Priya watches her for a moment, biting back a smile at the memory of last night's drunken passion.

She giggles to herself just as Pacious emerges from the bathroom, a towel draped over his shoulders. His glasses sit crooked on his nose, and his grin is just as lopsided. "Damn, a hot shower feels like heaven," he mutters, chucking the towel onto the floor. His nose twitches as he inhales deeply. "Smells amazing."

"Feel better?" Priya asks.

"Absolutely. Those patient beds downstairs are basically glorified cots. My neck was wrecked, but the shower helped."

She snorts. "I get that."

Pacious nudges her with his shoulder, flashing a knowing smirk. "Somebody had a good night."

Her stomach drops. She glances at him sharply. "Oh God, did you hear something?"

He chuckles, sipping his coffee. "Nah. But when you disappeared, and she told us to make ourselves scarce, we got the hint."

Priya's face heats. Her dark skin does little to hide the flush.

"So you just do whatever she says?" Priya asks, setting her fork down and eyeing him seriously.

"I do not," he replies, a little defensively. "I was about ready to pass out anyway. And honestly, that girl-on-girl stuff doesn't really do it for me."

"No?" she asks, genuinely confused. Usually it's every guy's fantasy.

"Not if I'm not involved," he says with a shrug.

"Ah, I see," she mutters, returning her attention to the bacon. "So, I wanted to ask you something—"

"Oh alright, I'll join you next time," he interrupts, grinning and winking. "Everybody needs a little D in their life now and again."

"Ew, no! That's not—" She groans and shuts off the burner. "Krishna, what did you do with that hand?"

Pacious's eyebrows shoot up.

Krishna pulls a plastic bag from the freezer. Inside—Lux's severed hand.

Priya takes it gingerly, peeling the frozen appendage from its bag. "Doesn't this look like what we saw at the hotel?"

Pacious sets down his coffee, adjusts his glasses, and leans in to examine it. The fingers are curled, frozen mid-motion, like Lux had been reaching for something when it was severed.

"Kinda," he murmurs. "But the limbs at the hotel were clean cuts. Like from a machete. This?" He rotates the wrist, pointing at the jagged edge. "This was done with a rough blade —maybe a saw. See the notches?"

Priya swallows back a wave of nausea. "But it wasn't chewed off. No bite marks."

"Nope."

Jesse enters the kitchen and stops short. "Dude, is that a hand?"

"It's Lux's," Pacious says flatly. "And it wasn't bitten off—it was cut."

Jesse frowns. "Shit."

"That's not even the weirdest part," Priya continues. "There was no body. No bones. Just the hand and a lot of blood. If it were Ronas, they would've torn him apart. This? This was deliberate."

Jesse exhales slowly. "So, what are you saying?"

"That someone out there is using the apocalypse to kill for sport. Like *The Purge*. Sick fuckers who've been waiting for an excuse to carve people up."

Pacious exhales sharply and gives the hand back to Krishna, who shoves it into the bag.

"And they're following us?"

Krishna shakes her head. "Not necessarily. We just keep ending up in the same places."

"What do we do?" Priya asks.

"Stay the hell away from them," Jesse says. "They were here first. This was a warning."

"But where do we go now?" Krishna asks, stuffing the severed hand back into the freezer.

"Honor needs insulin," Priya reminds them. "There's a big hospital in Denver. She said they had supplies."

"They've got a stockpile at the jail too," Tesslyn adds, suddenly behind them.

Jesse's eyes narrow. "And how do you know that?"

"That's where we were when we met Lux and Honor."

Pacious crosses his arms. "So why'd you leave?"

"They sent me to find more medical supplies. I'm a nurse." She doesn't hesitate.

Priya watches her carefully, unease prickling at the back of her neck.

"We'll have to wait for Honor," she says finally. "She won't leave until Gratian is stable."

"Fuck that," Pacious replies. "We should figure out who's doing this."

Krishna frowns. "And how do you propose we do that?"

Pacious sips his coffee, his expression dark. "I'll think of something. But running isn't the answer. This is a game to them."

"A fucked-up game," Priya mutters.

Pacious nudges Jesse. "Now's your chance to impress Honor."

Jesse grins and shoves past him toward the coffee pot.

Krishna turns off the stove. "Breakfast is ready."

Right on cue, Honor appears, looking worse than before. Dark circles smudge under her eyes, exhaustion evident in the slope of her shoulders as she leans against the island.

Priya softens. "Hey, love. Want some breakfast?"

Honor shakes her head. "No. I'm not hungry."

"How's Gratian?" Krishna asks.

"He's stable. Barely." She exhales. "I'm worried."

Tesslyn stretches. "I'll check on Janice."

Jesse steps closer to Honor as she rests her head on his shoulder.

"Do you guys really think he's still alive?" she asks, her voice hollow.

"Uh," Jesse replies, his voice cracking slightly, "yeah. Yeah, for sure."

Priya hesitates. "It's possible. Since his hand is the only thing we found, he could still be out there."

Honor straightens. "I need someone to go out and look for him today. I can't leave Gratian, but I need to know."

Jesse nods. "We'll go."

Pacious cracks his knuckles. "And maybe set some traps. See if we can catch whoever's been playing with body parts."

Honor's gaze sharpens. "You think someone's hunting us?"

"I don't know," Jesse answers. "But from what we saw at the hotel, and now the han—your husband's hand—it feels intentional. This kind of thing doesn't happen by accident. And it sure as hell doesn't come from those things out there."

"But who would do something like this?" Honor asks, glancing sideways at Jesse. "Out there, with those monsters? For what? What are they getting out of this?"

"I think someone's playing with us," Jesse mutters.

"And from what we saw at the hotel," Pacious adds, "I don't think they're done. Sometimes, the only way to survive is to become the thing you fear. Maybe becoming a monster is how they've coped with the end of the world."

"I appreciate you trying to understand their motives and

all," Honor says, "but my husband is missing. Probably dead. I want them dead too."

"I get that," Pacious says. "I'll run around today and gather what we need to go out there. When do you think we should leave?" he asks Jesse.

"After lunch?" Jesse suggests.

"Yeah, that sounds good. Gives us time to get shit ready."

"Thank you," Honor says softly.

"Of course," Jesse replies, offering her a gentle smile.

"What's going on, guys?" Michael asks, emerging from somewhere with Amy's hand in his.

Lux is Michael's friend, so this is going to be difficult.

Honor glances at him, holding her mug close, the sheen of unshed tears glistening in her eyes.

"Guys? What is it?" Michael asks, his eyes a worried gray.

"Lux is missing," Priya says as gently as she can.

"What?!" he exclaims, letting go of Amy's hand and moving toward Jesse.

"Calm down, please," Priya says, trying to keep things level. "Honor noticed he didn't come back last night, so she came up here. We told her he ran outside after the fight with Jesse—"

"He ran outside?" Michael interrupts. "Why didn't anyone tell me he ran outside?"

"We figured he'd come right back in," Jesse says defensively. "No sane person would stay out there unarmed."

"We thought he was going to retrieve the gun he dropped," Pacious adds.

"So then what happened?" Michael demands.

"We went out to look for him and—" Priya trails off. This is the hard part.

"And?" he presses.

"We found this," Krishna says, pulling out the hand again.

Amy's eyes go wide, and Michael's face sinks as he takes the bag being handed to him.

"What the fuck," he mutters, tossing the bag back to Krishna.

"But the thing is," Priya says as Michael turns and walks toward the living room, "we don't know if that means he's dead. It just means he's missing his hand."

"What the fuck?" he repeats, retreating to the windows. He drops to his knees, breathing hard, hands on his bald head.

Amy follows and rests her hand on his shoulder blades.

"They're going to go out and look for him," Honor says, wiping her tears with a sleeve and glancing back at Michael. "If you want to go."

Michael says nothing—just nods, standing slowly.

His eyes are glassy, but no tears fall.

"I'm going with," he announces.

"Okay," Pacious replies. "We should figure out who's going and who's staying. If we want to leave by lunch, we need to start getting things ready now."

Michael nods and stalks off, with Amy following close behind.

15

HEAP OF ASH

PRIYA

Pacious and Jesse move through the center, gathering supplies for the hunt—knives, rope, whatever will keep them alive out there. In the living room, Priya dips a chunk of bread into her soup, the warmth of the meal contrasting with the unease curling in her stomach. Across from her, Sariah watches in silence.

"And you're sure you want to go with them?" Priya asks, not wanting her to go but knowing she'll do whatever she wants.

"I do. I like going out there—in the wild, hunting things. It gives me a rush I don't often find in all this madness, you know?"

"I know. I just..." Priya trails off, not wanting to say too much.

It's a new fling.

Sariah turns, shifting so her legs brush against Priya's. "You just what?"

"I just... I'll be worried about you, is all."

Sariah lifts Priya's chin and kisses her, softly. "I like that."

"You like that I'll be worried?"

"Yes," she replies, kissing her nose. "It shows I'm more than just a fuck to you."

"Of course you are," Priya says quietly. "I haven't been with anyone since my wife. And I don't just... do that... with just anyone."

"Well, good. I'm glad to hear it—considering there aren't many normal people left out there."

"Look at you, calling yourself normal." Priya laughs as Sariah lightly kicks her leg.

"Hey, I try," Sariah says, fixing a dreadlock that's fallen loose from her ponytail.

"Just be careful out there, okay? I kinda like you."

"Kinda?" Sariah grins and winks.

"How long do you think you'll be gone?"

"Hard to say. Since we're on the Front Range, there aren't a lot of animals this far out, so we'll probably have to head toward the mountains. Maybe a day or two."

"Oh, okay. That's not too bad."

"But don't get all freaked out if we're not back for, like, a week. You never know what you're working with out there until you're out there."

"I'll try not to," Priya says.

Pacious strides in, slinging his spear across his back. "Ready to go?"

"Yeah, I just gotta grab my sword," Sariah says, standing.

Priya stands as well. "Did you guys pack some food and stuff?"

Shamus assembles his knives while Jesse grabs his bow.

"Yep, we grabbed some things," Jesse answers, gathering arrows and wiping off the tips of the ones he's retrieved.

"And who's all going, then?"

"Shamus, myself, Jesse," Pacious answers. "Sariah, Michael. I guess the three from the jail—Baxter, Jessica, and Tesslyn. Antonio and Juan."

"So that leaves me, Honor, Krishna, Amy, Maria, and Jesus to look after Gratian and Janice?"

"Yes. That cool?"

"Yeah. Should be fine. Please be careful out there."

"You got it, boss," Pacious says, tightening his canteen to the strap across his chest.

Priya follows him, Sariah, and the others down the steps toward the lobby, where the rest of the group gathers. Tesslyn, Baxter, and Jessica join them, faces set with the determination of people who know exactly what's waiting beyond those doors.

Jesse steps forward. "I'm going to check out where the Ronas are lurking—see if we can lure them away. If we can set a trap, lead them toward the mountains, we might get a better idea of whether Lux is out there, or if someone's pulling the strings."

Priya frowns. "What kind of trap? If they're going after the living, you'd need bait."

"I can do it," Baxter says. "I'll wait for those fuckers. Be my pleasure."

Sariah studies him. "You sure? No guarantee they'll even come for you."

"I don't mind. Just as long as you bring me food and supplies. I'll set up camp out there and keep an eye on things."

"We can do that," Honor says. "You're not worried about them forming a horde? Surrounding you?"

"Course not, ma'am," Baxter replies, shouldering his pack. "I've been around 'em enough to steer clear. Got my guns, got my gear. I'll be fine."

Jesse nods, and Baxter helps him pull the metal wall back up. "Alright. I'll go check things out and be back in a few."

The others watch as he moves to the door, peeking through a hole in the barricade to check for threats. Finding none, he unbolts the metal grooves and eases the door open. A warm April breeze sweeps in, sunlight stark against the dark interior.

No Ronas in sight—at least, not here. Jesse slips out, the door shutting behind him.

Five minutes later, he returns. "They're out there, but they're circling another building. We can move now, head west, and see if we find any signs of Lux. Baxter, pick a camp spot, but if you need back in, use a signal."

"Throw a rock at the second-floor windows," Honor suggests.

"Works for me," Baxter says. "I got my tent, fire-making stuff, and some canned food. I'll be fine for a night or two."

Jesse exhales. "Alright. Let's move."

As the group filters outside, Priya lingers, Sariah by her side. She pulls her into a tight hug, inhaling the familiar mix of sweat, dirt, and earth.

"Be careful, okay?" she whispers.

"I will, beautiful." Sariah's fathomless blue eyes sharpen, an edge of protectiveness settling in them.

Then she pulls Priya into a kiss, rekindling embers long extinguished in this cold, desolate world. It's a wonder how effortlessly Sariah ignites her—this clump of cold ashes she's become—into flames again, despite knowing her only a few days.

"Come back alive, okay?"

Sariah grins, stepping back. "You got it, boss." And then she's gone.

16

A GRIM DISCOVERY

PRIYA

The dark hallway echoes more loudly in the memory of Sariah kissing her. Priya touches her lips absently as they pass the room where Gratian is resting.

Honor slides open the glass door and peeks inside, most likely searching for the rise and fall of his chest.

"How's he doing?" Priya whispers as Honor quietly pulls the door shut.

"The same. In and out of consciousness. His ketones are still gradually coming down, and his blood sugar too. He's never been that high before, it'll take days for him to recover."

"Poor guy."

"I know. My poor baby."

"Does he need to eat anything?"

"Not yet. When he wakes up fully, he'll be starving, but that won't be for a while." Honor exhales, then turns her gaze toward the hall. "Has anyone checked on Janice?"

"Not me, no. Tesslyn was going to check on her this morning. Should we?"

"Yeah," Honor says, already heading toward the left hallway instead of the stairway leading to the apartment upstairs.

Priya follows, inhaling sharply as they step into the corridor's stale, oppressive darkness. The air is thick with the putrid stench of decay. It clings to the back of her throat, and she swallows hard against the rising nausea.

Janice's room is cold. Ice-cold. Their breaths mist in the air as they step inside. An IV tree drips fentanyl into the woman's unmoving arm. She is nothing but a still shape in the dim corner.

"Janice?" Honor murmurs, inching forward.

Priya stiffens. Something is wrong. "Wait," she says, grabbing Honor's wrist. "Don't go up to her like that without something to stick her with. She might be dead. Or one of those things."

Honor hesitates. "You're right."

Then, Janice's leg twitches. Just the smallest, almost imperceptible movement.

It's enough to send both girls scrambling back, tripping over each other as they tear from the room with strangled gasps.

They don't stop running until they reach the kitchenette, hearts slamming against their ribs. They spin, breathless, eyes locked on the hallway.

Waiting.

Listening.

Honor frantically scans the small space. "We need something sharp."

Priya yanks open a drawer, fingers shaking as she rifles through its contents. "Anything that can puncture a skull."

Cabinets slam, drawers rattle. The desperate sounds of their search fill the darkness with chaos. But it's the noise from the hallway that makes Priya's stomach clench with fear.

A slow, dragging scrape.

She freezes. The sound is getting closer.

Panic surges, shoving her back into motion. She sprints

across the hall to the nurse's station, barely sparing the shadows a glance before tearing open drawers.

Nothing.

Nothing.

Nothing.

Then. . . cold steel in her palm. A scalpel. Too small, but better than nothing.

She bolts back to Honor and presses the blade into her hand.

Honor exhales sharply. "It's tiny, but if you jab her through the eye—"

"That's what I was thinking."

Priya's gaze catches on an IV stand in the corner.

"What if we break one of the IV trees in half?"

Honor nods. "Yeah, that could work."

Priya grabs the nearest one and slams it over her knee. The metal bends but doesn't snap.

"Shit!"

A sound clatters down the hallway—shoes scraping against concrete.

Priya bends the pole back and forth, her hands slick with sweat, trying to snap it in half. The metal groans in protest.

The scraping intensifies, growing closer.

A chill slithers up her spine.

With a final, desperate twist, the IV stand breaks. One jagged edge, sharp enough to tear through flesh.

A breath of ice-cold air brushes the back of her neck.

The hair on her arms rises.

She spins—

Janice is right behind her.

Her skin is as pale as snow on the Rocky Mountains, her blond hair matted to her forehead. The clothes she'd been wearing are gone, replaced by an open-back hospital gown. Her eyes—so dilated they're nearly black—and her lips are white and cracked.

The only thing keeping Priya from shoving the pole into her skull is the lack of a telltale sign: her eyes aren't pale and milky like the Ronas'.

"Janice?" Priya says, backing away just a bit, still uneasy.

"Yes?" Janice replies, dazed and confused.

"Are you okay?"

"I think so," she says, her voice raspy. "I just came out for a drink of water and saw you guys. I thought you might need help with something."

"Thanks," Honor says, giving Priya a worried look. "Let's get you back to bed, okay?"

"Okay," Janice says reluctantly.

"I'll get you some water. Priya will help you back to your bed while I do."

Priya nods, setting the IV rod on the counter before gently turning Janice toward the hallway. Janice moves sluggishly, her steps unsteady, like her body is failing her in real time.

Priya guides her to the bed and eases her down, but the moment Janice's weight shifts, she winces.

"Oh, sorry, hon. Did I touch your bite?"

"No, that one's over here," Janice murmurs, pushing up the sleeve of her gown to reveal her left arm.

Priya gasps.

The original bite is worse, angry and swollen, the surrounding flesh tinged a sickly green. Black, spindly veins creep outward like cracks in marble, stretching toward her shoulder. But that isn't the worst of it.

Three fresh wounds gape along her forearm, raw chunks of flesh torn clean away. The jagged edges are dark—nearly black—as if the infection has already taken root.

"Oh my God," Priya breathes, stumbling back in horror. "What the fuck?"

Janice blinks up at her, confused. "What? What's the matter?"

Priya doesn't answer. Instead, she shoves up the sleeve on Janice's other arm.

Five more. Flesh missing in uneven patches, the wounds slick with congealed blood. Some look fresh—red and oozing—while others are mottled with sickly hues of yellow and black.

"Janice..." Priya's voice is a whisper. "What happened to you?"

"I got bit outside, remember?" she says, her tone light, unbothered.

"Yes, but you only had one bite. Now you have seven."

Janice grins—*grins*—as if she doesn't understand the words coming out of Priya's mouth. "No."

Glass shatters behind her.

Priya jumps, whipping around to see Honor standing in the doorway, water dripping from her trembling hands, shards of glass at her feet.

Honor's face is bone-white. Her mouth gapes in horror as her gaze locks on Janice's arms. "Oh my God..."

"What?" Janice asks again, blinking sluggishly.

"Janice," Priya says carefully, her pulse pounding, "how many bites do you have?"

Janice sighs and leans back against the pillows. "Just the one."

Priya swallows hard. "Can I... look at your legs?"

"Sure," Janice replies with an eerie sort of detachment.

Priya hesitates, then slowly lifts the hem of the hospital gown past Janice's knees.

Her stomach twists violently.

The flesh of Janice's legs is riddled with bites. Some deep, others shallow—all of them torn into her skin with gruesome precision. Some weep with pus. Others are crusted with blackened scabs. They run in irregular patterns, knees, thighs, calves, like something gnawed on her repeatedly.

A cold wave of nausea washes over Priya as she grips the fabric and lifts it higher, exposing Janice's stomach.

More bites.

Dozens of them, scattered across her abdomen like a grotesque constellation. Some are large, wide indentations of missing flesh. Others are smaller but no less vicious, as if made by different sets of teeth.

The realization slams into Priya like ice water.

Someone has been chewing on her.

"Janice, we're just going to turn your fentanyl drip up, okay?" Priya says, gently pushing the clothing back down.

"Okay," Janice replies, turning her head to face the wall.

Priya presses the button on the machine, up, and up, and up, the beeping layering over the rising tension. Grabbing Honor's hand, she pulls her from the room.

"Oh my God, what the hell," Priya breathes as they hurry down the hall.

"What the fuck was that?" Honor asks, wiping her brow with the back of her hand.

"Someone's been eating her," Priya answers, needing to force the words up and out before they consume her. Stating facts or not, it sounds insane.

"Yeah, but who? And why? And what the fuck?" Honor mutters, beginning to pace.

"I don't know. But we need to make sure she's out cold before we leave her down here with Gratian."

Honor cranes her neck to peer down the hall. "Can we lock her in there?"

"Let's go check," Priya says, walking back toward Janice's room.

The patient rooms are small cubicles with sliding glass doors—no locks on the inside or the outside.

"What are we going to do?" Honor asks.

"We can give her enough medicine to kill her. I mean, she's already dead anyway. Whatever's feeding on her isn't human."

"Alright. Do you know how much to give her?"

"I'd say just turn it all the way up. Then, when she's gone, we shove that pole through her skull and bring her body downstairs."

"Alright," Honor agrees, following Priya back into the room.

Priya presses the button and maxes out the drip.

"Are you sure that'll kill her?" she asks as they leave. "Aren't those machines supposed to keep patients from getting too much?"

"With fentanyl, that'll kill her," Honor says grimly. "The machines are meant for trained staff, but if you override them, it's just as easy to cause an overdose."

"You know about this stuff?"

"I was a patient care assistant in law school. Worked at a hospital. Sometimes nurses had me help with meds and saline drips. Picked up a few things, not much, but enough."

Honor hesitates, then asks, "How long will it take?"

"Not long." Priya exhales, glancing toward the hallway. "We'll check soon. In the meantime, we need to gather the others and figure out what the hell is going on here."

As they pass the nurse's station, Priya grabs the IV pole. "If whoever did this is still here, we need to be careful."

"I'm getting Gratian and bringing him upstairs with us," Honor says, slipping into his room. She gently scoops him up, cradling him against her chest. "Will you help me with his IV? I'll come back down for his chair later."

Priya detaches the insulin bag and follows her toward the stairs.

"This doesn't make any sense," Honor mutters as they climb toward the apartment.

Priya's grip tightens on the pole. "Do you think whoever did that to Janice is the same person who did it to Lux?"

Honor swallows hard. "I don't know, Priya. I have no idea."

17

THE HUNGER WITHIN
PRIYA

The comforting sounds of a movie drift through the air, a nostalgic contrast to the ominous hush of the stairwell. As Priya and Honor step into the living room, the warm glow of the screen flickers over Amy, Maria, Krishna, and Jesus, who lounge on the plush couches. Their relaxed postures shift the moment they take in the expressions on Priya's and Honor's faces.

Amy leans forward as Maria pauses the movie. "What is it? What's wrong?" Her eyes, wide and glassy, reflect Priya's own unease.

"It's Janice," Priya says, following Honor to the bed in the corner, where they gently lay Gratian down.

Maria frowns. "You mean from the bite on her arm yesterday?"

Priya shakes her head. "No... there's more. Bites. All over her."

A tense silence settles over the room.

"Like someone has been..."

"Feeding on her," Honor finishes grimly.

Amy swivels on the couch. "What the hell?" she breathes.

Her gaze follows them as they tuck Gratian in and set up his IV. "What the hell?" she repeats, more urgently.

"Exactly," Priya mutters. "We don't know how or why. But whatever did it is inside with us. It has to be."

Krishna's brow furrows. "But we searched this place, right?"

Priya nods, tying the IV bag to the bedpost with an old sock. "Yeah. Pacious, Jesse, and Shamus checked the basement. They said there was some weird shit down there. Maybe it's connected."

Maria pulls Jesus close. "You think someone's still down there?"

"Or something," Priya murmurs, leaning against the couch and gripping her jagged pipe.

A heavy silence hangs over them. Then Amy asks, "What do we do about Janice?"

Priya exhales. "We turned up her fentanyl. With how many bites she has... she wouldn't have lasted long anyway."

Amy lowers her gaze. "Understandable." A beat passes before she speaks again, softer. "Shouldn't someone be down there when she turns?"

"Yeah," Priya agrees. "We'll need to take her down to the basement. Lock her in with the doctor."

Maria shudders. "I can't believe we spent the night here with something... evil."

Priya taps a finger absently against the sharp edge of the IV pole. "What doesn't make sense is, if whatever did this to her is mindless like the Ronas out there, why didn't it go after anyone else? And if it's not mindless, why is it feeding?"

Amy rubs her arms. "None of this makes sense."

"What's worse," Honor adds, arms crossed, "Tesslyn's been in there with her. She set up her IV last night. Again this morning. She should've noticed the bites."

Priya frowns. "You'd think so. And if she did notice... why didn't she say anything?"

"Maybe she's the one doing it," Amy suggests.

The thought takes root in the group.

Jesus shivers. "Maybe she's some kind of cannibal."

"Still doesn't explain why," Amy mutters.

Krishna stands. "We need to take care of Janice before she turns."

"I'll help," Priya says, gripping her pipe.

Honor catches her gaze. "Be careful."

"We will."

Together, Priya and Krishna head down the dim stairwell, the silence pressing against them like a held breath. At Janice's door, Priya pauses, listening for movement. Nothing. She slides the door open a fraction, peeking inside.

"Is she...?" Krishna whispers.

"I'm not sure," Priya murmurs. "We need to check for a pulse."

"Or," Krishna suggests, "we just put that thing in her head and call it good."

"Let's be sure first."

Priya inches toward the bed. Janice lies still, her face turned toward the wall. No rise and fall of breath. Carefully, Priya reaches out, pressing two fingers to Janice's neck.

The second she touches skin, Janice moves.

With a guttural snarl, she lunges, grabbing Priya's wrist and snapping her teeth toward her arm.

Priya wrenches away as Krishna shoves Janice back. Teeth graze her skin—too close.

Too close.

Janice's eyes have turned white.

She's gone.

Her head jerks at unnatural angles as she staggers forward.

Priya stumbles, knocking her weapon beneath the bed.

Krishna shoves Janice, but she surges forward with renewed strength, knocking Krishna off balance.

They both go down hard.

Priya scrambles for the rod, fingers stretching just short of it.

Janice dives onto Krishna.

Krishna kicks her in the face. Blood splatters, but Janice doesn't even flinch.

She lunges again.

Priya's fingers close around cold steel.

With a desperate cry, she swings, driving the rod through Janice's skull.

A sickening crack.

Janice goes still.

Her body slumps over Krishna, blood pooling in a dark halo around her blond hair.

Chest heaving, Priya pushes Janice off and drops onto her stomach. "You okay?"

Krishna winces. "I think she broke my knee. Or tore something."

Priya's stomach sinks. "Shit. Let's try getting you up."

Krishna braces against Priya, but the second she puts weight on her leg, she screams.

"Yeah, that's broken," she gasps.

Priya exhales sharply. "I'll get Honor and the others. We'll get you upstairs."

Krishna nods weakly, her hands pressing against her knee.

Priya steps back, glancing down at Janice's lifeless body, the blood seeping like ink into the floorboards.

Whatever did this...

It's still in here with them.

18

THE PURIFIED

PRIYA

Priya, Honor, Amy, and Maria get Krishna to the stairwell, her arms slung around the two shorter women's shoulders—Amy and Maria—Priya and Honor merely supervise the human crutches.

The stairway leading up to the apartment is too narrow for three people to move side by side.

"Think you'll be able to get her all the way up those?" Priya asks Amy, staring up into the long, darkened flight of stairs.

"I'm good, boo," Amy says, setting a foot on the first step, allowing Krishna leverage to hop up.

"I'll spot them," Maria adds, taking position behind Amy and Krishna, bracing her bejeweled hand on their backs.

"Right, well then—Honor, do you want to help me get Janice to the basement while they take her upstairs?"

"Yep, let's do it."

Honor grabs her flashlight from the pack she'd left in the room Gratian was initially in as they return to Janice's death room.

"Wow," Honor murmurs, tiptoeing around the blood. "That's a lot of blood."

"Yeah," Priya replies. "Alright, you grab her ankles, and I'll grab her wrists. We'll just drag her."

Honor nods and moves into position. Priya grabs hold of her wrists and Honor her feet, and they toddle her through the room, tracking bloody footprints into the hall.

The weight of the dead body strains Priya's shoulders as she waddles backward, glancing over her shoulder for the basement door.

Her muscles are screaming by the time they arrive, and she drops Janice with a heavy thud.

"Do you remember what the boys said about where they left the key?" she asks, catching her breath.

Honor drops her feet. "They said they left it on top of the fire axe case," she replies, glancing around. "There," she says, pointing to the far wall.

Priya shoots over, feeling around on top of the case. Cold metal presses into her hand, and she scoops it up, returning to the door.

It opens with a click, and she shoves it open.

An even deeper dark yawns before them—the kind of dark death dies in.

"We probably shouldn't go down there unarmed," Priya says, remembering her pole is back in Janice's room.

"I have my .45 on me. You grab that axe."

"Good call."

Priya grabs the axe and sticks the handle down the back of her pants to free her hands. She grabs Janice's wrists while Honor flicks on her flashlight and holds it between her teeth as Priya carefully backs down the steps.

Even though Janice is a twig—maybe a hundred pounds soaking weight—dead weight is still heavy, and the dark, narrow staircase isn't helping.

Priya feels the weight worsening by the middle of the stairs. Maneuvering backward is becoming a strain.

When they reach the landing, Priya pulls with all her might to help Honor the rest of the way down. As Honor arrives, she lets go of the feet with a thud and leans against the wall, her chest heaving.

Priya drops Janice's wrists, and her head slams against the concrete.

Honor pulls the flashlight from her mouth.

Priya grimaces, closing Janice's milky-white eyes, her face frozen in a snarl. "Do we just leave her here, or..."

"I wonder where they put Dr. Mercer?" Honor says, shining the beam down the dark corridor.

"I don't know," Priya replies, shoving herself upright. She pulls the axe from her back, readying it in front of her.

The room before them is a wide-open entryway, with three hallways branching off in different directions. Most of the doors lead to storage, but as Priya steps into one hallway, a sinister feeling creeps over her.

Beyond the main entry, rooms filled with beds and bolted chains stretch before them. Shackles hang from metal loops, and empty saline bags, stained with mold, litter the floors. Cannulas are scattered about. One room houses Dr. Mercer's body, the flashlight casting shadows over his gnawed remains.

"What the hell happened down here?" Honor asks, gripping her .45 beside the flashlight.

"I have no idea," Priya replies, cautiously raising her axe.

Each room is darker, more disturbing than the last, filled with remnants of something unnatural. At the end of a long hallway, they find an office with a metal desk covered in papers, journals, and notebooks. A whiteboard looms behind it, listing names like:

Patient A, Patient B—all the way to Patient Z and beyond.

Priya picks up a journal. The scrawled notes are hard to read, but as she flips through, the pieces start falling into place.

And then, terror grips her.

Honor, sifting through another notebook, suddenly sinks into a chair. "Oh my God," she breathes.

"So this was all for 'Purifying' the Ronas?" Priya asks.

"That's what it looks like," Honor says, her voice tight.

"Then what happened to him? How did he end up dead?"

"Maybe one of them killed him."

They keep flipping through the journals until Priya finds something chilling.

"Look at this," she says. "Someone named Charlie took over after Mercer."

"What does it say?"

Priya squints at the spidery handwriting:

Dr. Mercer thought he could control them. He thought Purification was possible. I told him it wasn't. You can't cleanse what's already rotten. You can only change it... or let it consume you.

Honor tightens her grip on the notebook. "Change it?" she echoes, thumbing through more pages. "Oh my God, listen to this entry from Dr. Mercer:

The injections slowed the transformation at first, but then... something else happened. They started adapting. Thinking. Remembering. It wasn't just instinct anymore. It was something worse. Something aware."

A chill ripples through Priya. "He was experimenting on the Ronas," she murmurs. "But instead of curing them... he made them evolve."

Honor exhales sharply. "This goes deeper than we thought. And if any of these things are still down here—"

Priya interrupts, scanning another entry. "This one's from Charlie:

Today I killed Dr. Mercer. It felt wonderful, exhilarating. I have returned to my full self, yet the hunger remains. The most peculiar thing happened too. When I consumed his brain, his thoughts became mine. Memories that weren't my own flooded my mind, along with the brilliance of his discovery. By giving the Ronas chemo and puréed food, we return to life. However, while we regain human form, the hunger remains. But now, disguised as humans once more, we can blend in, gain trust... and strike. With his patients, I can create more. Now that his knowledge is mine, I can build an army of Purified. I am unstoppable."

She looks up. "That's where the first entry stops."

Honor's face is pale. "When was it dated?"

"Five years ago."

"So these things could be everywhere? Living among us?"

"That has to be who killed Janice."

"But who?" Priya mutters, flipping through the pages for more clues.

"There must be a way to tell who's been 'Purified,'" Honor says, air-quoting the word.

Priya's eyes widen. "Look at this—after Patient Z, he starts over: A2, B2... A3. He writes that the Purified have patches of new skin covering decayed flesh. One woman, Patient G6, had scars where she'd lost all hope of regrowing skin. Another, Patient D4, had a sunken chest from collapsed lungs—but after transformation, only a slight dip remained."

"This is fascinating," Honor whispers.

"Or horrifying," Priya counters. "This explains who's been killing people at the hotel, who hacked off your husband's hand, who ate Janice. But it doesn't tell us who in our group is one of them."

"My bet's on Tesslyn and her gang. They were the ones trying to lure us to the jail."

"If that's true, they're off with Pacious, Jesse, and the others. God knows what they're doing to them."

"And Sariah," Priya realizes. "Do we have time to stop them?"

"I can't leave Gratian," Honor says. "But Baxter's out there, supposedly scouting. We could question him."

Priya shakes her head. "Not safe. He's huge, he could overpower us. What if we drug him? Shackle him to one of these beds?"

Honor nods. "There are plenty of meds in the pharmacy. We could crush some into his food."

"That might work," Priya says, setting down the journal. "But it won't help Tesslyn's victims."

"Pacious, Shamus, and Jesse are strong. Sariah too. There are more normal people than Purified with them. Hopefully, they figure it out before it's too late."

A wet, unnatural noise echoes from the dark corridor.

Priya grips her axe.

"We're not alone down here."

19

LIAM

PRIYA

Priya's heart pounds in her ears as she stalks into the dark hallway, Honor behind her, shining the light down the different corridors.

The silence arrows through her shaky nerves, somehow heightening the ringing in them.

She concentrates on her breathing as she moves like the shadows, toward where the noise came from.

In. Then out.

In.

Then out.

Honor's breath behind her comforts her, but also solidifies the danger; the .45 points in every direction the yellow beam travels.

The pale yellow light illuminates the dark stone, even darker cells, until they reach the end.

Nothing.

"What—" Priya whispers.

A loud crashing sound.

Honor is running and Priya is following, the ground beneath her boots slapping with every step, chasing the noise instead of running from it.

This is what her life's become.

Honor fires a shot. The explosion of the bullet echoes through the stone dungeon, and Priya covers her ears as she dives under a metal desk.

Ragged breathing steeps her fear as she listens to the silence again.

"Hhh-hhello?" a small voice calls.

Honor's flashlight tracks over to the cell the voice came from. "Who's there?"

"I'm Liam," says the voice. It's high-pitched and tinny, but not like a child's.

Like a very scared and traumatized human being.

"Liam, are you armed? Bitten?" Honor shouts toward the distant cell.

It's in the corner—more like a cage than a cell.

Honor's light intensifies, and Priya sees it in full.

A dog kennel.

"I'm immune," Liam states, his voice shaky. "Who are you?"

"Immune?" Honor asks, stepping from the shadows. "What do you mean, immune?"

"Are you a Reset?"

The word, familiar in normal terms, but in this one muddles in Priya's brain. "Reset?"

The girls approach the kennel slowly, a shape of a very thin man taking form.

"Yeah. That's what the Redeemer called them."

"The Redeemer?"

A rustling. Wires clanging. Liam backs into a corner as they reach his cage.

Skin and bones. His legs curled to his chest, knobby knees dirty, bruised, and broken. A loose white muscle shirt, stained to brown, hangs on him, with similarly filthy shorts. Tube socks up to his knees. But it's his skeletal appearance that steals Priya's breath.

"Are you... one... of them?" he asks again, pure terror in his dark, saucer-like eyes.

Honor puts her gun in her waistband and kneels beside the cage, searching for the latch. "No. We're not."

She pops the door open and backs up.

Priya remains still as Liam hesitates.

"I can't."

"Can't what?" Honor chides. "Can't leave your cage? How are you not dead if you're not one of them?"

"I—I don't know. I'm immune to CoRona, but when the Redeemer did his experiments on me, I think I died. But I'm not a Rona. Not a Reset."

"What are you, then?"

"A fucking human," Liam spits.

Honor shines the light inside.

Amidst the dirty blankets is Liam's skeletal frame, his ankles and knees bent at unnatural angles.

"You can't walk?" Honor says, the realization hitting her— her own son likely flooding her mind.

His bony arms had been hugging his legs to his chest, but now he releases his grip, letting his legs part a little.

"I *can* walk! I just can't without my braces. That's why they left me. Now tell me about you. Who the fuck are you?"

Honor looks to Priya, and Priya nods.

We can trust him, she says with her eyes.

Priya can feel it.

"We're safe. We're traveling, looking for insulin for Honor's son. He's disabled too."

Liam's tension relaxes further. "He is?"

"Yes," Honor says softly, her motherly tone creeping into the darkness. "Let's get you out of this cage and upstairs with the rest of us. You need water and food."

Liam hesitates, still leery. "You'll need to carry me," he admits, a tinge of embarrassment in his voice.

"We can do that," Priya offers.

They'd just hauled Janice down here, and he looks about the same weight—maybe less.

Liam nods.

He gets on his hands and knees and crawls out of the cage.

***

It's more difficult than she'd imagined.

Because Liam had been in the cage so long, contractures have formed in his limbs—he can't straighten his legs or his arms.

Honor ends up doing all the heavy lifting, carrying him like a groom carries a bride across the threshold.

Priya grabs as many notebooks as she can on their way out of the dungeon.

The people upstairs are going to be blown away by everything they've just discovered.

When Priya, followed by Honor and Liam, bursts back into the apartment, a collection of reactions flashes over the faces of those present.

"What the…"

"Who the fuck…"

"How the…"

Liam flinches at the sudden noise, pressing his gaunt frame tighter against Honor, his fingers twitching in the fabric of her shirt. His breath is shallow, as if every new sight and sound is too much.

"Please," Priya says as Honor carries Liam toward the bathroom, "he's been through so much. He needs to soak in a bath for a while."

Liam's ratty hair is pressed against Honor's neck, his eyes squinting shut as the bright fluorescence likely stings. His skeletal fingers twitch once before going still. She disappears into the hallway while Priya addresses the others.

"We found him down there. He hadn't made a sound," she says, hauling all the books and journals to the kitchen island and spreading them out. "But there's more than that."

Amy steps closer and glances at the papers. "What's this?"

"This," Priya explains, settling onto a barstool, "is our worst nightmare come true."

***

Hot tea steeps in mugs steaming on the counter, wafting in lazy circles as the sounds of pages turning mingle with the drafty apartment breeze.

"I don't get it," Krishna says, flipping through the journals, squinting as she tries to wrap her brain around Liam and the mad doctor's notes. Or fully grasp the horror.

"How?" Maria asks, opening a musty, stale box of crackers. "How did he survive that long down there?"

"Right?" Krishna agrees, her red hair falling onto one of the pages. "The last of the entries ended, what, a year and a half ago? So that means he's been down there that long."

Priya, turning a journal in her hands, looks up at Krishna through the tea's steam. "Yes. The most recent one we found."

Honor, returning from the bathroom, picks up a thick black book.

Liam's absence is noticeable now. The silence where his frail breaths had been. The distant sound of water running.

"He definitely has a story to tell," Honor says, pouring water into a mug preloaded with a tea bag.

"I wonder what happened. Where they went. Why they left..." Krishna babbles, picking up a blue journal and flipping through its pages.

"Or how many of these Purified are out there in the world right now," Priya adds, setting her book aside and grabbing her tea, leaning back into the hard wood of the barstool.

Maria, a look of utter bewilderment plastered across her face, flips through some of the loose papers strewn across the faux marble countertop. "And you think Tesslyn is one of those Resets, like Liam called them?"

"That's the only logical explanation," Honor says, sitting next to Priya. "We met them out on the road near the jail. They were very adamant we go back with them, but when I protested because of Gratian's condition and mentioned we had more people, she changed her tune. She had to come with us. Dumbass Lux, smitten by her big boobs—he's always been a tit man—agreed to let them come. I was too distraught over Gratian to protest. Anything to get us moving again."

"She's also the one who was down there with Janice the most," Priya adds, sipping her tea.

Jesus, rummaging through the cabinets for a snack—teenagers—asks, "So you think there's a colony of them at the jail, luring people in and eating them?"

Priya shudders. "I bet that's exactly where they are. What better place than to lure a bunch of regular folks, lock them up in cells, and eat them bit by bit? What unimaginable pain those poor people must be in."

From the bathroom: a faint noise. Water sloshing. A muffled cough. A reminder that Liam is real. That they pulled him from that nightmare.

Amy moves to the kettle whistling on the stove and removes it from the burner, pouring herself a fresh cup. "And then what? After we drug Baxter?" she asks, steeping her tea. "Drag him in here, question him... and then what? Go save the people at the jail?"

"No," Honor responds.

Priya shoots her a questioning look.

"I have Gratian to look after," Honor explains. "I don't have Lux to protect us anymore. I have to get to Denver—be where the insulin is. I don't have time to save the world."

"Do you really think getting that large, dangerous man back in here is the best idea?" Maria asks skeptically.

"Better to have him chained up in here than out there, finding his own way in and killing us all," Amy adds.

"This is true," Maria concedes. "And if we have him in here and lock him up, when the others come back, we'll have some leverage."

"That is, if they don't kill our people first," Krishna adds grimly.

"I don't think those two women will overpower Jesse, Pash, Shamus, Sariah, Michael, and Antonio," Priya says. "And whatever concoction we whip up for Baxter, we can pre-make some for Jessica and Tesslyn too."

"What are we going to drug him with?" Maria asks.

"We could use the fentanyl Janice was on," Honor says.

"Or Diladud," Krishna offers. "It's more powerful than fentanyl."

"Alright," Priya says, standing. "I'll work on the food. Honor, if you want to grab whatever you think will knock out a six-foot-five, 250-pound man..."

"Okay," Honor replies, rising.

"I'm going to go read through the doctor's notes," Krishna adds, nodding toward the desk and whiteboard in the corner. "See if there's anything else in them that can help."

20

THE LOST TIME

PRIYA

By the time Liam begins to talk, the tea on the table has gone lukewarm.

He's bundled in clean, oversized clothes, a blanket around his shoulders, and propped up with pillows on the couch. Honor sits cross-legged on the floor beside him, close enough that their shoulders brush whenever he shifts. The others have gathered nearby in varying degrees of casual curiosity—Priya perched on the arm of a chair, Maria curled into one corner, Krishna thumbing absently through a book she's not reading.

They've been talking for a while. Nothing heavy. Just the sort of light, meandering conversation that happens when no one wants to push, but everyone is waiting for something.

Eventually, Liam sets his untouched tea back down and exhales.

"I was lured here by a handsome man," he says, like it's the start of a joke. "He promised me a colony of survivors holed up in a medical facility. Running water, heat, food... the works."

Maria arches a brow but says nothing.

"I fell for it. For his schoolboy charm and soft eyes." He

shakes his head, almost smiling. "What I really walked into was a nightmare."

Liam shudders at the memory. Priya and Honor sit close to him, Honor grabbing his hand.

"The Redeemer's name is Charlie, but we weren't allowed to call him that. He's got an ego, that one. But a genius nonetheless. However he got his genius is foul, though—it's hard to think of him as anything but a monster."

"He consumed Dr. Mercer's brain, right?" Honor asks.

"Yes."

"However gruesome that is, it's still miraculous in a morbid way," Krishna agrees.

"Absolutely. He basically had a concentration camp set up. He had people for food and people for experimentation. Since I've always been skinny, I wasn't their first choice for food, so he thought killing me and turning me into a Rona would be their best bet. He likes Resets to look vulnerable, people survivors would most likely take in. He tried killing me multiple times, trying to turn me into a Reset, but something in my physiology —possibly tied to my disability—caused the process to fail. Instead of dying or transforming, my body entered a near-suspended state, drastically reducing my need for food, water, or even oxygen.

"It made me uniquely resistant to Charlie's methods. Possibly even immune to the virus."

Honor shifts. "Interesting. And what's your disability, if you don't mind my asking?"

He shakes his head. "Not at all. It's something I've learned to be proud of. I have amyoplasia arthogryposis, a really rare disease that causes curved or reduced muscle mass.

"See?" he says, shoving his bony arm out from under the towel-like blanket. Instead of the limb going out straight, it curves to the right.

"I underwent the Ponseti method to correct it as a

newborn," he says, pulling his arm back in, "which untwists the joints slightly, casts them, then repeats the process until fully corrected. Then a surgery with an Achilles tendon to release and promote mobility.

"My ankles are permanently fixed, so I'll forever have flat feet and wear leg braces to keep them from re-clubbing. My knees dislocate randomly, which is incredibly painful, and I can't lift my arms over my head. Lifting heavy things is virtually impossible. When I was a kid, my bones would break easily. I broke my arm falling on carpet.

"The worst part was being able-passing before CoRona. People didn't realize I was disabled at first, which is how I got lured here. They don't think anything is different at first glance, and when they do, they don't understand why I do things differently. Even my mom didn't. When my knees were dislocating, I'd push them back in myself instantly, so even though I was screaming on the ground in pain and telling her they'd dislocated, I'd always be told to stop being so dramatic. My entire family would make fun of me for limping around on a freshly dislocated knee. It took six years for my mom to be present when it happened. I sat on my hands to stop myself from pushing it back in, told her to take one look at my knee and tell me it wasn't dislocated—and she finally took me to the hospital. They did an MRI. I have permanent damage in the tendons around my knees because no one believed me for so long.

"Which is why the Redeemer left me. I had dislocated a knee and wasn't allowed to put it back into place. They shoved me into the cage."

"And why did they all leave you here? Where did they go?" Amy asks.

"This place was getting too small for them."

"And why was there all this food leftover?"

"Because they didn't eat people food. Even the prisoners,

who were only kept for feeding the Resets, were fed the puréed vegetables. He kept a massive garden out back."

"So Charlie's experiment could've inadvertently made you a disruptor to the Reset virus," Priya states.

"Immune to even the original virus," Krishna adds.

Honor leans back. "So you could potentially figure out which ones are Resets, or as we call them, Purified, and which ones aren't?"

He nods solemnly. "Possibly. I wasn't here for very long—maybe a week or two. I ended up in that cage a month or so ago."

"A month ago?" Priya asks, confused.

"Yeah. It has to have only been a month," he states, his eyes colliding with Priya's.

Honor shakes her head. "No, Liam. You were in that kennel for a year and half."

His eyes widen in shock "What?"

Priya runs to the kitchen, grabs the last journal with the most recent date, and shoves it at him.

He slips his arms out of the towel and holds it, flipping to the last page.

Liam's hands tremble as he grips the journal, his breath coming in sharp gasps.

"No. That's impossible," he whispers. "I would know."

The silence in the room is deafening. No one knows what to say.

Because if Liam doesn't remember a year and a half passing...

What the hell happened to him?

21

POISON

PRIYA

The savory aroma of simmering herbs and slow-cooked meat fills the air as Priya stirs the large pot of stew, the wooden spoon scraping softly against the cast-iron bottom. Wisps of steam curl around her face, warming her cheeks. She hums under her breath, lost in the rhythmic motion, when a shadow shifts beside her.

"Priya."

She turns to find Honor standing close, her fingers curled tightly around a small glass vial. The liquid inside glows faintly, swirling as if alive.

Priya arches a brow, wiping her hands on her apron. "What's that?"

Honor hesitates, glancing over her shoulder before leaning in. "Something that might make this stew a little more... interesting," she says, a sly smile tugging at her lips.

Priya eyes the vial warily. "Define interesting."

Honor merely smirks, tipping the vial slightly so the liquid catches the light, flickering between deep crimson and molten gold.

"Trust me," she murmurs. "It'll be worth it."

She unscrews the top and watches as the liquid coats the glass like syrup before glancing back at Priya. "I found Polymetaline. It's one of the chemo drugs they used to give me. It always made me so sleepy, and I was thinking... if we mixed this with some morphine, it would probably get him nice and catatonic. Enough to keep him sedated—won't kill him, but it'll make sure we can get him in and tie him up."

Priya exhales through her nose, thoughtful. "Good call." She taps the wooden spoon against the rim of the pot, then holds out her hand. "Let me get this portioned out so we have one batch of drugged stew and one batch of edible stuff. You know, so we can eat too."

Honor grins. "Smart thinking." She tucks the empty vial into her pocket and takes a step back. "I'm gonna go check on G. I'll be right back."

As Honor slips away, Priya finishes adding the final ingredients to the stew, stirring in slow, deliberate motions. Her mind races as she scours the cabinets, searching for containers to separate the portions. The plan was set. Now, all they had to do was hope it worked.

Finding two large containers, she takes the one with the black lid, pours the stew into it, and then dumps the contents of both vials inside. In the other one, the one with the neon green lid, she simply adds the stew and closes the lid.

"Alright," she says to the group in the living room, "the soup in the black container is bad. Just remember that. The stuff in the container with the bright green lid is good."

"Got that, Jesus?" Maria says to her son. "Don't eat the stuff with the black lid."

"Got it, Mom," he says, agitated.

Liam, stretched out on one of the couches with blankets piled on him, merely sniggers at the mother-son interaction.

"Honor, ready to do this?" Priya asks, ladling the thick stew into a bowl.

Honor exhales sharply. "Better do it now while I have my nerve."

She grips the canister of poisoned soup like it's scalding, her fingers tense around the edges as she carefully makes her way down the stairs. Priya follows close behind.

At the door, they hesitate. Honor cracks it open just enough to peek outside. "Alright. Coast is clear—at least out front."

Priya nods, unholstering her .45 and readying it in front of her as they step into the daylight. The wind tugs at their clothes, and the empty space around them feels unsettlingly vast. No Ronas in sight. The hunting party must have done its job, drawing them away. Still, every step toward the back of the building feels heavy, each breath measured.

"Where do you think he's camping out?" Priya murmurs.

Honor points past a row of storage sheds. "There. His tent."

As they approach, a bald head peeks out from the tent flap. Baxter watches them for a second before stepping out, stretching his broad shoulders.

"We brought you some soup," Priya calls as they reach him, offering the bowl.

Baxter grins, wiping his hands on his pants. "That's mighty nice of you, ma'am." He takes the bowl, glancing around before tilting his head toward the compound. "No sign of Ronas for miles. The hunting party did good coaxin' 'em away. Y'all are safe—for now."

His voice carries a weight, a quiet warning they can't quite decipher. Does he suspect something? Or is he talking about the danger still lurking out there?

"Well, enjoy your soup," Priya says smoothly. "Let us know if you need anything else."

Baxter gives a small nod before retreating into his tent.

Without a word, Honor and Priya turn on their heels and head back toward the building, their pace quicker now. Once inside, Honor exhales, pressing her back against the door.

"How long should we wait to check on him?" she asks.

Priya thinks for a moment. "Let's give it a good while. We don't want to look suspicious."

They return to the apartment, passing the time sifting through old notes, searching for anything new. The minutes drag.

"I think it's been long enough," Krishna says from the couch, her injured knee propped up on the coffee table.

"Alright," Honor says, standing. "Who's coming to help drag him in?"

"We can help," Maria offers, nodding toward Jesus.

Amy cracks her knuckles. "You got me too—"

A sudden bang echoes from downstairs, followed by the frantic thud of footsteps racing up.

The room stills. The air thickens. Hands inch toward weapons.

Jesse is the first to emerge, and a collective sigh of relief ripples through the group. Honor rushes forward, visibly eager to see Jesse again.

"You're back early," she murmurs.

But Jesse's face is hardened. Agitated. He steps aside.

Honor's expression mirrors Jesse's as Michael and Pacious enter, supporting a familiar figure between them.

Her husband.

Pale. Weak. Barely able to hold himself up.

And suddenly, everything feels colder.

22

MONSTERS WITHIN

PRIYA

Lux looks absolutely worse for wear. His left hand is missing, wrapped tightly in a filthy flannel he cradles against his chest. His left eye is swollen shut, his lip split and bleeding, and scratches mar his skin.

"Oh my God, Lux!" Honor gasps, breath rushing from her as she hurries toward him.

He only glowers at her, limping past with Michael still supporting most of his weight.

Honor's face falls, her shoulders curling inward. If her dark skin could flush, it would. Instead, she presses herself against the wall, slipping through the crowd to disappear into the background.

Across the room, Priya's pulse stumbles when she spots Sariah. The second those brownish-green eyes lock onto hers, she has to fight the urge to close the distance and kiss her. They're still... a situationship. New. Undefined.

Sariah, freshly returned from battle, sets her swords down with a metallic clink. Then, with a slow, deliberate stride, she closes the space between them.

"Miss me?" she murmurs, her voice low enough that only

Priya can hear. Before Priya can answer, Sariah reaches up, brushes her fingers along the collar of Priya's shirt, and flicks it. "You always this wrinkled, or do I make you nervous?"

Priya exhales a soft laugh, shaking her head. "You're insufferable."

"And you're adorable when you're flustered." Sariah grins, then winks before stepping away like nothing happened.

Across the room, Tesslyn drops her weapon onto the counter and yanks open the fridge. "Anyone got food? I'm starving."

"Just don't eat anything with a black container top!" Honor calls over, brows furrowing. It's odd—that's exactly what Tesslyn seems to be reaching for.

They hadn't even been gone a full day.

"What happened?" Priya asks Sariah as she slithers onto one of the barstools, pouring herself a glass of water from the crystal pitcher. "You weren't gone very long."

Sariah slams back the water in a few loud gulps, wiping her mouth with the back of her hand. Priya wordlessly pours her another glass, and Sariah takes it with a nod of thanks.

"Yeah, we made it to the Fossil Creek area," Sariah starts, her voice still rough from thirst. "Jesse and Pash were following a trail of blood when we spotted an antelope. Jesse got a clean shot with his bow, and we were getting ready to dress it when Michael saw something—boots he recognized, sticking out from a bush near the marshlands." She pauses, her eyes darkening. "Lo and behold, it was Lux. He was dazed, confused... didn't even seem to know what had happened. He doesn't remember the argument with them."

Priya frowns, sliding onto the barstool next to her. "That's... odd. I wonder what that's all about."

Sariah leans in slightly, lowering her voice to a whisper. "That's not even the strangest part, Priya." She swallows. "He was eating... *Someone*."

Priya stiffens.

"There were... pieces," Sariah continues, her voice barely above a breath. "All around him. And he was just... passed out."

Priya's eyes widen. She covers her mouth with her hand. "Do you mean... he's a Rona?"

Now isn't the time to get into the whole story—the doctor's notes, what they discovered. But could Lux really be one of the Purified?

How?

When?

"I don't know, Priya. It's the damndest thing. He doesn't look anything like them. Jesse and I were talking on the way back, and we were thinking... maybe he bled out after losing his hand. But wouldn't his eyes be white? Wouldn't his mind be gone?"

"Right?"

"And when Michael ran up to him, he seemed completely unaware of the body parts around him—like he had no idea what they were doing there. He's been dazed and confused ever since."

Priya's gaze drifts to Lux, lying on the couch. Michael and Nikki crouch in front of him, speaking in hushed tones, while Honor stands against the wall, watching.

"I have to tell Honor," she whispers to Sariah. "She needs to keep Gratian safe."

Sariah nods. Priya rises and slowly makes her way to Honor, leaning in close.

"We need to talk," she murmurs in her ear.

Honor catches the gravity in Priya's expression and nods, following her out of the apartment and down the dim stairwell.

Once inside one of the patient rooms, Priya slides the door closed.

"What's up?" Honor asks.

Priya doesn't waste time. "Honor, I think Lux is one of those monsters."

Honor blinks, the weight of the words sinking in. She processes it the same way Priya has—wrapping her mind around a thought that refuses to fully take shape.

"What? How?"

"I have no idea. Sariah said when they found him, he was unconscious, surrounded by body parts. He claims he doesn't remember anything. He doesn't even recall arguing with the boys or losing his hand."

"But... how? If he doesn't remember, why was he so cold to me when I came in?" Honor frowns.

"And he's been with us the entire time," she continues. "According to those notes, it takes months to turn a Rona into one of those things. How could he have changed so quickly?"

"I don't know," Priya admits. "But we need to keep him away from everyone. We can't trust him."

"How do we do that without alerting everyone? Michael won't let us lock him up."

"First, let's get Baxter in here. If the soup worked on him, we might be able to use it again, maybe he'll have some insight." Priya clasps Honor's hands. "We need answers."

Honor nods solemnly, the gravity of the situation sinking in. "We also need to tell Jesse, Pash, and Shame. They have to know what we found."

"Okay. You stay down here. I'll send them to you. I need to be with my son. I don't trust Lux anywhere near him."

Priya nods, and as Honor leaves, silence creeps in, filling the room with an eerie, suffocating dread.

A few minutes later, Pacious, Jesse, and Shamus enter, shutting the door behind them.

"Hey, what's up? You good?" Jesse asks.

"No," Priya replies honestly. "We have a problem."

She explains everything—Janice, the discovery, the suspicions about Lux, and how they poisoned Baxter, who is likely passed out in his tent right now.

"So you think Lux is one of them?" Jesse asks.

"We're not sure. But if it takes months to create one, we don't see how this is possible. And yet... there's no other explanation."

"I don't know the guy," Jesse says, "but when we found him —just lying there, surrounded by body parts, acting clueless— it didn't sit right. What do we do?"

"Honor and I think we should use the same concoction we used on Baxter, if it worked, to drug Michael and Lux, then restrain them. There are enough beds with shackles down there."

"Can do," Jesse agrees.

"First, we need to get Baxter in here before Michael or the others realize he's drugged."

"Tesslyn was acting weird the whole way to the marsh," Pacious adds. "Not that I know her well, but man... something was off."

"How so?" Priya asks.

Pacious glances down at his boots, as if the answer might be written there. "She reminded me of Janice."

"In what way?"

"Whiny. Complaining about absolutely everything. Negative comments. Even her mannerisms. It's hard to explain, but yeah... like Janice."

"That's enough for me," Priya says. "Okay, we need enough 'soup' to knock out Lux, Tesslyn, and Jessica. What about Michael?"

"I'm not worried about him," Shamus says. "We can take him if we have to. Amy can distract him before dinner while we handle the rest."

"Sounds like a plan." Priya stands. "Now, let's move Baxter before the drugs wear off."

"On it," Jesse says, cracking the door open. He pauses, his eyes narrowing. "Oh yeah, by the way, who the fuck is that skinny kid up there? I almost didn't even realize it was a person under all those blankets."

"Oh," Priya says, brushing her hair back. "Yeah, that's Liam. Long story, but he's a good guy. He may have information to help us as well."

Jesse wrinkles the bridge of his nose. "You sure?"

Priya holds his gaze. "I'm sure. C'mon. Let's go."

The four of them move toward the tent, scanning the darkness for any lurking Ronas. The cold air is thick with rot, the only sound their careful footsteps.

Jesse crouches near the entrance, tilting his head. Inside, someone breathes—ragged, uneven. He unzips the flap an inch, peering in. The heat hits them first, thick and humid, like stepping into a sauna. A small, battery-operated space heater hums in the corner, its orange glow casting flickering shadows across the crumpled tent walls.

Baxter lies sprawled on his sleeping bag, one arm draped over his stomach. A newspaper, its pages creased and smudged, rests on his chest, as if he'd fallen asleep reading. An overturned bowl of soup lies beside him, the broth seeping into the fabric, mixing with dirt and the scent of stale sweat. Scattered around him are a few ration wrappers, a half-empty water bottle, and his weapons—two knives and a battered handgun—lined up within arm's reach.

Jesse inches the flap open a little more. "Alright, he's out cold. Let's move."

Pacious and Shamus step inside first, carefully navigating the mess. They grip Baxter's wrists while Priya and Jesse take his ankles. His body is limp, his breathing slow and steady. But as they lift him, his head lolls to the side, lips parting in a soft groan.

The group freezes.

A long second passes.

The heater hums.

A droplet of condensation slides down the tent wall.

Then—nothing.

His breathing evens out again.

Moving quickly but cautiously, they haul him back to the compound, straining under his dead weight. Once inside, they descend into the basement, the cold stone walls pressing in around them.

Priya and Jesse secure Baxter's arms and legs into the shackles bolted to the ground. Jesse tightens the last restraint with a sharp click.

Then—

"What the hell are you guys doing?"

They freeze.

A shadow moves in the doorway.

Turning, they find themselves face-to-face with Tesslyn and Jessica.

Jessica's arms are crossed, her eyes flicking from Baxter to Jesse. Tesslyn's hand hovers near her knife, lips pressed into a thin line.

No one speaks.

Priya's heart pounds.

Shit.

23

BLOOD AND BETRAYAL
HONOR

The warmth radiating from Gratian seeps into Honor's side as she strokes his hair, waiting for the ketone glucometer to register.

5. 4. 3. 2. 1.

Beep.

3.4.

Okay. His ketones are coming down.

Relief washes over her, loosening the tension coiled in her muscles. She shoves the meter back into the pokey pack, discarding the strip somewhere inside.

She'll clean it out later.

Gratian stirs as she pulls the covers up around his shoulders. Her gaze drifts to Lux, sprawled on the couch, snoring loudly. The sound doesn't seem to bother Michael and Amy, who are speaking quietly with Liam on the other couch.

Honor is about to shift Gratian off her lap when the sudden scrape of barstool legs against the floor startles her.

Sariah bolts toward the bathroom, one hand clamped over her mouth. The door slams shut, followed by the unmistakable sound of retching.

Must've eaten something bad.

Gratian's breathing is leveling out, the fever breaking little by little. Honor brushes his hair off his damp forehead and exhales, the tension still lingering but softer now.

After some time, Sariah reemerges, looking pale and drained. She wipes the corner of her mouth with the hem of her shirt before shuffling toward the counter.

Honor's gaze lingers on her. Sariah's stomach is smooth, untouched by stretch marks, her belly button an in-between of an innie and an outie, like a little button at her navel. But that's not what catches Honor's attention.

A scar, swirling like a burn, stands out in lighter milk-chocolate contrast against the deep mocha of the rest of her skin.

Sariah pulls out a barstool and slumps onto the island, resting her head against the cool surface.

After a few minutes, Honor carefully moves Gratian's head off her lap and walks over. She places a hand on Sariah's back.

"Hey, you okay?"

Sariah lifts her head slightly. "Yeah, I'm alright. Just been feeling a bit off. Probably something I ate." She rubs her temples, then looks at Honor. "Have you seen Priya come back up?"

"No, not yet. She and the boys were talking about what happened with Lux," Honor says, not eager to dwell on the nightmare of monsters lurking among them.

"I should check on her." Sariah shifts forward like she's about to stand.

"No, it's okay. You rest." Honor squeezes her shoulder. "Do me a favor—keep an eye on Gratian while I go check on her?"

"You got it." Sariah nods and gets up, moving over to the bed where Gratian is still sleeping.

Honor turns and heads for the basement. As she descends

the stairs, the air grows colder, the scent of damp stone thick around her. Voices echo from below—angry, heated.

Tesslyn's sharp southern accent cuts through the space.

"Get off me, you psycho!"

Honor quickens her steps, emerging into the dimly lit room just as Jesse and Shamus finish tying Tesslyn to the bed. Her lip is busted, her hair a wild mess from some kind of struggle.

"What's going on?" Honor demands.

Tesslyn's wild eyes lock onto hers.

"Honor! Help!" she screams, thrashing against the restraints. "These psychopaths are trying to detain me for absolutely insane reasons! Tell them! Tell them what they're accusing me of!"

Jesse tightens the last shackle around her ankle, then moves toward Honor, ushering her toward the door.

"WAIT!" Tesslyn shrieks, her voice raw with panic. "Don't you dare leave me in here, you asshole! I'll starve to death! I am STARVING!"

Her screams fade as Jesse closes the door, and they walk toward Dr. Mercer's office with Shamus.

Honor shakes off the unease. "What the hell is going on?"

Shamus exhales. "We were chaining up Baxter when Tesslyn and Jessica ambushed us. We didn't have a choice but to subdue them too. Priya told us what they are. It makes sense now. Tesslyn's been acting strange from the start. She's the one who's been gnawing on Janice. She's acting just like her."

A cold chill slithers down Honor's spine. "And what do you propose we do with them?" she asks, as Priya and Pacious enter the room.

"We chain them up, feed them some of the soup, and wait for Baxter to wake up. If anyone's gonna give us answers, it's him."

Before Honor can reply, a voice rings out from the stairwell, frantic and sharp.

"Honor!"

Panic slams into her chest.

Gratian.

She takes off, heart hammering, her feet barely touching the ground as she races toward the sound.

Sariah meets her halfway, wild-eyed.

"Oh my God, Honor! I—I tried to stop him—I tried—"

"Stop who?!" Honor seizes Sariah's shoulders. "What happened?"

Sariah's breath shudders. "Lux. He's gone mad. He went for Gratian—I couldn't stop him—I'm so sorry!"

Honor doesn't wait for more. She shoves past her, sprinting up the stairs.

Jesse is right behind her, his face twisted in fury.

When they burst into the apartment, chaos greets them.

Lux is pinned to the ground beneath Michael's knee, thrashing violently. Maria cowers in the corner with Jesus, their eyes wide with terror. Juan, Antonio, and Amy are helping Michael hold Lux down.

And Krishna—

Krishna is on the bed, cradling Gratian in her lap.

A white pillowcase is pressed to his tiny arm, the fabric soaked through with deep crimson.

Honor's knees give out. She collapses beside them, hands trembling as she strokes her son's ashen face. He doesn't stir, but he's breathing.

"My baby," she whispers, her voice cracking.

A numb, icy void consumes her.

Lux attacked her son.

Her husband, the man she once loved—

She will kill him.

Honor kisses Gratian's forehead, then rises, her movements slow and deliberate. She crosses the room to the counter, where a .45 rests. She picks it up, chambering a round as she turns back toward Lux.

Jesse is already there, pummeling Lux's face, his knuckles bloodied. But Lux—Lux isn't even reacting. His eyes, milky white, stare blankly up at the ceiling. His lips curl, smeared with blood—Gratian's blood.

Jesse steps back as Honor approaches.

The room stills.

Lux meets her gaze. His face is a ruin of blood and bruises, but he's still grinning.

She doesn't hesitate.

She raises the gun, presses the barrel to his forehead—

And pulls the trigger.

The blast shatters the silence.

Lux's head snaps back, his body going limp as blood and brain matter spray the wall behind him.

His lifeless form collapses in a heap.

24

PETECHIAE

HONOR

The ragged breathing sawing in and out of Gratian's little chest has Honor stifling her sobs. She rocks him slowly as he lies unconscious in her lap, the bed, sheets, and his clothes all covered in blood. The old shirt she'd found is pressed against his neck where the bite wound is, saturated with crimson. It's stopped bleeding—for now—but the severity of the bite and what it means is not lost on her.

Strong hands massage her shoulders as she rocks, a mystic sort of comfort in a foggy fucking world. The grim palpability undulating around them constantly seizes Honor's existence, her will to live narrowly edging on the sharp point of a cruel world and a hard death. Tears stream down her face as she focuses on her own breathing, trying only to concentrate on the here.

The now.

The last moments she will have with her son on this earth.

Jesse clears his throat, switching to her other shoulder. "How the fuck did this happen?" he utters.

Normal thoughts are viscous, bending and bleeding and morphing into a language indecipherable. The only thing she can be right now is Gratian's mother, holding him as he inches closer to death.

The IV tube drips into the silence, Lux's brains spattered on the wall spelling out the ending of something.

Whether or not they were a loving, happy couple at the end, he was still part of her story. His chapters were filled with love and laughter at the beginning, more heartache and pain in the middle, and absolute betrayal at the end. But the pages of their story will be dog-eared for the rest of hers—pages she'll revisit and smile upon remembering.

Batting a tear away, Honor tries to focus on the rhythmic dripping of the IV pump, but the hard padding of boots on linoleum pulls her attention. She glances sideways just in time to see Sariah bolting for the bathroom again, her shoulders hunched as if bracing for the next wave of nausea.

Jesse's hands still against Honor's tense shoulders, his fingers digging into the knots he's been working out. His gaze follows Sariah as she disappears down the darkened hallway. "What's up with her?"

"I think she ate something bad," Honor says, though doubt flickers in her voice. The sound of retching echoes down the hall, sharp and wet, cutting through the sterile air.

Silence follows, broken only by muffled coughs and the IV's steady drip. Honor tries to focus on anything else—the way the fluorescent lights hum above them, the worn leather of Jesse's jacket pressing against her back—but worry needles its way in.

The bathroom door creaks open.

Footsteps shuffle.

Sariah emerges, pale and damp, her breaths shallow.

"Are you okay?" Honor asks as she watches her sit heavily on the bed, her elbows braced on her knees.

"I don't know," Sariah admits, rubbing her face. "I feel just awful. I think I may be coming down with something."

She absently lifts her pant leg to scratch at an itch, and

that's when Honor sees them—the red dots scattered across her skin like tiny pinpricks of blood bursting beneath the surface.

"What is that?" Honor asks, leaning forward.

Sariah frowns and pulls her pant leg higher, revealing more of the rash-like spots. "I don't know. They started showing up last week, maybe longer. I figured it was poison oak or something."

Honor's chest tightens. "Sariah, how long have you been feeling fatigued? Like, really exhausted?"

Sariah exhales slowly, sifting through memories. "Same, about a week or two. Why?"

Honor swallows hard. "I think you may have leukemia."

The words land like a punch, sucking the air from the room.

Sariah's face is blank, her lips slightly parted as though the thought refuses to register. "What?"

Honor gently grips her shin, pressing her thumb lightly against one of the dots. "These are called petechiae. It means your blood vessels are breaking open and leaking into your skin. It happens when your blood counts are too high or too low to stop it. You're bleeding internally."

A long silence stretches between them. The air feels heavier, thick with something neither of them can name.

Sariah blinks, her throat working around a response. "But... that doesn't make sense. I mean, I—I just thought I was run-down." Her voice trembles.

"I know. That was my reaction when the doctor told me the same thing," Honor says, her voice softer now, like a thread stretched too thin. "I'm no expert, but based on everything I've seen from you—Sariah, it fits."

Sariah stares at her, searching for a way to make this untrue. "What am I supposed to do with that now?" she whispers. It's not anger—it's fear, raw and real.

"I can help," Honor says immediately. "I remember some of

my treatment regimen. We can go downstairs, hook you up to the machines, get you started on chemo. Krishna was in pharmacology school—she can help with the medicines. We just—" She exhales, steadying herself. "We just have to act fast."

Sariah's gaze flickers toward Gratian, curled up on the couch, oblivious to the weight pressing down on them. Her eyes turn glassy, rimmed with unshed tears. "I'm sorry you have to deal with this after—" She stops, her voice cracking.

"It's not your fault," Honor says, standing. "Honestly, it gives me something to focus on. To process."

Jesse, silent until now, exhales sharply and straightens. "What do you need?"

"Have Pacious or Shamus stay with Gratian," Honor replies, already moving. "I need to find the medicine I had. Krishna can help me set everything up."

Jesse whistles low, motioning Pacious over while Honor strides toward Krishna, still resting her leg on the coffee table. The urgency in her steps makes Krishna sit up straighter, her eyes sharp with understanding.

They don't have time to waste.

Honor swallows hard, her throat dry despite the lingering metallic tang of blood in the air. Someone—probably Michael—has taken Lux's body somewhere, but remnants of him still stain the walls, dark patches of his existence clinging to the floor like ghosts. She refuses to look at them.

Instead, she anchors herself in the present, perching on the table across from Krishna, who shifts her injured leg with a wince.

"I need your help with something," Honor says, her voice quieter than intended.

Krishna lifts her head, weary but attentive. "Sure, love. Anything. What's up?"

Honor exhales. "I think Sariah has leukemia. I need to start her on chemo, but I need your help mixing the chemo."

Krishna's brows furrow, but she nods without hesitation. "Of course."

Jesse steps forward, already offering Krishna an arm. "Come on, I'll help you downstairs."

They move together, Honor shadowing them, her pulse quickening as they descend toward the center's medicine stockpile. At the landing, the door ahead creaks open, and Priya steps out, brushing dust from her sleeves.

She stops short, her eyes flicking between them. "What are you all up to?"

"We need to talk," Sariah says from behind them, her voice steadier than Honor expected.

Priya hesitates, then nods. "Alright."

Honor watches the two step aside before following Krishna and Jesse into the medicine room, the stale air thick with antiseptic and decay.

Krishna exhales sharply, scanning the rows of glass vials and IV bags. "Do you remember exactly what kind of chemo you had?"

Honor doesn't hesitate. "Vincristine, Cisplatin, Cytarabine, Methotrexate. And there was a daily pill—6MP."

Krishna hums as she shifts on her feet, reaching for a worn cardboard box. "They weren't all at once, right? You cycled through them?"

"Right, one each week," Honor confirms, picking through a row of vials, checking labels. "But we don't have that kind of time. If we wait, the cancer could progress too fast. I'm thinking we hit her hard—one today, one tomorrow, and so on."

Jesse stiffens beside her, arms crossed. "That doesn't sound safe."

Honor glances up, jaw tight. "Neither is doing nothing."

Silence. Jesse presses his lips together but doesn't argue further. He turns, rifling through a crate before pulling out a saline bag. "Alright," he mutters, setting it on the counter. "Let's do this."

They work in silence, gathering the necessary supplies before heading back out. The moment they step out of the room, Honor sees Priya wrapped around Sariah, silent sobs shaking her shoulders. Sariah rubs her back, her own expression carefully composed, though a flicker of fear lingers behind her eyes.

"It's gonna be okay," Sariah murmurs, her voice a thread of steel. "I'm in good hands." She pulls back just enough to meet Priya's gaze. "You might just have to help me shave my head when the time comes, yeah?"

Priya swipes at her tears, nodding. "Yeah."

Krishna exhales. "Alright, let's get you hooked up."

They move toward the room with the chemo chairs, the old leather creaking as Sariah sinks into one. She adjusts, shifting uncomfortably.

"So," she says as Krishna preps the IV, "anyone figure out what's up with these Ronas?"

The room tenses. Krishna's gaze flicks to Honor, who glances at Priya, then Jesse. No one speaks at first, each waiting for the other to step up.

Finally, Priya sighs. "It's... complicated."

As she starts explaining what they found in the office—about Lux, about the disturbing truth lurking beneath their feet—Honor forces herself to keep breathing, to not get lost in the grief pressing against her ribs.

Sariah listens, her face unreadable until Priya finishes. Then, slowly, she shakes her head. "But how? How could Lux have been one of them?"

Honor swallows hard. "We don't know."

Priya shifts her weight. "We were thinking of drugging Baxter and getting him to talk. Since we're pretty sure he, Tesslyn, and Jessica were trying to lure us into a trap, it makes sense that they'd know more. We managed to chain Baxter up in the basement, and when those two Purified girls showed up looking for a fight, we locked them up too."

Sariah raises an eyebrow. "So that's what happened to Tesslyn." She winces as Krishna slides the needle into her arm, blood blooming for a second before Krishna flushes the line with saline. "I was wondering."

"We should check on Baxter," Jesse says, tightening the strap on his bow. "See if he's awake yet."

Honor nods, adjusting the chemo bag. "Alright. Priya, Krishna, you good staying here?"

Krishna gestures toward her injured leg. "Not going anywhere."

Priya nods, but her focus lingers on Sariah. "Yeah. We'll be fine."

Jesse presses a hand to the small of Honor's back, guiding her toward the stairs. The air is heavy between them as they descend into the dark, the distant clang of metal making her stomach twist.

"Think he'll talk?" she asks.

Jesse pulls the key from above the fire ax case. "Doubt it. But it's worth trying."

The deeper they go, the stronger the scent of sweat and something sour becomes. The low groans of someone stirring reach their ears.

Jesse tightens his grip on his bow. "Sounds like he's waking up."

Honor grips the .45, the cold metal grounding her. They step through the door together.

Baxter is slumped forward, heavy chains bolted to the concrete floor keeping him anchored. His head lolls to the side, his lips dry and cracked. The stench of old sweat and soiled fabric makes Honor's nose wrinkle.

Jesse approaches first, nudging his shoulder.

Baxter stirs, a low groan rumbling in his throat as his eyes flutter open. One, then the other.

The room goes deathly silent.

Honor tightens her grip on the gun.

Jesse raises his bow.

Baxter smiles.

And then he starts to laugh.

25

MINDFUL MONSTER
HONOR

"What the hell is this?" Baxter grumble-laughs, trying to lift his arms. When he realizes they're chained, he swings his body violently from side to side. "What the fuck!" he yells.

"Baxter," Honor says softly. "We know what you are."

Jesse throws her a quick look, but she ignores it. There's no time to ease into this.

Baxter stills, his breath coming hard through his nose. Then, just as suddenly, he scoffs. "I don't know what you're talking about."

"That's bullshit," Jesse snaps, stepping closer, his bow still clutched in his hand. "We know what you were trying to do to us."

Baxter's eyes narrow as he glances between them, calculating. "Did one of those bitches cave?" His lip curls. "It was Jessica, wasn't it? That bitch. I knew we couldn't trust her."

Jesse doesn't bother to correct him. Instead, he leans in slightly. "She did. And now we know." His voice sharpens. "But there's one thing we don't get. When was Lux made into one? We thought the process took time."

Baxter tilts his head, lips twitching like he's considering whether to indulge them. Finally, he shrugs. "I'm not privy to all the ones the Redeemer makes. I only do what I need to do to survive and bring more people in." His fingers twitch at the chains around his wrists. "But I didn't notice anything that would make me think Lux is one of us, if that means anything."

Honor barely breathes as he speaks.

Baxter lifts his gaze back to her. "All I know is that Sariah is one."

The room tightens.

Honor feels something inside her ribs splinter. The breath she takes is sharp, jagged. "What?"

"Yeah," Baxter says, watching her carefully. "She's definitely one of us."

"That's not possible." Jesse's voice is rough, like he's swallowing broken glass. He turns away, raking a hand through his hair before pacing toward the door. "That's not fucking possible."

"I saw the patchwork scarring on her stomach," Baxter continues, like he's enjoying twisting the knife. "The telltale sign of where rotten flesh has healed into new skin."

Honor's knees threaten to buckle. Her mind reels back to earlier—when she saw the scars. When she didn't question them. Didn't think about them.

"No." Her voice is barely above a whisper.

"She's never—" Jesse shakes his head violently, turning back toward Baxter, then toward Honor. "She's never done anything that would make us think she's one of you. She's not one of you."

Baxter grins, lazy and cruel. "Maybe she's just been at it longer than the rest of us. Maybe she's smarter. Maybe she knows how to hide what she is."

The words crash into Honor like a tidal wave. Her breath stutters in her throat.

She had trusted Sariah.

Poor Priya.

Her hands tremble. She balls them into fists.

Jesse's eyes find hers, wide with something between anger and fear.

"I've been with her for years. She's never given any indication…"

Baxter shifts, the chains rattling. "That may be because she's been conditioned far longer than us. She can control her hunger and hide her eating habits. She's never been to the compound though, I'll tell you that much."

"What does that even mean?" Jesse asks, his voice rising in frustration. "So you people just infiltrate groups, gain their trust, and then lure them to this 'compound' where you tie them up and eat them?"

"Hey, Charlie saved me from being a mindless monster. He's a genius! We could be out there, roaming with those mindless shells."

"And what are you now? A mindful monster?" Jesse retaliates. "You gain people's trust, befriend them, then lead them to their most excruciating death? Have you ever been eaten alive, Baxter? Doesn't sound like fun to me."

Jesse's face flushes with rage. His voice quivers with anger.

"We do what we have to in order to survive." Baxter retorts.

"Oh, and eating people is just a bonus?" Jesse's skin burns red. He's by the door but turns back, pointing his bow at Baxter as he strides toward him, arrow pressed against his forehead. "I should just kill you now. Put you out of your misery."

Baxter's expression is a mixture of annoyance and amusement, but he doesn't seem scared. "Nice try, kid. But I've seen real monsters, and you're not one of them."

Instead of making Jesse mad, the words draw a slow smile to his lips. "What is it you get out of eating people?" His voice is low, probing. "If you don't need to—what is it? The kill? The hunt?"

A wicked smirk forms at the corners of Baxter's mouth. "It's the sweetest high," he states. His gaze slides to Honor. "I bet you taste sweet. Like candy."

Before he can say another word, Jesse cracks him over the head with the back of his bow. Baxter's head jerks to the side, and when he rights it, blood—a shade too dark, almost brown—seeps from the wound.

Baxter smirks through the pain. "And I bet you taste salty. Like your attitude."

Before Jesse can strike again, Honor rushes up, grabbing the bow. "He's trying to piss you off. Don't let him."

Jesse looks at her and nods, though his breathing is heavy.

Honor turns back to Baxter, her voice quieter. "I don't care about any of this. All I care about is my son, who is now bitten. I need to know if Lux was one of you, and if my child is about to suffer the same fate." Her voice shakes. "Please, just help me figure this out. And then we'll release you—if you promise to let me and my people go."

"I didn't see anything that would tell me Lux is one of us, if that's what you're asking."

"But he bit my kid," she presses. "He was found near severed limbs, eating them, and yet still coherent. If he was one of you... then my son is bound to the same fate. And if that's the case, I need to know how to save him. No matter the cost."

A heavy silence falls.

Jesse looks at Honor imploringly. "Honor, you don't want him to be one of... these... things, do you?"

Her eyes shimmer with desperate longing. "I don't care how he comes back. I just want him to come back. And I'll do what-ever it takes."

"If you let me take him to Charlie, he can turn him," Baxter offers. "He knows the method."

"And we're just supposed to walk in there and trust we won't get eaten?" Jesse scoffs.

"I wouldn't ask that of you," Honor says. "I would go with them. Willingly. To have them save my child."

Jesse's jaw tightens. "But what about you? Wouldn't you just be sacrificing yourself?"

"I don't care," Honor says, her voice resolute. "My child is my world. I'd do anything for him."

Jesse pulls her away from Baxter's watchful eyes, his voice urgent. "This is what he'll turn into." He gestures at Baxter. "A mindful monster who hunts people and eats them."

"Jesse, I don't care at this point. I just want him to survive. If he turns, at least he won't be mindless. He'll learn, adapt. He could become something else entirely."

"That's a nice thought, but you can't be sure."

"I'll teach him," she insists. "If they let me live."

Jesse rubs his stubble, his eyes darting as he thinks. "Maybe... maybe if we keep Tesslyn and Jessica for leverage. You, Gratian, and one of us go get Charlie to save Gratian. Then we use the others as bargaining chips."

Honor nods. Then a new thought hits her. "What about Sariah?"

Jesse exhales sharply. "Maybe she's important to Charlie. We tie her up before she realizes we know."

"So don't tell Priya yet?"

"Not yet." Jesse's expression hardens. "Let's go back and see what else Baxter can tell us."

26

WARRING THOUGHTS

SARIAH

As the chemotherapy medication flows into her veins, Sariah starts to feel a strange wooziness—not the kind that makes her lightheaded, but as if a dense fog is slowly lifting from her mind. It's difficult to describe, but the relentless hunger that gnaws at her day and night, the insatiable craving for human flesh, begins to wane—if only just a little.

Once Charlie had molded her into one of his top-ranked soldiers and granted her the freedom to recruit more Ronas, she discovered an unexpected thrill in the hunt. She reveled in the chase—the art of earning someone's trust, drawing them in, only to savor their slow demise. The rush of consuming human flesh, the intoxicating high that came with each drop of blood, was unlike anything she had ever known.

It was a stark contrast to her past life, where she had been a physical therapist, dedicated to healing rather than harming. But after clawing her way back from death's grasp, she emerged as someone entirely new. Each person she consumed altered her, reshaping her mind in ways she couldn't fully comprehend. Their memories, their emotions, their very essence fused with her own, and with every different kind of human she devoured, she felt herself shifting, evolving.

Every day became an experiment—a question of who she might become next. But after she consumed the rabid man, the one who took pleasure in slaughtering the innocent, something within her changed permanently. Though she absorbed pieces of everyone she fed upon, carrying fragments of their identities long after their flesh had been stripped away, it was his darkness that left the deepest imprint.

The person she was today wasn't just herself. She was an amalgamation of countless others, a patchwork of souls stitched together by hunger.

She never did take orders well. While she respected Charlie and knew he'd make a damn good king of the monsters, she preferred to play her own game of cat and mouse. From the moment she un-became a dead-ass Rona, she knew she wasn't going to follow his plans.

Charlie had fallen in love with her, but she liked pussy, so that was never going to work.

After consuming the brain of a genius doctor, Charlie had become a super-genius himself—though he'd always been something of a mad scientist. He'd successfully created a serum that, when injected into someone bitten by a Rona but not yet dead, bypassed the entire enlivening decay process. Instead, they went straight to being Purified—undead but unalive, craving human flesh and blood, like vampires. She hated it. It took all the fun out of the process. So, she struck out on her own, determined to live life on her own terms.

That's when she found Pacious, Shamus, and Jesse. They were proving to be entertaining company while she hunted for humans to eat, but she was already getting sick of most of them. Jesse thought way too highly of himself, acting like God's gift to the world. Pacious was a closeted gay man—still refusing to admit it, even though everyone around him could see it plain as day. And Shamus... ah, Shamus was her kind of people. She liked Shamey.

None of them knew what she was really up to, but sometimes, after returning from a late-night snack, she got the sense they could tell she was up to no good. Charlie and she had parted ways before he went over to the jail, and while the departure left a bad taste in his mouth, it had been sweet serendipity to hers.

It all began one night when they didn't see eye to eye about running the medical center. He was running out of places to put all the monsters he was creating, and she was clashing with some of the other women and men among them. He and another Purified, Axel, had decided they would make their way to the jail and set up shop there. While they created their plan, she made a new one: to part ways. Charlie was still salty about the departure, and she knew that if she ran into him—or anyone she recognized—it wouldn't be a sweet reunion.

It was almost as if this were fated, for her to end up back at the same medical center where she'd first come to as a Purified. While she remembered everything from her life before CoRona, she wasn't the same person she used to be. Not at all.

Even though she still craved flesh and brains and blood—and consuming them gave her the sweetest of highs—she absolutely loved watching the life drain out of someone. Seeing the terror in their eyes as she took a bite out of their arm, hearing them gasp in horror when they realize she was one of the world's worst monsters. She played the part of innocent survivor so well that none of them saw it coming.

It has come surprisingly easy to hide the monster in her. To adapt to the apocalyptic nature of the world and pretend like she was one of the survivors just trying to make it. What made it even more enjoyable was that she wasn't afraid of the monsters in the dark.

Because she *was* one of them.

The Ronas don't bother her at all. She's learned, from months of being among them, that they just *know* she's one of them. She can stand in a horde and not be touched.

It makes her invincible.

It gives her power.

And power is a fragile thing to hold in a world like this.

It wasn't until she met Priya that her thoughts began to change. This woman—this beautiful, soft, tanned goddess—has awakened something long dead inside her, something warm. And while there's a large part of her that wants to know what Priya's insides taste like, she fights against that urge every day just to see what this newfound feeling might become.

Up until a few weeks ago, when she started feeling like shit —after she'd snuck away from Jesse, Shamus, and Pacious's camp one night and eaten a woman who hadn't put up much of fight—she now knew why. The woman had leukemia.

And now *she* has it too.

It was also after consuming that woman that the hunter in her began to fade, just a little, and slivers of empathy started creeping back into her bones. She didn't know why it worked that way, only that it *had*. And now she was dying from a goddamned blood cancer—of all things.

The irony.

This must be karma.

When she watched Lux take a bite out of Gratian, she'd had to bite down on the saliva that pooled in her mouth at the sight —on the instinct to consume. But then something else stirred in her. She *felt* for Honor. For Gratian.

The killer in her is warring with the empath in her.

And it's hell.

First, she'd decided to run and get Honor—to let *her* kill Lux.

Then she would go down and eat some of Lux herself, like she'd been enjoying pieces of Janice.

But the vomit overtook her.

She'd thrown up instead.

Now that Lux is dead, and now that she knows she has leukemia, Charlie is probably their only chance to save Gratian.

And who the hell is this voice in her brain telling her to save someone?

Even when she *was* a killer, kids had been off-limits.

Even in this limbo state between unalive and undead, she'd never take the life of a child.

"How are you feeling?" Priya asks from the chair beside her, rousing her from the reverie.

"Scared," Sariah answers quietly. "I knew I wasn't feeling great starting last week. Felt more and more tired. But I never expected this."

"This is just...so..."

Priya trails off, and Sariah knows exactly what she was going to say.

"I know. Unfair."

Priya takes her hand, and at her touch, the monster in Sariah wants to bite it—but the empath in her leans into the tingles blooming in her gut.

Even the other night, when they'd fucked, she'd felt *real* arousal—the heat in her clit that sang down her legs, the orgasm Priya gave her with her fingers and tongue. That had been *real*.

It still surprises her that even in the heat of passion, the monster hadn't come out to play.

"Honor knows what she's doing," Priya says, and the sound of her voice is like butter on a hot pan—melting some of the deranged demon away.

"It does seem that way. It's crazy she went through this and knew what to look for. I just thought they were some kind of poison oak. Or hives."

"Even luckier we're in a place with medicine. God knows how long you would've had left if you..."

The last words hang in the air. They don't need to be spoken.

If I were still out there. With the Ronas.

Priya looks up at the chemo bag and swipes a stubborn tear from her eye.

The more medicine that drips into her, the quieter those other voices become.

It's like the chemo isn't just killing the cancer—it's killing the echoes of the people she consumed. The ones she *became*.

They sit in a comfortable silence that's almost peaceful, until Honor and Jesse come running into the room...weapons drawn.

27

A PRETTY WHITE LIE

HONOR

"Honor, Jesse," Priya says, her face a mixture of worry and confusion.

"Priya," Honor starts, her heart aching. She knows this will shatter Priya—but there's no time. "Your girl here is one of those monsters."

Priya's face sinks, her head tilting as if the words don't register. "Um... what?" she asks as Honor and Jesse step fully into the room, their weapons raised, aimed directly at Sariah.

"No," Priya says, shaking her head. "There's got to be some sort of mistake. Sariah?"

Sariah looks sick—pale despite her dark skin, lips nearly white, her body weak and slumped. Still, her eyes lock with Honor's, and the glare in them makes her pause.

"I don't know what you're talking about," Sariah says flatly.

"Sariah, Baxter told us everything," Honor replies, her voice quiet but firm. "There's no need to lie. I saw your stomach earlier. The scar—it's where your new skin grew in."

Priya drops Sariah's hand and shifts, subtly moving her legs so they no longer touch her.

Sariah remains in the chemo chair, the IV still dripping into her arm. "Priya, please listen," she says, her voice cracking as her eyes turn pleading. "It's not what you think."

"What. The. Actual. Fuck," Priya seethes, standing up and backing away from Sariah.

"Priya. Please. Just listen."

Priya moves to stand beside Honor as Jesse approaches, his bow still trained on Sariah's head.

"No sudden movements," he warns.

"Bro, do you think I can even *move* right now?" she snaps, gesturing weakly toward her IV. "I'm sick as fuck. You can kill me if you want—but at least hear me out first."

"Alright," Jesse says, unmoved. "Spill it."

"I was a Rona. Yes," she starts, and Priya's face crumples, tears brimming in her eyes. "I was killed by my girlfriend. I wandered for a while—mindless, like the rest of them. But then Charlie found me. He gave me this concoction that brought me back. My flesh, my brain, everything started regenerating. I remember waking up in one of the rooms downstairs."

She swallows hard.

"I don't remember *dying*. I remember getting bit. Getting really sick. But not the part in between. Not being one of them. Not really. But after Charlie 'cured' me, I still craved... human flesh. Like an addiction. But I didn't *want* to do what Charlie wanted. I didn't want to be one of his soldiers or play his sick little games. I knew I had to get away.

"At first, I tried not to eat human flesh, but the hunger—it's wired into me. No matter how much I fought it, my body still thought it needed it. And for a long time, I gave in. I had to. Until I got high enough in Charlie's ranks to go on missions alone. That's when I had some control.

"Charlie wanted us to lure people back here—to torture them, to kill them for sport. I couldn't do that. I played along just enough to survive, to make him think I was loyal. But I was never one of them. Not really.

"When he and Axel decided to move to the prison, I knew I wasn't going. I cut ties. Walked away. I found my own way, learned how to live with what I'd become. That's when I met Pacious, Shamus, and you, Jes. I finally had a family that wasn't built on bloodshed. I don't want to hurt anyone. I never did. Priya, please."

Her voice cracks as she looks at Priya, desperate.

Jesse doesn't say anything at first. He just stares, his bow still trained on her head, knuckles white around the grip. Then, in a voice quieter than she's ever heard from him, he says,

"What the fuck, sis?"

Sariah flinches. She's heard him angry before—seen him kill with that fury. But this is different. It's not rage. It's betrayal. Deep, cutting, personal.

Honor watches Jesse, but she doesn't lower her weapon. She doesn't have the luxury of doubt. "I don't care what you were or what you say you are now," she snaps. "I just want my son to live."

Priya paces, a deep frown etched into her face. "Why the hell didn't you say anything, Sariah? If you're not a threat, why keep this from us? And if it wasn't you eating Janice, then who the hell was? Do you know Jessica, Tesslyn, and Baxter are Purified?"

Sariah shakes her head, her eyes wide. "I was going to tell you. I swear. But you and I—we were just starting to trust each other, Priya. I haven't had something real like this in so long. I didn't want to lose it. And no, I didn't know about them, but I figured someone in the group had to be, with how Janice was being bitten. But it wasn't me. I swear. I learned how to control the hunger."

Jesse laughs bitterly. "Control it? You mean you *hid* it. From me. From us." He swallows hard, jaw clenched. "We bled together, Sariah. We saved each other. And all this time, you've been lying to my face."

Sariah looks down. "I was afraid."

Jesse doesn't answer. His silence is heavier than words.

"I say we lock her up," he finally says, spitting the words like they taste bad. "Throw her down there with Baxter and the others. Fuck her, Priya."

"Wait," Sariah pleads as he moves to grab the IV stand. "I can help you. I can talk to Charlie. He's the only one who can help Gratian."

"Don't fucking say my son's name," Honor snarls, stepping closer, pressing the barrel of her gun to Sariah's forehead. "You lying, two-faced monster."

"Wait." Priya steps between them, shielding Sariah. "Maybe she's telling the truth, Honor. And she's right—Charlie is the only one who can save Gratian." She turns to Jesse. "I say we have to trust her."

Jesse scoffs. "Trust? That ship fucking sank." He glares at Sariah. "You don't get to call me brother anymore."

Sariah's face crumbles, and for the first time, real tears fill her eyes. But Jesse doesn't care.

Honor grips her gun tighter, fighting every instinct telling her to pull the trigger. "Fuck that. Just kill the bitch. I'll deal with Charlie myself."

Sariah straightens, forcing herself to meet Honor's gaze. "Charlie is a monster, Honor. He won't listen to you. He doesn't care about your son, he'll see him as an experiment. As a recruit. He'll use him." Her voice trembles, but she pushes through. "But listen to me. I know you don't believe me, but I have to tell you anyway. This chemo, it's doing something to me. I can feel it. The hunger, that itch—it's fading. I don't know why, but I think this medicine is curing me. It's breaking the Purified conditioning."

Honor doesn't believe her. Not for a second.

But she's right about one thing; they can't walk into Charlie's den without leverage.

And if Sariah really did leave the way she says she did, Charlie might be more than happy to see her again.

If only to kill her for good.

Jesse glances at Honor, reading the conflict in her face. "We can still lock her up until we're ready to move. If you still don't trust her." He glares back at Sariah. "I know I fucking don't."

Priya sighs, pressing her fingers to her temple. "She also needs more medicine. If you want her to help you save Gratian, you need to keep her alive long enough to do it."

Honor grits her teeth.

She doesn't care if Sariah dies of leukemia.

But not before she helps save her son.

28

A CURE TO THOSE DEMONS

PRIYA

Priya's head spins as Honor and Jesse haul Sariah up by the elbows, dragging her toward the basement. The IV tree rattles behind them, its tubes slithering through the dark like veins trailing a ghost.

This whole time?

This whole time, Sariah had been one of *them*—one of those monsters. She wormed her way into their group, earned their trust. Priya had let her get close. She'd *touched* her.

A wave of nausea rises, sharp and fast, acid clawing up her throat like a firestorm. She swallows hard, but the sickness lingers, coiling in her gut.

Sariah looks back at her with those wide, pleading eyes, and Priya wants to believe her. Wants to believe that she isn't one of those Purified, twisted, evil fucks. But there's no telling.

The truth is, she barely knows her.

There's something unsettling about it—something that keeps her from fully dismissing Sariah's story. But what if she's wrong? What if she lets her guard down, trusts the wrong person, and it gets them all killed?

She didn't survive this long—didn't claw her way through hell—just to let her bleeding heart make a fatal mistake.

Gratian is all that matters.

She loves that little boy like her own, and he doesn't deserve this fate. He's ten. He shouldn't be one of those mindless, flesh-eating killers. The thought of losing him—of watching him turn—gnaws at her worse than anything.

But what if this Charlie doesn't cure him? What if they walk straight into a trap? What if he locks them all up and throws them to the Purified like scraps of meat?

As they descend the stairs, Sariah stays quiet. A few glances back, but she's too weak to put up much of a fight. Sweat beads on her pale skin, her breath shallow. She looks sick—really sick. Like she's barely holding on.

They reach the basement, and Jesse and Honor shove her onto a metal table. She doesn't resist as they secure the heavy chains bolted to the floor.

In the background, Baxter, Jessica, and Tesslyn shout, their voices a chaotic hum of anger and desperation.

"Alright," Honor says, wiping her hands on her jeans. "Let's get upstairs and figure out how we're getting into that prison. We don't have much time."

Sariah shifts weakly, her voice barely a whisper. "Even if he dies..." Her breath hitches. "Charlie can bring him back. That's how we were all made. After we died."

Priya watches as Honor stiffens at the word *dies*. For the briefest moment, her mask slips—just enough for Priya to see the raw, gut-wrenching fear underneath. But in an instant, she steels herself again, shoulders squaring like armor locking into place.

"I don't want it to come to that," she says, her voice cold and final.

Then she turns and stalks toward the door. Jesse follows without a word.

Priya stays rooted in place.

Honor pauses, looking back. "You coming?"

"I just need a minute with her," Priya murmurs, not even sure what she's going to say.

Honor studies her, as if questioning whether she's sure. Priya gives a slight nod, and after a beat, Honor turns and disappears into the darkness. Jesse follows, their footsteps fading beneath Baxter and the others' distant, desperate yelling.

Priya exhales, finally alone with Sariah.

And she has no idea where to start.

Priya looks at Sariah, the beam of her flashlight turning the woman's green eyes into glowing emeralds.

Under normal circumstances, she would be terrified, knowing exactly what kind of monster Sariah is. But despite everything, there's a pull she can't ignore.

She takes a deep breath, waiting to see if Sariah will speak first. The only sounds in the room are Baxter's deep, booming voice, still demanding to be let out, threatening death if they don't. The weight of it all presses down on Priya's chest. Finally, she pulls a chair from the corner and sits—not close enough to get bitten, but not far enough to escape the space they share.

"I don't even know what to say to you," she starts, letting her heart guide the words.

"Priya, I—"

"No. Let me speak." Her anger coats her voice like venom. "Whatever lies you're about to spew, save them. I don't want to hear your bullshit excuses—about waiting for the right time, about how you were going to tell us but didn't. That's over." She stops, folding her hands in her lap, letting her dark hair fall forward like a shroud. She steadies herself. She won't shout. She wants every word to cut. "I don't know who you think you're dealing with, but I'm a lawyer. You can't bullshit a lawyer, Sariah.

"You knew about Charlie. You knew he was making monsters. You knew what you were. And still, you didn't tell us. Not even when Janice was being eaten alive. You let us trust you. And now, here we are."

Her words hang heavy in the silence. She surprises even herself with her harshness, her relentlessness. Any feelings she had for Sariah don't matter anymore.

This is the apocalypse.

There's no time for foolish attachments.

Sariah stares at her, something flickering in her expression. Shock, yes. But something deeper too.

"I'm afraid if I tell you the truth, you'll think differently of me."

"I already do."

A slow breath leaves Sariah's lips. She shifts, leaning her head back against the wall, eyes fixed on the ceiling. "I'm a monster," she says, her voice flat. "And I like killing people. I love the high, the taste, the anticipation. When I consume someone, their memories become mine—I take pieces of them into me. And I enjoy it."

Priya clenches her jaw, bile rising in her throat.

"But," Sariah continues, "the person I was—the real me—she's still in there. Buried under it all. And when I met you, she started screaming at me to let her out." Her voice softens, breaking at the edges. "I never wanted to hurt Pacious, Shamus, or Jesse. They became my family. I learned how to live with them, how to feed and still be with them. But then I met you."

She shifts again, her eyes finding Priya's.

"You quieted the monster in me. For the first time since I turned, it stopped clawing at me, screaming for more. You did that. And when they started this chemo, it got even quieter. I don't know what that means, or if it's curing the monster the same way it's curing the cancer, but... Priya, you are my chemo. You silenced the darkness inside me."

Priya's breath catches.

"I don't expect forgiveness. I don't expect you to believe me. I'll sit in this cell, go to the jail, and face whatever Charlie decides. Even if that means my death. But honestly?" Her lips curve into a sad, broken smile. "If I can't have you in my life—now that I know what love feels like—I'll gladly take that death."

Priya stares, stunned.

She had feelings for Sariah. She knew that much.

But love?

No.

She wants to believe her.

She really does.

But she can't.

"I'm glad I helped you see the light again, Sariah," she says, her voice steady. "But after what you just told me—about how you enjoy killing, about how you take people's memories—I can never be with you. I won't be with someone like that. It's wrong. It's evil." She shakes her head. "Regardless of what this chemo is doing, whatever we had is done. Thank you for telling me the truth. But you're staying in here until we take you to the jail. Then Charlie can do whatever he wants with you."

The pain in her own words feels like a blade in her chest.

She wishes—more than anything—that Sariah wasn't one of those things.

"Priya, please—"

Sariah reaches for her.

Priya jumps back, knocking over the chair. The clatter echoes in the dark, loud as a gunshot.

Silence.

Baxter and the others are quiet.

Too quiet.

They were listening.

Priya swallows hard.

"No. I don't want to hear any more." She turns, walking toward the door. "I'm done."

She steps out, Sariah's desperate voice chasing after her into the dark.

29

SIT IN DARKNESS
HONOR

"You good?" Jesse asks as he and Honor leave Priya alone in the dark with her monster, climbing the stairs to check on Gratian.

"No. I'm not. I don't even know what the fuck is going on anymore."

Jesse exhales and switches his bow to his right hand so he can slip his left arm around her shoulders. "Hey," he says softly. "I know this whole thing is fucked up. But if there's one silver lining, it's that these monsters exist."

Honor gives him a look like he just grew a second head. "I'm sorry—how the hell is that a good thing?"

"Because at least now we know there's a way to save your boy, right? That's how I'm choosing to see it."

Honor sighs. "Yeah, you're right. It just feels shitty either way. My son either dies and becomes a mindless monster, or he dies and becomes a mindful one. I know which is the lesser of two evils, but it's hard to see through the fire I'm in right now."

"I know." Jesse squeezes her shoulder. "But Gratian's got you for a mama. We can teach him how to curb his appetite, make sure he isn't out there like some evil fucking jack-off preying on innocent people." His voice wavers on the last few words, like his mind has drifted to Sariah.

"Are *you* good?" Honor asks, slipping her arm around his waist.

"I'm fine."

"Jesse, you don't have to be fine all the time. You're allowed to be hurt by her betrayal. I know I would be."

He lets out a bitter laugh. "I'm just so fucking pissed I didn't see anything weird with her. Like—now that I look back? She'd get all hangry after a few days without 'eating,' sneak off, then come back all… different. Even her eyes would be lighter." He shakes his head, jaw tightening. "There was this one time, we were all sitting around the fire, just bullshitting, you know? It was pitch black around us. She got all weird—ears perked up like she heard something. Said she'd be right back, made up some excuse about an upset stomach —classic code brown, don't follow me type situation."

Honor frowns. "And?"

"And she came back, like, half an hour later, acting different. Subtle shit. Her posture, her voice—hell, one time, she came back with a subtle lilt in her voice, like she was trying to suppress a cockney accent. I thought she was just fucking around, being weird. But now? Now I know she was different. Whoever she killed that night, she took something from them. And I just sat there, laughing along like a fucking idiot."

"You couldn't have known. There's no way you would have. Don't blame yourself for not seeing it sooner. You had no idea what these *things* even were, let alone that someone in your inner circle was one of them. I definitely would've never guessed, and I wouldn't have believed it if I didn't find those notes."

They stop walking. She meets his eyes—those fathomless blue depths—and something inside her surges. Jesse calls to her soul like he was forged from the same fire, the same stubborn, reckless material as she was. Cut from the same cloth. She's only just met him, yet it's as if she's known him across lifetimes.

The first time he looked at her like this, she slammed the door on what stirred in her chest, because of Lux. But now Lux is gone. The walls she built quake and splinter, and Jesse is the only one she wants crashing through the ruins.

"Do you think we should believe her?" she asks him, as the darkness around them swallows them whole. It takes on a tangibility, swaddling them in night, until it feels like they're the only two in the whole universe. The amber beam from the flashlight stutters, making shadows dance along the wall beside them. Their voices echo with the shadows, shifting and warbling along the concrete stairwell.

Jesse's features are enhanced by the melancholic light. "Believe the chemo is magically curing her lust for flesh the minute she starts getting it? No," he answers curtly, his tone infected with anger. "We can leave her chained up down here and keep her tied up when we go to the jail. I don't trust her as far as I can throw her."

"Yeah, me neither. Poor Priya. Do you think there's anyone else in our group who's one of these things?"

He thinks on this for a moment, his gaze shifting to the wall behind her. He's so close now that his warmth caresses her skin, needling her hairs to stand on end. "What did that dipshit say—Baxter? How you can tell if they're one of them?"

"The patchwork scars, where new flesh has healed over rotting skin."

"Good to know. Everyone is all bundled up, so it's hard to tell, but definitely something to keep an eye on."

Honor starts up the stairs again, needing to check on Gratian, to see for herself that he's okay.

"Hey," Jesse says, catching her wrist before she can leave.

His grip is firm but gentle, grounding her. "I know this shit sucks. But it's going to be okay. I just know it is."

"You seem so sure." Her voice is raw. "I'm having a harder time convincing myself of that."

He steps up onto her stair, close enough for her to see the array of blues in his eyes. His smile is sincere, enough to weaken her knees. There's a slight gap between his front teeth, something imperfect that makes him seem even more perfect. He lifts a finger under her chin, tilting her gaze to his.

Her heart stammers.

He's going to kiss her.

She hasn't kissed anyone but Lux in eight years.

What if she's forgotten how?

His breath is warm, sweet. "All you have to do is speak it into existence," he murmurs. "If you think negatively, you'll bring that shit right to you. And we don't need any more of that in the world. Think positive. Your boy is gonna be the one to save the world."

His words settle into her bones, soothing like an elixir. He's right. Gratian will make it through this.

It's what she told herself when he was born—when the doctors said he wouldn't make it off the ventilator.

They were wrong.

He made it then.

He'll make it now.

"You're right," she whispers, and the tension in her shoulders melts. She exhales, unsteady but lighter.

Jesse's face dips closer, the space between them vanishing—

Then the door swings open.

Light from the hallway slices through the dark stairwell as Maria pokes her head in, her thick Spanish accent breaking the moment. "There you are. I was just about to come find you."

Honor's heart sinks.

"What is it?" she asks, dread curling in her stomach. "Is it Gratian?"

"Yes, but he's okay. He's awake. He's asking for you."

Honor looks to Jesse, who nods, and then she's rushing up the rest of the stairs, brushing past Maria.

Gratian is sitting up in bed, IV still secured to his arm, his sweet little face streaked with tears. He looks so lost. So scared.

She sits beside him, wrapping him in her arms. He clings to her, sobbing into her chest.

"What is it, baby? What's wrong?"

"Daddy bit me," he chokes out, his tiny body trembling. "I'm gonna turn into those scary things, aren't I, Mommy?"

Her heart shatters.

He pulls back just enough to meet her eyes.

Jesse sits on the other side of the bed, silent but solid. Even without asking, he's there. That's what she needs most.

Honor turns to Maria, silently asking *how*? How does he even know? He was unconscious.

Maria shakes her head. "He just knew. He woke up screaming and crying for you, saying his dad was a monster and bit him. He was holding his neck."

Honor swallows hard and forces herself to meet Gratian's gaze. "How did you know, love?"

His lip wobbles. "I—" He hesitates, brows scrunching tight. "I don't know. It just... it happened. Like a bad dream, but real. I think I woke up for a second. Everything was fuzzy, but I saw him. And I—" He sniffles, voice small. "I thought if I didn't move, he wouldn't... wouldn't keep eating me."

Vomit crawls up the back of her throat.

She swallows it down, pulls Gratian closer.

She has to be honest with him.

"Yes, love. Daddy did bite you. He was turned into a monster at some point. We just don't know when. But it's going to be okay. You're going to get some medicine, and it's going to make you better, okay?"

"I am?" He sniffles again, taking a shaky breath. "Can Daddy have some of the medicine too?"

Her stomach twists.

Oh good, he didn't see me blow his dad's brains out.

She forces herself to steady her voice. "No, honey. Daddy isn't going to get better."

The words are a knife to her chest.

So this is what it feels like—to tell your child their other parent is gone.

It sucks.

It's the worst feeling she can imagine.

"He's not?" Gratian's sobs return, and he buries his face against her shoulder.

"No, baby." Tears burn her own eyes, her voice shaking. Because this is her loss too. No matter how distant they'd grown, there was a time when she had loved Lux enough to marry him. Enough to create a life with him. There was something to mourn there—what they had been, what they lost. The life they built. The child they made.

"Daddy isn't coming back now."

Gratian wails, and she holds him tighter.

Together, they sob into the silence.

Jesse and Mariah stay with them in the dark. Jesse rubs Gratian's back, Maria his leg.

Even though they aren't touching her, she feels their comfort.

Now, all that's left is to get Gratian to the jail—and hope they can save him.

30

WHAT MONSTERS LURK
PRIYA

This cannot be happening.

Any of it.

Finding out her crush is a monster. Gratian teetering on the edge of becoming one too. And now, his little heart breaking because he knows his daddy is gone—and that he's the reason he's dying.

The past few hours feel like some kind of fever dream. The idea that monsters have been living among them, disguised as real people, only to be revealed as Purified Ronas, is beyond comprehension.

But knowing that the one person she'd started to have feelings for is one of them?

That's something else entirely.

Priya sits cross-legged on the floor beside the bed where Honor rocks Gratian, her mind racing.

How long do they have to get him to the jail? What's their plan?

As if reading her thoughts, Jesse speaks. "We need to figure out how we're getting to the jail."

Honor nods, quickly wiping away a stray tear. "Yeah. Let's get some rest and leave at first light. It's too risky to go now."

"Yeah, that's probably best," Jesse agrees.

Priya hesitates before asking, "Do you think we could wait a few days? Just to give Sariah more time with the chemo?"

Honor's head snaps toward her, eyes filled with disbelief. "Priya, we can't—"

"It's not like that," Priya interjects, shifting to sit on her knees. "It's just... if we take her the way she is now, I don't know if she'll make it. And I think she's our best shot at getting Charlie to help us."

Jesse's expression softens. "She has a point. The way she is right now, she ain't gonna make it far."

Honor stays silent, looking down at Gratian, who has somehow drifted back to sleep. Her voice is quiet when she finally speaks.

"I just don't know how much time..." Her words break off from her mouth, as though too painful to give them full shape.

Jesse's strong hands knead the tension from Honor's shoulders, and she leans back into him with a sigh.

It's obvious—something is blooming between them.

And Priya is here for it.

But standing there, watching them, she suddenly feels like a third wheel.

"I'm gonna check on Michael and Amy," she blurts, pushing to her feet. "Haven't seen them in a while."

Honor lifts her head. "Okay. Be safe."

Priya nods and heads out, leaving them to their moment.

The living room is a grim display of normalcy in the wake of horror. Jesus, Maria, Juan, and Antonio scrub brain matter off the walls and floor. Krishna has her injured leg propped up on the coffee table, watching something on TV. Pacious and Liam sit by the fire, sipping whiskey from rocks glasses, Liam laughing at something Pacious just said. The flickering flames catch the lenses of Pacious's glasses, turning them into twin glimmers of gold. Across the room, Shamus sits at the kitchen island, nursing a beer, eyes scanning a book.

No sign of Amy or Michael.

Priya has no clue what time it is—maybe dinner? It's hard to tell anymore.

She drifts toward the kitchen, wondering if Jesse told the others about Sariah.

"Hey," she says, sliding onto a tall chair.

Shamus glances up. "Hey, you. Beer?" He nods toward the fridge. "Found some in dry storage. They're kinda warm, but we've got more chilling."

"Yes," she replies. She doesn't care how warm it is, a beer sounds divine.

Shamus hops up, grabs one, flicks off the cap with a lighter, and hands it over.

She downs several deep gulps, relishing the bitter fizz. The bubbles pop wickedly against her tongue, sending a tiny rush through her. God, she's missed this—even if she was always more of a wine drinker.

Pacious notices her and murmurs something to Liam. Since Liam can't walk without leg braces, Pacious—without hesitation—lifts him, carrying him effortlessly to the kitchen. He sets him down gently before sitting beside him.

"You okay?" Pacious asks.

"No," Priya says bluntly. She takes another swig before meeting their eyes. "Has Jesse told you yet?"

"Told us what?" Shamus asks, taking a slow, deliberate gulp of beer.

"Sariah is one of those monsters."

Silence.

Then—

"What?"

"What the fuck?" Pacious leans forward, elbows on the counter, hands covering his face. His glasses slip slightly, stretching his eyes behind the lenses. "How the hell did you find that out?"

"Baxter told them. I just found out too."

Shamus whistles sharply, calling Jesse over.

Across the room, Jesse looks up from where he's still comforting Honor. He murmurs something to her, then strides over.

"Yeah, what's up?" he asks, eyeing their drinks. "You got more of those?"

Shamus pulls another beer from the fridge, pops the cap, and hands it over.

"Were you going to tell us about Sariah?"

Jesse exhales, rubbing his jaw. "Of course. I needed to make sure Honor was okay first. I figured Priya was telling you."

Shamus scowls. "Kinda important information to share, considering she's been with us for almost a year."

A year?

Priya's stomach flips.

Sariah's been with them for an entire year, and no one suspected a thing.

Maybe she isn't lying when she says she hates what she is.

Then—

A thunderous boom rattles the floor beneath them.

"The fuck was that?" Pacious is already on his feet.

Shamus grips his gun. "Sounded like it came from the main floor—not the basement."

The others in the living room freeze.

Maria rushes Jesus behind the couch while Juan and Antonio scramble for their weapons.

Honor is at Jesse's side in seconds. "What was that?"

"We're not sure," Jesse says. "Stay here with Gratian. We'll check it out."

Priya grips her gun, following the men into the dark stairwell. Pacious leads, flashlight and spear in hand. Shamus is just behind, gun drawn.

At the landing, they pause—listening.

Silence.

Pacious signals to Shamus and Jesse to check the basement while Priya follows Antonio and Juan toward the lobby.

Her pulse hammers as she sweeps her flashlight through the patient rooms. Shadows lurch and stretch, every corner a potential hiding place. The knowledge of what monsters lurk in the dark makes her skin prickle.

Juan yanks open curtains with sharp, practiced movements, gun poised. Priya's light cuts through each space, searching for movement.

Ahead, Antonio rounds the hallway toward the lobby, gun raised.

Then—

A blur. A shadow. A thing lunges from the darkness.

Heidi.

Her teeth sink into Antonio's arm, just above his gun hand.

His scream rips through the hallway, echoing off the walls...

A gunshot explodes into the air.

Blood splatters.

And everything erupts into chaos.

31

CRIES OF HORROR
JESSE

A gunshot rings out, followed by cries of horror, freezing Jesse and the rest of the group in their tracks.

But what's even eerier is the silence down here.

Part of him wants to run up and see what happened, but another, stronger part tells him to keep moving forward.

Something isn't right.

It's too quiet.

Then more screams.

More gunshots.

Pacious doesn't hesitate—he turns and bolts toward the chaos.

"Fuck," Jesse mutters, taking off after him.

Priya's yelling.

Antonio's screaming.

Juan's fighting.

Jesse can hear all of it as they bound up the dark staircase.

The moment they shove open the door, they're thrown straight into the middle of a battle.

Priya's flashlight has fallen to the floor, its beam casting frantic shadows. Jesse barely registers it before his eyes lock onto the horror unfolding before them—Heidi is devouring Antonio. Blood and torn flesh coat her face as he writhes beneath her, screaming. Meanwhile, Juan and Priya are locked in a brutal struggle with two more figures Jesse can't make out in the dark.

No time to hesitate.

Jesse rips his knives from their belt holsters and charges, slashing at the woman attacking Priya. Light blond hair peeks from beneath a scarf covering her face. He grabs the fabric, yanking her head back, and slices her throat clean through.

The sickening sound of flesh splitting is followed by a wet gurgle. She collapses, blood pooling beneath her nearly severed head.

Juan is still grappling with a man who refuses to go down, landing punch after punch that barely fazes him. He must've lost his gun.

Pacious fires a shot into the man's shoulder, and he staggers back before fleeing toward the stairwell.

Juan scrambles to find his weapon, chasing after him as Jesse turns his attention to Antonio's attacker.

Heidi.

Jesse drives his knife deep into her trapezius muscle, wrenching her head up from Antonio's mangled body.

She looks up, and his stomach drops.

Priya's flashlight illuminates her face, revealing the impossible—her throat, which had been slashed open before, has healed. The skin is an uneven patchwork of scar tissue, a grotesque mockery of regeneration.

"Ouch, you fuck," she snarls, blood dripping from her lips, bits of Antonio's flesh still caught in her teeth.

She staggers to her feet, clutching her neck where the knife wound gushes dark, almost brown blood.

Then she lunges.

Jesse dodges and slashes across her face as she passes, the blade biting deep.

Shamus doesn't hesitate.

A single gunshot.

Brain matter and fragments of skull splatter across Jesse's face, warm and wet, some landing in his mouth. He spits it out with a gag as Heidi crumples to the floor, this time truly dead.

Antonio is still alive—but barely. His body is a wreck, chunks missing, intestines spilling onto the ground where Heidi had been feasting. His screams are agony made manifest, each one clawing at Jesse's nerves.

There's only one thing to do.

Pacious is faster.

Without hesitation, he drives his spear into Antonio's skull, silencing him for good.

Pacious turns, urgency in his voice. "The others."

No one argues.

Priya, Shamus, and Jesse sprint after him, taking the stairs two at a time.

When they reach the apartment, all hell has broken loose.

The man who escaped is locked in combat with Juan.

Another figure—someone Jesse doesn't recognize—lies dead next to an also dead Maria.

She's lifeless. Chunks of flesh are missing from her neck and face.

Jesus kneels over her, sobbing, screaming at the man Juan is fighting.

Honor crouches in the corner, shielding Gratian. Her grip on her gun is tight, the barrel trained on the chaos.

Shamus doesn't hesitate. He steps forward, presses his gun to the stranger's head, and pulls the trigger. The man drops, lifeless.

Juan rushes to his family, pulling Jesus away from Maria's

body. Jesse spots the bite, deep and ugly, torn into Jesus's arm. He's clutching it, blood seeping through his fingers.

Jesse crosses to Honor, who looks shaken but intact.

"You okay?"

Honor exhales sharply. "I think so. What the fuck just happened?"

"I don't know," Jesse admits. "But I think someone let those fucking things in."

Honor's eyes drift to Juan, now weeping over Maria. Her voice is low. "Do you think we can save Jesus?"

Before Jesse can answer, static crackles through the room.

A walkie-talkie.

"Cody?" a voice rasps through. "Cody, come in. Are you there?"

Everyone freezes.

That voice.

Too familiar.

"Cody? We got Baxter, Jessica, and Tesslyn. Sariah was too sick to move. We're heading back to base. If you can hear me, meet us there."

Honor's eyes widen. "Was that Jerod?"

Priya nods slowly. "I think so."

"What the actual fu—"

Gunfire erupts outside, cutting Honor off.

"Oh my fucking god," Jesse growls, slinging his bow off his back. "What now?"

Shamus reloads his gun. "Let's go."

Jesse follows Pacious and Shamus to the door. Juan storms past them, pure fury etched across his face.

On the main floor, a low, ominous rumble vibrates through the building. Then the sharp splintering of wood. Bullets tear through boarded windows, spraying shards of glass like shrapnel. The metal wall at the entrance groans under pressure but holds—barely.

Then they come.

Rotters pour through the breaches, their encroaching decaying gait louder than the gunfire.

Juan doesn't waste a second, he's already firing, taking them out one by one.

Shamus, Pacious, and Jesse follow suit, knifing, shooting, smashing.

The hallway turns into a bloodbath.

At the front, Juan and Pacious shove furniture against the broken windows, makeshift barricades forming in seconds.

"Left," Jesse shouts, sprinting with Shamus into the fray.

"Right," Pacious calls, and he and Juan break off, clearing clusters of creatures.

At least thirty—maybe forty—had gotten in. Probably during Jerod's escape with Baxter, Tesslyn, and Jessica.

The last Rotter finally drops with a sickening thud.

Jesse exhales sharply, wiping blood from his blade onto a corpse's tattered shirt.

Juan, panting, glances at the broken windows. "We gotta seal these up before more get in."

Pacious nods, already grabbing a nearby table and shoving it against the largest opening. "Shamus, help me with this."

Shamus yanks a board from a busted doorframe, wedging it against a window. "This won't hold for long," he mutters. "We need to reinforce it."

Jesse turns to Juan. "Check the storage room. See if we've got more nails, wood—hell, anything that'll hold this shit together."

Juan doesn't argue, disappearing down the hall. Within minutes, he's back with salvaged boards and a hammer.

The group works fast, boarding up the shattered windows. Jesse and Shamus drive nails into the wood while Pacious and Juan stack heavy shelves in front of the barricades for extra support.

Finally, the last plank is secured.

Jesse steps back, assessing their work. "It's not perfect, but it'll do."

Juan wipes sweat from his brow. "Good enough to buy us some time."

A heavy silence settles over them. The only sound is their own ragged breathing, until a faint rustling comes from the corner, behind a shelf.

Jesse raises his weapon, stepping forward cautiously. Juan stays close, covering the angles Jesse can't.

Jesse shoves the shelf aside—and freezes.

Michael is cowering in the corner, bloodied and beaten, arms covering his head like he's expecting another hit.

"Michael?" Jesse asks.

Michael flinches, then looks up.

"What the hell are you doing? Are you one of them?"

"No!" Michael stammers. "No, I'm not one of those fucking things!"

Jesse grabs him by the elbow and shoves him into a chair.

"Then what the fuck is going on?"

Michael groans, rubbing his face. "Amy, man. Amy is one of them. Goddamn it."

Jesse and Juan exchange glances as Shamus and Pacious cross the room.

"That should be all of them," Shamus says. Then he nods toward Michael. "What the hell is he doing here?"

"We found him hiding," Jesse replies. "Still trying to figure out why."

Pacious exhales sharply. "Let's get him upstairs. This place is clear, but I'll feel better once we're locked in again."

"We can't trust that anyone else isn't a fucking Rona," Jesse mutters, yanking Michael to his feet and pushing him forward.

As Michael walks, his arms fall to his sides, revealing deep bite wounds.

Jesse eyes Pacious. "If a Purified bites you, does it turn you into a Rona?"

Pacious hesitates. "I don't know, dude. Guess we'll find out."

The group ascends the stairs in silence. When they reach the upper floor, all eyes land on Michael.

"Sit," Jesse orders. "I don't trust you yet."

Michael slumps into a chair, his expression empty.

Honor leaves Gratian's side and approaches. "What happened?"

Michael runs a shaking hand over his bald head. "Fucking Amy," he mutters. "She's one of them."

The room falls silent, waiting for him to explain.

"We were downstairs... making out. Just wanted to be alone for a bit. Then she got real quiet, like she was listening to something. I pulled back, and her eyes were... wrong. Almost all white." His voice cracks. "She started kissing me again, but this time, she tried to bite my lip. When I jerked away, she took a chunk out of my arm."

He holds it up, revealing the raw, gaping wound.

"I freaked out. She punched me in the face, hit me over the head with a lamp, then ran to the front door and let Jerod and some others in. I wanted to warn you, but the Ronas came with them. They just started pouring in. So I ran. Hid. Hoped they wouldn't find me."

"Amy?" Honor whispers, like she can't believe it.

Pacious narrows his eyes. "The real question is... who else in here is one of them?"

He stands and points his gun at the group.

Juan throws his hands up. "I am not one of those fucking monsters," he snaps.

"Neither am I," Krishna says.

"How do we tell?" Priya asks.

"The skin," Honor says. "Baxter said the patchwork scars were a dead giveaway. That's how I knew Sariah was one."

Jesse scans the room. "Everyone strip."

The group stares at him in disbelief.

"You don't have to get naked," he clarifies. "But I want everyone in their underwear. Now. I don't trust any of you."

Honor gives him a look. "Seriously?"

He smirks. "Yep. You too, missy."

"You first," she challenges, unbuckling her pants.

Jesse grins and sets his bow on the counter. He pulls off his shirt first, revealing lean muscle and old scars.

One by one, the group strips down. Jesse grabs a flashlight and runs the beam over Honor's arms, shoulders, and stomach. His gaze lingers on the curve of her waist, the glint of her navel ring, the perfect roundness of her ass. His boxers tighten, but he forces himself to focus.

Once satisfied, he hands her a second flashlight.

"Help me check," he says.

Honor catches the way his boxers strain and smirks as she takes the light.

They move through the group—Honor checking Priya while Jesse inspects Juan. He moves on to Pacious and Shamus while Honor searches Krishna.

Michael is last.

Pacious checks Jesse in front of everyone, and by the time it's over, Jesse's hard-on is long gone.

"All clear," he announces. "No monsters."

Priya pulls her pants back on. "I should check on Sariah."

"I'll come with you," Honor says, slipping on her shirt. As she passes Jesse, she winks.

32

THE HUNGER THAT REMAINS
PRIYA

"So, what's going on with you and Jesse?" Priya asks once they slip into the dark stairwell.

"Nothing yet," Honor replies, her voice a little shaky.

"But you like him?"

"I do. There's something about him I can't shake. Like I've known him before... in another life. He doesn't feel new to me. If that makes any sense."

It does make sense.

"That's how Sariah felt to me." The words feel heavy on Priya's tongue.

"I'm so sorry she turned out to be one of them, Pri," Honor says softly, slipping an arm around Priya's waist as they reach the landing.

Priya exhales sharply. "I'm just so angry with her. I have so many questions. The last time I was alone with her, I told her to quit the bullshit, and she just... told me everything. That she's a monster. But she also said I sat her demons down and told them to relax." She lets out a bitter laugh. "Poetic, considering the macabre setting."

"Do you believe her? That the chemo she *just* started is making her better in her head?"

"I don't know, Honor. I want to believe her, but after what we just saw—Amy, of all people, being one of them—how can I ever trust her? How could I let her walk around, knowing she could snap and eat one of us at any moment? Nope. Not gonna happen. We'll keep giving her the medicine, take her to the jail, and leave her there for all I care."

Honor sighs. "That has to be so hard. But I get it. I wouldn't feel safe either." She shudders. "I still can't believe Amy. I keep thinking about all the things she might've done that I didn't notice. And Michael had sex with her! I wonder what that was like—"

Priya shoots her a smirk.

"You had sex with Sariah?"

Priya hesitates. "Yeah... we fooled around the night—" She stops short, the memory clearly painful.

"Oh. *That* night."

"So much has happened since. I would've told you sooner, but... it's hard to believe that was only two nights ago."

"Is it night now?"

"I think it's early morning."

"Yeah, I've completely lost track of time," Honor mutters.

"We should check on Sariah, then try to sleep before we head to the jail."

"Good plan."

When they reach the basement, Sariah is still in her cell. The chains are gone, but she lies motionless, as still as a corpse.

For a moment, Priya isn't sure how she feels. If Sariah is dead... would she be relieved?

Just in case, she kneels and re-secures the chains around Sariah's ankles. Still, she doesn't move.

"Is she—"

"Dead?" Sariah finishes for her, eyes fluttering open. "Not yet. But close, I'd imagine."

Something in Priya's chest cracks, but part of her still thinks: *It would be easier if she died.*

Honor removes the empty chemo bag. "I'll go get the next round."

Priya nods. "Do you want some water?"

Sariah swallows. "Yeah. Water would be wonderful."

Priya pulls a bottle from her pack and hands it over. Sariah's fingers tremble as she tries to twist the cap.

She's too weak.

Priya takes it back, opens it, and hands it over. Sariah drinks greedily before passing it back.

"Why didn't you go with your friends?" Priya asks.

Sariah wipes her mouth. "Firstly, I didn't want to." She exhales and stares at the ceiling. "And second, look at me. I can't even open a damn water bottle."

"Do you think that's from the cancer or... from not eating?"

Sariah glares at her. "Pretty sure it's the cancer, Priya."

"My bad," Priya mutters, screwing the cap back on.

Honor returns and hooks up the next chemo drip.

"When are you guys leaving for the jail?" Sariah asks.

"Early tomorrow," Honor replies.

"And what time is it now?"

"Dawn. Probably five or six."

Sariah nods, then hesitates. "How's Gratian?"

Honor shoots her a sharp look, as if warning her not to go there.

"He's... as well as can be expected," Priya answers instead.

Honor secures the IV. "Let this finish. I'll come back later to disconnect it. Try to eat if you can, but you'll probably puke. We'll do the next round before we leave. You can sit here with the drip while we go."

"What? I'm not coming?"

Honor snorts. "Can you? You look like shit."

"Honor," Priya says, shooting her a warning look.

Sariah forces herself to sit up straighter. "I should come. You don't know Charlie. I do. If he sees a bunch of strangers rolling up, he'll kill you all on the spot. Listen." She exhales sharply. "I know you don't trust me, and I don't blame you. But I care about this girl right here, and I want to help save your boy. I'm done preaching about how I'm changing. I just have to show you. But you have to let me. Otherwise, you all might die."

She has a point.

Honor crosses her arms. "How would you even go? You can barely hold your head up."

"Leave that to me. You don't know me. I'm resilient."

Honor looks at Priya, wordlessly asking her opinion. Priya nods.

"Fine," Honor says. "We leave after your drip."

"That's all I ask."

Honor turns to go. "Coming?"

"I'll be right there."

Honor eyes her, then stalks off, her heavy boots echoing down the hall.

Priya sits on the edge of a chair. "Did your friends want you to go with them?"

Sariah exhales. "Yeah. They said Charlie would be thrilled I'm still alive and 'out here doing the Lord's work'—or whatever the fuck Jerod said."

Priya tilts her head. "Did you know about Jerod? Or Amy?"

Sariah's brows shoot up. "Fuuuuck. Amy's one?"

"Don't bullshit me."

"I'm not. I had no idea."

Priya studies her. "So you can't sense when one of them is near, but you can hide among the dead ones?"

Sariah sighs. "We don't have, like, a sixth sense. The Ronas can tell when we're near—probably by smell or something—but no, I can't just *know* when someone is one of us." She shakes her head. "But Amy? Damn. She hides it well. Jerod... I had suspicions. Especially at the hotel. I thought I saw some patchwork skin on his chest when he got hit with arrows. But I wasn't sure."

Priya's stomach tightens. "Did you do that to those people at the hotel?"

Sariah scoffs. "God, no. That was Axel and his cronies. They like the taste of brain."

Priya clamps her lips shut, fighting the bile rising in her throat. "They *like* doing that?"

"Oh yeah." Sariah's voice is grim. "They enjoy taking people apart. Bit by bit."

Priya swallows hard. "You said you liked killing people."

"I *liked* killing certain people," Sariah corrects, emphasizing the past tense. "There were times I had to do what I had to do. But I never killed kids. Never hurt innocent women. I only went after the bad apples."

"How did you know who was bad?"

Sariah exhales. "I got in with their groups. Observed. Picked them out." She hesitates. "I was going to kill Jerod... if he hadn't gone mad and thought you killed Heidi."

Priya stills. "Did you kill Heidi?"

Sariah looks her in the eye. "I did." Sariah's voice is steady, almost indifferent. "I was going to stash her body with the others the boys found and eat her quietly that night. But when I slit her throat, I realized she was one of them. I knew she wouldn't stay dead for long." She shrugs. "Didn't like the way she treated you and the others."

Priya clenches her jaw. "Why didn't you take Jerod out when you killed her?"

"I didn't have time. And I didn't want to rouse suspicion."

"No, instead, you made him think *I* killed her."

"That was an accident. I didn't see that coming."

"Jesus fucking Christ, Sariah." Priya's body trembles with barely contained rage. "Every time I talk to you, I get angrier than when I started. I just—UGH." She shoves up from her seat and slams her fist into the wall, instantly regretting it as pain explodes through her knuckles.

"Babe, what—"

"Don't fucking call me that." Priya jabs a shaking finger at Sariah, then cradles her injured hand to her chest. "Was it you? Were you the one feeding on Janice?"

She already knows the answer. She just doesn't want to hear it.

"Yes. But I think Tesslyn was too—because the last time I went down there to take a bite, she'd already been in the room, saying she was setting up the fentanyl drip."

"What the—"

"Janice was already dead, Priya. What does it matter? It's not like *I* killed the bitch. I just fed the hunger I can't ignore."

Priya's stomach churns. "And what happens if you do ignore it?"

"We turn back into those mindless monsters."

"How do you know that?"

Sariah exhales, her expression darkening. "Because I saw it happen. There was a kid—Randy. I helped Purify him. When he came to, when he realized what he was, he didn't want any part of it. Used to be a preacher—the good kind, you know? The kind that actually believes what they preach and doesn't touch little boys." She shakes her head. "He refused to eat, which got him beatings from Charlie. Eventually, Charlie chained him up down there and tried to force-feed him human flesh and brains, but Randy wouldn't touch it. After two weeks without food, I went to check on him... and he was a Rona again. Full-blown. Charlie tried to Purify him again, but there was no saving him. He was gone. So Charlie shot him and buried him out back." Her voice turns hollow. "It was sad. But it's also what keeps me feeding. I don't ever want to be one of those things again. I'd rather die."

Priya swallows against the lump in her throat. "You keep saying that, but how are you any better than those mindless fucks outside? They don't understand what they're doing. You do. And you *still* kill and eat people."

"I know how it sounds." Sariah's gaze locks onto hers, unwavering. "But I will *not* be that again."

The pain in Priya's hand is unbearable now, throbbing with each heartbeat. But it's nothing compared to the ache in her chest. She doesn't want to hear any more of this.

"I need a drink." She turns for the door. "I'll be back later."

Sariah starts to say something, but Priya doesn't hear it.

She doesn't want to.

33

UNBECOMING A MONSTER
SARIAH

Sariah listens to Priya's angry footfalls fading into the distance, the echoes trailing down the empty halls that now serve as her cell. With a sigh, she leans back, staring at the chemo bag dripping poison into her veins.

It's dark as hell down here, but luckily, in her monster form, she can see through the blackness. It's strange, but she finds it comforting as her old human emotions creep back into her bloodstream with each slow drip.

The last time they locked her down here, at least she had company. Even though she had nothing in common with Baxter, Jessica, and Tesslyn, their whining and bickering had been mildly entertaining. They'd spent hours formulating a plan that never had a chance of working, and she humored them, agreeing with every idea they threw her way.

When all hell broke loose, and Jerod and Axel came down to free them—including her—she knew she wasn't going with them. She may have pretended to be weaker than she was, knowing they'd never take her if she became a burden.

Still, she really does feel like shit, there's no faking that.

The chemo is hitting hard, and though it should worry her

that Honor isn't a doctor and has no clue what she's doing, Sariah knows it won't kill her. Being a Rona makes her sort of immortal.

But the cancer?

That will kill her for sure.

And then what?

Would she rise again, only to be cured and thrown into an endless cycle of death and resurrection?

What happens when Ronas get old? A hundred years from now, will they be shuffling around in wheelchairs, wobbling after their prey like decrepit monsters?

The image makes her chuckle as she shifts, trying to get comfortable.

After Jerod and Axel found her, they asked what the fuck was wrong with her. She showed them the chemo bag, and they debated hauling her—IV and all—over to the jail. But when Jerod tried to help her up, she played weak, making it seem like she'd need to be carried the whole way. She knew those assholes wouldn't go for that.

Her plan worked. They left her behind, promising to send someone for her later.

She didn't care either way.

But once they were gone, the silence became unbearable. Minutes stretched into hours, and the emptiness threatened to swallow her whole. She tried singing, telling herself stories—anything to push back the nothingness. None of it helped.

Now that she's alone again, she almost wishes she'd gone with them.

Almost.

Because something is changing. The longer the chemo drips into her system, the more normal she feels. The killer inside her slips away, floating like a balloon from her grasp. And she doesn't fight it. She enjoys watching it go.

What does this mean for her? Who knows.

Priya hates her. She doubts she'll ever be forgiven, but Priya saved her in ways the chemo never could. If she had the chance, she'd spend the rest of her life making it up to her.

But time is running out. They need to get Gratian to Charlie—soon. If the boy dies, Purifying him will be far harder than simply giving him the serum. Not that they even know about the serum yet. She hasn't had a chance to tell them.

Of course, to Priya, it'll look like she's keeping more secrets.

Not that she knows much about it herself. Charlie has probably perfected it by now, made it stronger—better than the alternative.

But what kind of monster would it make Gratian?

Sariah has no idea what kind of teacher she's about to become.

And then—

Wait.

An idea sparks in the back of her mind, tingling at her senses.

What if they give him the chemo *after* the serum?

If it's working on her, making her less of a monster, maybe it could work for him too.

Next time Honor comes down, she's going to tell her.

It has to work.

Doesn't it?

34

THE BREAKING
PRIYA

As they arrive back upstairs, Honor goes over to Gratian, and Priya heads to the kitchen to start making food and get a drink to help with the pain.

The grumble in her stomach reminds her she hasn't eaten in a while, and she wants to get some nourishment into the group before they head to the jail.

Lords know what adventure that will be.

"How'd that go?" Shamus asks as she makes her way to the fridge.

"Oh. You know. Shitty," she admits. "Any meat left?"

"Yeah, there's some rabbit in there from the snares outside. Jesse and I just got done skinning it. What you gonna make?"

"I was going to see if there was enough to hodgepodge something together for tonight's dinner. I can't wait until we're settled somewhere enough to have a garden."

"Wouldn't that be the shit?" Shamus answers from the barstool.

Priya pulls the bottle of rum from the freezer and takes two large swigs.

"Priya," Shamus says, shooting her a sideways glance.

The liquid burns on the way down, settling heavily in her empty stomach—but at least her knuckles start to feel better.

"What?" she hisses through the sting. "Last time I checked, one—we're in an apocalypse, and two—I'm not married to you. So I can drink whenever the fuck I want."

"I was just going to say," Shamus replies, standing up, "pass it this way." He smirks as he plucks the bottle from her hands.

Priya rolls her eyes and rummages through their meager supplies for something edible. There's still some un-poisoned stew left from the last batch she made—good enough for anyone desperate enough to call it breakfast.

The rattling pots stir Pacious, who's curled up on the couch, the big spoon to Liam's little spoon. He grunts and peers over the edge, squinting before reaching for his glasses.

"What time is it?" he mumbles as he gets up and stretches, making his way to the kitchen.

"Early," Shamus answers, flipping the page of a yellowed newspaper. "Not that it matters. The world's still over, in case you missed the headline."

Priya snorts but moves on. "Have you thought about going down there to talk to Sariah at all?" she asks, glancing at Pacious as he pours coffee into a chipped white mug.

"No," he says flatly. "I have nothing to say to her."

"I hear you. But if you feel so inclined, I'd appreciate someone who knew her better than I do going down there to listen. She talks like the chemo is really changing her, and I want to believe her. But at the same time, I don't know her well enough to tell if she's lying."

"Look, Priya," Shamus says, exhaling sharply. "I don't mean to be rude, but you should just consider her dead. The bitch ran with us for a year and lied to us just as long. Even if she is telling the truth, I wouldn't trust her as far as I could throw her."

"He's right," Pacious adds. "Even if she *is* telling the truth, could you really sleep at night knowing one of those fucking imposters is in the same building, the same tent—hell, even the same space as you? Knowing that at any minute, she could walk up and take a chunk out of you?"

They're making sense, and deep down, Priya knows the answer. But a small part of her refuses to let go—the part that still believes in the woman she once knew, the part that wants to see that version of her again.

It's like every time she asks, she's hoping someone will say the words she's desperate to hear: *Yes, you can trust her. She's your shieldmaiden in shining armor. She's going to sweep you off your feet, and you're going to live a hundred more years together on a porch swing, watching your babies and grandbabies play at your feet.*

HOURS LATER, Priya jolts awake, heart pounding at a noise she can't place. She must've dozed off on the couch next to Liam after forcing down her breakfast of stew.

The apartment is silent, everyone still asleep—except Juan, who left to bury Maria with Jesus and hasn't returned.

It's probably just him coming back.

She shifts, turning toward the back of the couch, and lets her eyes drift shut again. But before sleep can take her, a sharp yank at the back of her hair rips her upright. In an instant, she's airborne—then crashing down hard on her ass.

Panic surges as she scrambles to her feet, shoving hair out of her eyes.

The apartment is swarming.

Purified.

"Honor!" she screams as hands grab at her, rough and relentless. Two—no, three of them—wrench her from the couch, forcing her arms behind her back, ropes biting into her wrists.

Shouts explode as Pacious, Shamus, and Jesse snap awake, lunging into the fight.

Someone yanks Gratian out of bed, oblivious—or uncaring—that he can't stand on his own.

"He can't fucking stand, you dickfuck!" Honor roars, struggling against her own captor.

How the hell did they get in?

Was it Sariah?

A massive man—easily 240 pounds, all muscle, with long hair and a beard—grabs Priya by the hair, yanking her head back so she's forced to meet his gaze. His dark eyes gleam with something sickening.

"Mmm," he hums, lips curling into a grin. "You look tasty. I think I'll save you for last."

"Fuck you, you stupid fucking—"

SMACK.

His palm collides with her face so hard her vision flares white-hot. Her ears ring. The room tilts.

She barely gets her bearings before he slams her backward, her nose cracking against the wall with a sickening crunch. Pain detonates across her face. Warm blood gushes instantly, spilling over her lips.

She tries to lift a hand, instinctively reaching to stop the flow, but rough fingers clamp around her wrists. A zip tie cinches tight, biting into her skin.

Then he yanks her forward by the plastic restraint, sending her stumbling.

"On your knees," he orders, shoving her down.

Before she can even brace herself, the butt of his gun swings toward her temple.

CRACK.

Agony explodes through her skull as her eyebrow splits open. Blood spills down her face, blinding her. She gasps, trying to blink it away, but with her hands bound, she's helpless.

35

AND HER WORLD GOES DARK

HONOR

Chaos swirls around Honor as she begs the Purified to leave her son alone. A massive man pins her down, his knee crushing the back of her neck, the floor biting into her cheek. She can barely breathe, her vision blurred by pain and dust. Just beyond him, she sees Gratian, crawling, trying to get away.

"PLEASE!" she screams, sobbing, spittle flying from her lips. "Let my child go! He's been bitten—he needs help!"

Tesslyn appears, shoving away the men gripping Gratian. "He can't stand, you idiots! Let me handle him."

They scoff but relent, turning instead to where Jesse, Pacious, and Shamus are bound together in the kitchen, their hands wrenched behind their backs.

"Good job, team," rumbles a deep voice from behind Honor. She doesn't need to see him to know—it must be Charlie, their leader.

"Alright, looks like we got everyone. Did someone go down and get my wench yet?" His tone is casual, dismissive.

So it wasn't her who let them in?

Honor was certain it was.

"No, she ain't down there," a woman answers.

Charlie's voice sharpens. "She's not? Where the fuck else would she be? She can't have gone far."

"We'll look around, sir," the woman replies before her boots clomp away.

Honor seizes the moment. "Sir—please—" She chokes, barely able to form words under the weight of the man's knee. "I just need to see my baby."

A sharp blow to the back of her head sends nausea rolling through her.

"Shut the fuck up," the man growls.

"MAMA!" Gratian cries.

Honor fights to turn her head, but the pressure only intensifies, crushing her into the floor. "It's okay, baby," she soothes as best she can. "Just stay calm. Do what they say."

"I said shut—"

"That's enough, Axel."

The command stills the violence, and Honor hears heavy boots approaching. "Let a mother soothe her child," Charlie says, his voice dripping with mock sympathy.

The weight on her neck vanishes, but before she can react, Axel yanks her upright by the hair. She clamps her hands over his, trying to ease the pain in her scalp.

A man crouches in front of her, his face weathered, salt-and-pepper hair neatly trimmed. Cigarettes and cinnamon taint his breath.

"You're a feisty one, aren't you?" he muses, his eyes gleaming. "We could use someone like you."

"I'll never be a monster like you," Honor spits.

A second blow crashes into her skull, blinding her with pain.

"MAMA!" Gratian sobs, desperation thick in his voice.

From behind her, Jesse snarls, "Don't you fucking touch her!"

A sickening thud—flesh and bone colliding with metal. Jesse grunts in pain.

Charlie chuckles. "All you have to do is behave, sweetheart. Then we won't have to do that anymore."

"What do you want from us?" Honor demands.

Charlie's laughter starts as a quiet shake of his shoulders, then builds into a full-bodied cackle. He tosses his head back, as if she's just told the funniest joke in the world.

"What do we want?" He leans in, his dimpled smirk inches from her face. "You're the ones who fucked with us first. We want our girl back. And we want you to pay for poisoning my boy Baxter and those two bitches, Tesslyn and Jessica. See, we don't take kindly to people who don't take kindly to us."

"You eat people," Honor retorts. "How the hell is that taking kindly?"

She braces for another blow. But instead, Charlie inches closer, his foul breath mingling with her own.

"I like you," he murmurs. "You've got fire."

"Fuck you," Jesse snaps.

Charlie's attention shifts. "Oh, he likes you, doesn't he?" He glances toward Jesse and the others, his smirk widening. "Baxter told me you killed one of ours for another man in your group. I'd wager it's him, huh?"

Honor stiffens. "One of yours?"

Lux was one of theirs?

Questions swarm in her mind.

Charlie studies her, then chuckles. "You really didn't know, did you?"

"What the hell are you talking about?"

He strokes his stubbled chin, savoring the moment. "Interesting. I figured he'd slip up at least once."

He reaches into his pocket and pulls out a syringe with an orange cap. Honor recognizes it—insulin syringes.

"I took Dr. Mercer's brilliant work," Charlie says, biting off the cap, "and improved it. Mixed it with a few other geniuses I ate, and boom—one of the greatest creations in the world."

Her pulse hammers. "What does this have to do with my husband?"

Charlie grins. "Late husband, don't you mean?"

The words sting. She forces a nod. "Yes. Late husband."

"I caught him and that other one—Jerod—out hunting. They were my first test subjects. We kidnapped them, injected them with my serum, and waited." He twirls the syringe between his fingers. "Twenty-four hours later, they turned."

Honor's world tilts.

Charlie grips her arm, wrenching it forward despite her bound wrists. The needle's tip glints in the dim light.

"I perfected it. A serum that initiates the immortal side of being a Rona—without the rot. No need to die and rise again."

Honor's breath comes in short, sharp gasps.

"MAMA!" Gratian's scream cuts through the haze. His small face is twisted in terror.

Charlie presses the needle to her skin.

"No—" She thrashes, but Axel clamps down on her neck.

The needle punctures her flesh.

Charlie smiles.

"You shall be one of my monsters."

The plunger depresses.

And her world goes dark.

36

BALL BITES ARE A BITCH
PRIYA

Priya doesn't know what to think when her heart suddenly drops.

Jerod, Baxter, and Tesslyn stride into the room. Baxter has Juan by the shirt, gripping him like a ragdoll, while Tesslyn drags Jesus by the hair, his arm still oozing blood from the bite wounds he endured.

Jerod saunters toward her and kneels, his ugly face blotchy and red from the effort of running up the stairs. Bald, overweight, and reeking of sweat, his crooked yellow teeth flash in a sinister grin. His dead, emotionless blue eyes bore into her.

"Thought I was dead, didn't you, bitch?" His deep voice booms through the room.

Priya stiffens as he pulls a syringe from his back pocket, flicks off the cap, and holds it up so the silver glint of the needle catches the dim light.

Her death.

Around the room, other Purified close in, each holding their own syringes, caps flicked off in unison. The ones surrounding Jesse, Pacious, and Shamus are ready, as are those near Michael and Krishna. The plan is clear—they're going to turn them into monsters all at once.

Priya's gaze locks onto Jesse. He's gripping a knife in his left hand, having already sawed through the zip ties binding him. He winks at her—a silent instruction—before slipping the blade to Pacious.

She knows they have weapons hidden on their bodies, but will it be enough to take down a group this large?

Honor's head is bowed, her chin touching her chest.

Passed out?

Unconscious?

Priya has no idea, but she doesn't have time to worry about that now.

Her gaze flicks to Gratian. The kid is on the floor in tears, staring at his mother with a hollow expression. He looks scared, but also... dead.

Not dead dead.

Rona dead.

This might be their chance.

She waits for Jesse's signal, heart pounding. No plan forms in her mind, except for one. If nothing else, she'll bite Jerod as hard as she can between the legs and run.

Jerod smirks. "I'm going to enjoy this part."

"You know I didn't kill your wife, right?" Priya says, stalling. "I mean, she was a fucking monster. Just like you."

"I don't give a fuck about that. I just don't like you, brown bitch."

"Oh, so it's a race thing now?"

His backhand slams into her face before she can react. Pain explodes through her already busted eyebrow, and warm blood trickles from her nose. She wipes it on her shoulder, then catches something in her peripheral vision.

A shadow shifts in the hallway—someone backing into the darkness.

Watching.

She blinks, shakes her head.

Anxiety?

Hallucination?

She doesn't have time to dwell on it.

Jesse nods.

And all hell breaks loose.

In a flash, Jesse springs forward and buries his knife in the brute's jugular. Blood erupts like a geyser, spraying his face. Pacious drives his own blade into a man's skull, dropping him instantly. Shamus slashes the throat of a nearby Purified woman.

Jesse lunges for his bow on the counter.

Charlie, realizing the chaos, grabs Honor by the hair and yanks her toward the hallway. Jesse lets an arrow fly—it narrowly misses. Shamus fires his gun, a single shot exploding through the room as Axel drops dead.

Priya doesn't hesitate. She lunges at Jerod, sinking her teeth into his crotch with all her strength. His agonized scream shreds the air. She releases him and stumbles toward Pacious, who slices through her zip ties.

Shamus struggles with another Purified, missing his strikes as the man dodges each blow.

Priya makes a break for Gratian, but the man holding him presses a knife to his throat.

"Whoa, don't do that," she says, her hands raised.

Jesse is already chasing Charlie down the stairs with Honor, while Pacious works on freeing Michael.

Shamus takes out another Purified, but Jerod is limping toward her, his face a furious shade of red. He pulls out a gun.

Priya's breath catches. She has no weapons. No time.

Jerod raises the barrel and aims at her head.

Then, a piercing scream.

The man holding Gratian howls in agony as the child sinks

his teeth into his hand—hard. Flesh tears. A finger comes clean off.

Jerod pauses, eyes flicking to the commotion.

It's all the distraction Priya needs.

But before she can move, he refocuses, gun locking back onto her. His finger tightens on the trigger—

A blur of movement.

Sariah bursts from behind the couch, throwing herself in front of Priya just as the gun fires.

The shot rips through her chest.

Priya barely has time to register what's happening before Sariah crashes into her, both of them hitting the floor.

The world spins.

Then everything erupts into chaos again.

37

I WAS FEELING EPIC
JESSE

Jesse chases Charlie down the dark stairwell, loosing arrows every chance he gets. Not wanting to run out, he ducks into the nearest room, quickly reloading while gathering the fallen ones from the floor. He retrieves his gun from his boot, chambers a round, and tucks it into the front of his waistband.

Charlie has gone to the basement.

The torture chamber.

His playground.

Jesse's heart pounds against his ribs, his only thought to put a bullet in Charlie's head and free Honor from his grasp—even though he has no idea what that means for her now that she's been injected with the serum.

He takes a steadying breath and moves out from behind the curtain, listening for any noise that might give away Charlie's location. Avoiding his flashlight so he doesn't reveal himself, he steps into the stairwell leading to the dungeon. The darkness is absolute, swallowing every trace of light until he can't even see his own hand.

This isn't a good idea.

He hesitates, then turns back toward the main floor. Confronting Charlie down there would be suicide—Charlie will see him first, and that advantage could mean Jesse's death. Better to wait. Charlie will come for him.

Won't he?

Honor is already injected. There's nothing more Charlie can do to her.

A gunshot echoes from above, yanking Jesse's attention upward. Someone just died.

Chaos reigns upstairs, and he wrestles with the decision—stay and wait for Charlie or go help his team. If he heads into the basement, it could mean both his and Honor's deaths. He needs to be smart.

Moving quietly, Jesse starts up the stairs. If Charlie thinks he's still after him, all the better. He'll regroup upstairs.

The commotion from the apartment suggests his group is gaining the upper hand.

"Sit the fuck down!" Pacious yells. A low, guttural grumble follows—either Baxter or Shamus. They're both grumbly.

Jesse peeks around the corner at the wreckage. Most of the Purified are subdued, but a few of his own look worse for wear.

Emerging fully, he spots Pacious and Shamus tying Baxter up—again. Priya is bruised and bloodied, cradling Sariah in her lap. Gratian crawls toward Jesse, his Rona-infected eyes eerie and blank, blood dribbling down his chin.

The man who once held Gratian down is missing a finger, now being restrained by Michael. Krishna limps toward Priya, while Juan helps Jesus with his bindings.

Jesus sits eerily still on the couch, looking dangerously close to turning Rona himself.

Liam, still not strong enough to stand, is curled up with his knees to his chest against the far wall.

Dead Purified litter the floor—Tesslyn, Jessica, Jerod, the latter with a bullet hole clean through his forehead.

"Pash," Jesse calls.

Pacious looks up from tying one of the Purified women. "Dude." He hurries over, wrapping Jesse in a quick, one-armed hug. "You get Charlie?"

"Nah, he disappeared into the basement. I don't wanna go down there without light."

Pacious shoves him aside. "Whoa—watch out."

Gratian lunges for Jesse's leg.

"Poor little dude," Jesse mutters, eyeing the Rona version of Gratian.

"Here," Pacious says, handing over a confiscated syringe. "Shoot him up with this."

Jesse takes it, turning it over in his hand, skeptical.

"It's alright, Jesse. It's his only chance." Pacious claps his shoulder, reassuring. "It's what Honor would want."

"Do it, Jesse," Priya urges, her voice thick with pain. Blood trickles down her face, mixing with her tears. "Save him."

Jesse pulls off the cap, kneels beside Gratian, and holds his forehead steady to avoid getting bitten. With a steady hand, he drives the needle into Gratian's neck and presses the plunger.

"We'll have to tie him up," Shamus says, kneeling beside them. "Until the mindless Rona passes."

Jesse nods, holding Gratian down with Pacious while Shamus secures the restraints. Gratian snaps at them, but they dodge his teeth.

Lucky for them, he can't walk.

"Should we go after Charlie?" Pacious asks, loading a fresh clip into his Glock.

"Yeah, one sec." Jesse makes his way to Priya. Sariah lies in her lap, still breathing but barely. Her chest is a mess of blood, a bullet wound at its center. Her eyes, half-lidded, track his movement.

"Hey," he says softly, kneeling beside her.

Even after all the lies, he still loves her. He doesn't want to see her die.

"Hey, you," she rasps.

"What'd you go and do, huh?" He takes her hand, squeezing gently.

She musters a faint smile. "I was feeling epic," she whispers, quoting *The Vampire Diaries*. "Saw my love needed a maiden in shining armor. So I was one."

Jesse shakes his head.

What kind of villain catches a bullet for someone?

Maybe she was telling the truth. Maybe the chemo is changing her.

Priya strokes the back of Sariah's hand, her swollen eye blinking slowly, tears spilling freely.

"Is there anything I should know about Charlie before I go kill him?" Jesse asks.

Sariah's breath hitches. "He's strong. Super strong. It'll take all three of you to take him down. He can see in the dark. He's ruthless. If he gets ahold of you, you're dead."

Jesse exhales sharply. "Right. So—night vision, super strength, extra side of dickhole. Got it."

Sariah grips his wrist as he moves to stand. "Jesse." Her voice wavers. "I would tell you to be careful, but I know you won't be. So don't be stupid. If it looks like you won't win, accept that and walk away. Don't get yourself killed." She hesitates, then adds, "She's already gone."

Priya scoffs. Jesse clenches his jaw.

"I won't accept that," he says, his voice low. "But I won't be stupid." He squeezes Sariah's hand one last time. "Don't die."

He gets up and walks away before she can say anything more.

38

TAKE AWAY THIS DEATH
HONOR

Darkness surrounds her. Honor hears Charlie breathing beside her, still clutching her neck. Static, warmth, nausea, and swirling sensations overwhelm her as whatever is happening to her body wreaks havoc on her system.

She thinks of Gratian, and a sadness more profound than anything she's ever felt tightens around her like a chokehold. She hopes someone saved him, that someone had the decency to inject him with this awful thing—because then, at least, he wouldn't be a mindless Rona.

It feels like she's dying. Like every atom and cell inside her is on fire, multiplying, dividing—every nerve buzzing, as if she swallowed a bolt of lightning and it's making a home within her.

Dizziness washes over her, and she doesn't dare move too fast for fear of throwing up. She hasn't eaten in—she doesn't know how long—so she isn't sure what she could even vomit. Still, she fights back the urge, trying to orient herself in the darkness.

Whatever is happening to her body, she imagines she's

becoming a Purified without turning into a Rona first. Even though, technically, she *is* dying.

As she focuses on her breathing, the room sharpens around her, as though the darkness is seeping into her soul, making her one with it.

If this is her fate, then she'll accept it.

She just needs to hold on long enough to reach her child, to make sure he's safe before she succumbs to whatever waits for her.

A sound echoes down the hall—faint, like the scrape of a shoe against the floor. Normal ears wouldn't catch it.

But she does.

And it sounds close.

Even her hearing is sharpening in this monstrous state.

Charlie tenses beside her. He hears it too.

She doesn't know what's coming, but she assumes Jesse is on his way. There's no plan—only instinct. She slumps further down the wall, pulling Charlie with her, knowing he won't let go until Jesse is in sight.

Charlie crouches next to her, his eyes locked on the darkness, waiting.

A large machete glints in his hands. It wasn't on him upstairs. Maybe he stashed it down here before—when this was their home.

Her hands are still bound behind her back, leaving her with only one option. She takes a deep breath and unleashes an earth-shattering wail, letting their pursuers know exactly where they are.

Everything happens at once.

She screams. She collapses, dragging Charlie with her. Heavy boots slam against the cement—three sets, running straight for them.

Chaos erupts.

Charlie releases her and starts swinging. Pacious, Shamus,

and Jesse barely dodge the blade. Jesse's flashlight flicks onto her, and in the split second of illumination, she throws herself sideways, sweeping Charlie's legs out from under him.

Charlie falls forward. The machete slices into Pacious's arm, and the sound is sickening. His scream shatters the air, throwing everyone off balance. Jesse unloads his clip into Charlie.

The scent of blood slams into her senses.

It's intoxicating.

She wants to lick it, to drop to her knees and lap it from the floor. It's more than a craving—it's a need. A hunger deeper than anything she has ever felt. She wants to sink her teeth into the flesh, chew, devour—

Charlie doesn't flinch. He rises and lunges at Jesse.

Shamus fires, his gun emptying as fast as his trigger finger allows.

Pacious, blood gushing from his wound, grips his spear and charges. The weapon spears straight through Charlie's middle. His blood is different. Wrong. It smells foul, like rotting sludge, disrupting the cloying sweetness of Pacious's wound.

Jesse nocks an arrow and releases. It strikes Charlie through the skull.

He stills. Falls. Motionless.

Jesse rushes to Honor and slices through her zip ties, freeing her wrists.

"You okay?" he asks, hauling her up.

"I'm fine," she gasps, breathless. "But my son—where is my son?"

"Honor—" Jesse starts, but she doesn't hear him.

She's already gone.

Her child is all she can think about.

She bounds up the stairs, her body threatening to betray her with every step. Nausea claws at her throat. The world spins. But she forces herself forward.

She reaches the main landing and stops, her vision flaring white. The ground tilts.

Jesse catches up, placing a hand on her lower back as she bends over, bracing her knees.

"Honor," he says. "He's not good. He's a Rona right now—but we gave him the serum."

"I have to see him."

She smells Pacious's blood creeping up the stairs behind her. The temptation is unbearable. Before she gives in, she lurches forward, staggering toward the stairwell leading to the apartment.

Jesse steadies her as best he can, but she barely registers his help.

She has to see her child.

Every step is a mountain, each one steeper than the last. Her limbs burn. Fire tears through her veins. She could collapse at any moment—but something else fuels her. A fury. A desperate, unyielding fire.

She reaches the top.

And then she sees him.

Gratian.

His eyes are white. Blood drips from his chin.

A mindless Rona.

Her heart plummets.

Her baby.

She rushes to him, getting as close as she can. He doesn't see her. Doesn't react. It's like he's looking through her.

"I thought you said someone gave him the serum," she sobs, wanting nothing more than to gather him in her arms and take this nightmare away.

"That's not how it works," Sariah croaks, her voice weak.

Honor turns. Sariah lies against Priya, looking deathly pale, blood pooling around her. Priya is barely recognizable—bloody, beaten, broken.

"What do you mean?" Honor demands. "I thought you said—"

"I said to get him the serum before he died," Sariah rasps. "Now he has to be Purified first. From what I know, the serum only works if they haven't already died from CoRona. It skips the dying and decay and goes straight to the vicious villain part."

"Shit," Honor breathes, collapsing to her knees. "What do we do now? We just killed the only man who knew how to Purify him."

"I know what you can do," Sariah says, her tone grim. "But you're not going to like it."

Honor already knows what she's going to say before she even says it.

"What?" Jesse asks.

"She's going to have to eat his brain and do it herself."

39

THERE ARE DEAD PEOPLE EVERYWHERE

HONOR

Honor is sweating. Her mind is swimming, fever burning through her. Her child is tied up, trying to bite people, mid-transition into a monster. There are dead people everywhere.

She sits as close to Gratian as she dares, careful not to let him bite her. Not that it would matter at this point—who knows what's happening to her own body?

Priya is still cradling Sariah, who's barely clinging to life. Jesse drags corpses into a pile by the door, while Juan rifles through pockets, desperately searching for a syringe—he needs to hurry, because Jesus doesn't look good.

Shamus never came back up from the basement, likely stashing Charlie's body somewhere. Krishna is nursing her injured knee, and Michael is securing the ropes on the surviving Purified, making sure none of them escape.

Then, the stairwell door slams. Everyone looks up, tense, until they see it's Shamus. His brow is furrowed, either in concentration or frustration.

"What is it?" Jesse asks, dropping Tesslyn's lifeless hands mid-drag. If Shamus looks like that, something's very wrong.

"Either he wasn't dead, or he can't be killed."

Honor's heart plummets. "What?"

"I was moving him—dragging him up here—when he woke up. Bullet hole in his head and everything. He was sluggish, like he was drunk, but he still managed to fight me. And then he ran."

"Ran?" Honor echoes, forcing herself to her feet. "What do you mean, ran?"

"Tried to tie him up, but he's strong. Fought like hell. Then the bastard bit me and bolted—straight up the stairs and out the door."

Fucking hell.

What the fuck are they going to do now?

Jesse meets Honor's gaze.

He's thinking what she's thinking.

"We'll have to go to him," she says, her voice hollow. "Beg him to Purify my child."

"Anybody got a syringe?" Shamus asks, inspecting the fresh bite on his arm.

Pacious, who's in the middle of stitching up a nasty gash on his own arm, clears his throat. "Yeah, there's some over here in these assholes' pockets."

Shamus heads for the dead Purified in the kitchen, searching them.

Jesse nudges Tesslyn's body with his boot. "So... does that mean all of these fools are about to wake up too?"

"I don't know," Shamus grumbles, "but I wouldn't take that risk."

"We can't die, you idiots," a voice pipes up from the corner. It's one of the tied-up Purified. "They're just sleeping. They'll wake up soon."

Either he's too stupid to realize the advantage of surprise, or he's trying to trick them into moving the bodies—giving him a chance to escape in the chaos.

"Welp," Pacious says, finishing his stitches. "Time to move them outside."

"If they're gonna wake up," Priya says slowly, "then Sariah should be fine in a bit... right?"

But Sariah's eyes are closed, her breathing faint.

"She definitely needs more chemo," Honor mutters, fighting the surge of heat rolling over her.

The scent of blood overwhelms her senses, a war raging in her mind. One part of her wants to devour everyone in the room. The other part fights back, desperate to smother that instinct, to shut it down and never feel it again.

Another wave of fresh blood fills the air. Her hunger surges, and she squeezes her eyes shut, reaching deep within herself. So deep, she nearly loses consciousness.

And then—there it is. A switch in her mind.

She flips it off.

The hunger disappears. The blood scent fades.

When she opens her eyes, Gratian lunges at her. She sidesteps just in time, setting him upright before he faceplants again.

He really is a cute little zombie.

A fucked-up thought, but maybe she's delusional.

She steadies herself and moves to Jesse, who's preparing to haul Tesslyn's body out.

"Do you really think that guy's telling the truth?" she whispers, making sure the Purified man can't hear.

Jesse exhales sharply. "How else did Charlie just get up and walk out of here?" He nods toward Tesslyn. "Pash, grab her feet."

Honor shakes her head and walks over to Priya, sliding down the edge of the bed to sit beside her.

"Hey," Priya says. "How are you holding up?"

She manages a tired smile. How kind of Priya to ask, when she looks like *she's* the one who just got mugged in a dark alley.

"I'm alright. How's Sariah?"

"Passed out. I don't know."

"And you?"

"Splitting headache," Priya mutters, eyeing the bottle of rum on the counter.

Honor follows her gaze. "You want some?"

"Yes, please."

As Priya shifts Sariah's weight, the woman suddenly jolts upright, gasping like she's been drowning.

Honor's first instinct is to run.

What kind of monster is she now?

Sariah blinks, looking around in confusion.

Priya scrambles away, crab-crawling across the floor. But before she can get far, Sariah grabs her leg.

"What's wrong?" Sariah asks, bewildered.

Honor's heartbeat steadies.

"You good?" Priya asks warily.

Sariah frowns. "Yeah. I feel... weird. But good."

"Let me see your chest," Priya says.

Sariah smirks.

"Not like that, weirdo."

But she pulls down her leather vest anyway.

The bullet wound—right through her heart—is gone. In its place, fresh skin, like patchwork.

"Interesting," Sariah murmurs.

"Told ya," the Purified man chimes in.

Honor sighs. "What's your name?" she asks, tired of calling him "the Purified man" in her head.

"Zane," he answers. He's a massive, tattooed brute, tied up but still dangerous-looking.

Sariah tilts her head. "Zane... how much Purifying did you help Charlie do?"

"Oh, tons. I'd like to think I was his right-hand man, aside from Axel over there. Charlie trusted me more than him."

"I see, I see..." Sariah muses. "And if we asked for your help Purifying our little buddy over there, could you do it?"

Honor narrows her eyes.

What is Sariah up to?

"By the way," Sariah adds, her voice dangerously casual, "did you eat someone recently? Someone you probably shouldn't have?"

Zane's eyes widen. "What do you mean?"

"You know, like a sweet old lady? A good person?"

"Well, yeah, but that's what—"

Sariah lunges.

Her teeth tear into Zane's throat. He screams, blood gurgling in his mouth as it sprays across the table. Shamus is on him in an instant, tearing into his shoulder like an animal unleashed.

Jesse and Pacious burst through the door—freeze.

"What the hell—" Jesse breathes, backing into a wall.

Honor can't look away. She should feel sick. But all she feels is stillness.

Zane thrashes in the chair, eyes wide, blood pouring from his neck.

Sariah doesn't hesitate. She grabs a large knife off the table —something salvaged from the hotel kitchen—and jabs it straight down into the top of his skull. The sound is sickening, like cracking a melon. His body seizes. Then slumps.

"Shamus, help me," she mutters, wiping blood from her face.

Without a word, he lifts the limp body by the shoulders. Sariah grabs his feet.

"What are you doing?" Priya asks, her voice sharp with shock.

Sariah glances back, wild-eyed. "Taking him downstairs to open his skull and eat his brain."

Silence.

"So *you* don't have to go to the jail," she adds, locking eyes with Priya.

Jesse collapses into the couch, staring at the blood trails on the floor. "And you still say you've changed?"

"I did this for Gratian," Sariah says, quieter now. Her face is pale.

Honor doesn't know what's worse—the horror she just witnessed... or the fact that this might actually be her child's only chance.

40

NOT IN THE ZOMBIE WAY

PRIYA

Seeing Sariah murder that man was, without a doubt, one of the most disgusting things Priya has ever witnessed.

Her feelings for Sariah have shifted—twisted into something unrecognizable. She knows Sariah did it for Honor, for her child. But Jesus fucking Christ, that was brutal.

Even knowing the man was already dead—a killer himself, who'd admitted to eating someone he shouldn't have—it doesn't make what Priya just saw any easier to stomach.

It was horrific.

How could she ever be with someone like that?

What if, years from now, they're sleeping in the same bed and she wakes up to find Sariah gnawing on her leg?

Priya's head throbs. She needs that rum.

Pushing off the couch, she strides to the counter, grabs the bottle, and takes two—no, three—huge swigs. The burn sears her throat, stinging all the way down. She winces at the tart bite, then twists the cap back on and heads toward Honor, who's sitting beside Gratian. He's gone white-eyed and snaps at the air like some kind of rabid turtle. The whole scene is unnerving.

Juan has given Jesus the serum, which seems to be holding off the worst of the virus, but they still need to keep an eye on him.

Priya passes the bottle to Honor, who takes it, loosens the cap, and downs a swig of the brown liquid.

"Well, now that he's gone," Priya says, watching as Jesse, Sariah, Shamus, and Pacious haul more bodies out of the apartment, "we need to get Gratian started on the Purification."

Honor hisses at the burn of the alcohol, then looks over at her son. "Yeah. And what do you think about Shamus being one of the Purified now? And Jesus?"

"And you," Priya adds, making Honor scowl. "Not that I don't trust you, but we just watched Sariah murder a man and go eat his brain. I'm not putting anything past anyone anymore."

Honor grins and pinches Priya's side, making her squeal. "I'm gonna eat you first."

"Please do. Put me out of my misery."

"Aww, boo, I'm sorry." Honor pouts, then shrugs. "If it's any consolation, I don't want to eat brains. I did at first, but then—I don't know—I flipped some mental switch, and the craving just disappeared."

"What do you think that's about?"

"No clue. Maybe the chemo I got before? Maybe Sariah's onto something."

"Maybe." Priya takes another swig, then passes the bottle back. "Bigger question is, how do we kill them if a headshot doesn't work?"

"Taking out their brains seems to do the trick."

"Yeah, but realistically, if we run into more of them on the road, how are we supposed to get to their brains?"

"Burn them," Jesse says, suddenly appearing beside them.

His hands are streaked with blood from dragging Axel's body outside. "We're piling them up and setting them on fire. We'll see if they rise then."

"That's a good idea," Priya replies.

"If you wanna help get these fuckers outside," Sariah calls over her shoulder, dragging Jessica's corpse toward the stairs, "we can get started on Purifying your boy there."

Honor nods, stands, and offers Priya a hand up.

***

By the time the last body hits the flames, hours have slipped by. The scent of burning flesh fills the air.

Jesse, Honor, and Pacious stand back, watching the bodies burn. They got all of them—Janice, Jerod, Heidi, Axel—every last one.

"Hopefully this keeps them from coming back," Jesse says.

"And if it doesn't," Pacious adds, "we'll be ready this time."

Honor watches the flames dance, her fingers laced with Jesse's. His hands are cold and clammy but grounding.

"I'm going to mix up the serum," Sariah says, turning toward the building.

"How long does the process take?" Honor asks.

Sariah shrugs. "Depends on the state of decay. The worse they are, the longer it takes. But someone like Gratian? A few days. We can add the leukemia chemo to speed up the healing process—keep him from turning into a mindless monster first."

"Yeah, uh, about that..." Honor trails off.

Sariah sighs. "Look, I know you don't trust me. That's fine—I wouldn't either. But I'm telling you, I'm not the same as before. Whatever's in that chemo you gave me? It changed me. I don't crave blood like I did. It's a miracle."

"We still need to give you more rounds," Priya says. "You're not done."

Sariah nods. "You can hook me up while we're down there."

As she and Priya head inside, Jesse stops Honor with a hand on her arm. "How's it going for you?"

"Surprisingly fine. There was one moment when I smelled Pacious's wound and wanted to lick it. But then—the weirdest thing happened."

Jesse's blue eyes hold steady on hers. "What?"

"I—I don't know how to explain it. I dove deep into my own mind and found a switch. A literal light switch. I flipped it off, and ever since, the craving hasn't come back."

Jesse smirks. That tiny gap in his teeth makes her stomach flip.

"That's interesting," he says, edging closer.

Her heart pounds. She wants him to kiss her. Wants it more than anything.

But not here. Not now.

"You think it has something to do with the same chemo I'm giving Sariah?" she asks.

Jesse clasps both her hands in his, his voice low. "I had the same thought."

"Maybe Sariah isn't completely full of shit," she muses. "But I don't know if I can trust her yet."

"Same with Shamus," Jesse says. "I never fully trusted him, with his shady past. But I still feel like he won't hurt us."

Honor frowns. "I'm not so sure. He needs the chemo immediately. He's the type who wouldn't hesitate to kill someone."

Jesse chuckles. "Yeah, he does seem like that."

"What was he in jail for again?"

"Robbery. Some real *Criminal Minds* type shit. He stole millions from big corporations. Swore he'd never touch a mom-and-pop shop."

"Well, that's... something."

Jesse grins. "Remember when Sariah murdered that guy and ate his brain?"

Honor snorts. "Yeah. It was literally hours ago."

They enter the building, making their way to the back rooms, where Sariah is busy mixing medicine with puréed vegetables.

Honor eyes the containers. "Where did you find those?"

"Charlie had a stash in the freezer downstairs. I thawed them in the microwave. He made thousands of these before we hit the jail."

"Why didn't he take them with him?" Jesse asks.

"I think he planned on coming back. Or using both places. But apparently, the jail had a vegetable garden and a stockpile of canned goods, so he didn't need them."

"So what's next?" Honor asks.

Sariah straightens. "We need to hook Gratian up to a feeding tube. It goes through his nose and into his stomach. Once I add the medicine, we'll shackle him to one of the beds. You don't want to watch this part."

Priya glances at Honor, who shakes her head. "No. I have to help him however I can."

"We need to make sure he doesn't bite anyone," Sariah warns. "Someone will have to hold him down while we insert the tube."

"I can help with that," Jesse offers.

"How do we stop him from biting?" Pacious asks.

"We gag him," Sariah says simply.

Jesse sighs. "Let's just get him down there first."

Honor nods. As Jesse, Pacious, and Shamus leave to retrieve Gratian, Sariah exits to gather the medicine.

And the real work begins.

41

DYNAMITE

JESSE

"Alright, you grab his ankles and tie them up," Jesse says as he and Pacious creep toward Gratian, who's still snapping at them like a rabid turtle. "I know he can't walk, but these things sometimes have crazy strength. I'll gag him so he can't bite. Then we hogtie him and get him downstairs. Try not to let Honor see him like this if we can help it."

"You really got a thing for her, huh?" Pacious smirks as he grabs Gratian's feet, pulling him flat and binding them tight with rope.

Gratian thrashes weakly. Even in death, his muscles aren't as strong as most.

Jesse shrugs. "She's cool. Hot. She's got this grit I like. Hard to explain."

"Yeah, yeah," Shamus mutters, used to Jesse's aloofness by now.

"Just be careful," Pacious warns, nodding toward Shamus with a knowing look. "She's one of them now."

"Fuck you," Shamus shoots back with a smirk.

"Dude, just don't eat me in my sleep," Pacious jokes,

holding up his hands in mock surrender. "I wanna get my dick sucked at least one more time before I die—preferably not by a Rona."

"Maybe Liam will do it," Shamus quips, glancing at Liam, who's pulling himself onto the couch. "He probably needs a good fuck after being down in the dark for so long."

"It's true, I do," Liam says jovially, finally settling into a comfortable position.

Jesse chuckles as Pacious grins and winks at Liam.

"Alright," Pacious says, refocusing. "You keep his head still," he instructs Jesse, "and I'll tie this around his face. Ready?"

"One, two, three."

Jesse grabs Gratian's head as Pacious quickly works to tie the bandana around his mouth, dodging the snapping teeth.

"Maybe we should've had Shamus do this part," Pacious mutters, narrowly avoiding Gratian's lunge as he drops the bandana. "He's already Purified—maybe he's immune to their bites now."

"Let me try," Shamus grumbles, taking the cloth from Pacious as Jesse readies himself to hold Gratian's head again.

"Okay, ready? One, two, three."

Jesse pins Gratian's head while Shamus moves swiftly, wedging the bandana between his teeth and looping it around his head. Jesse lifts his chin, and Shamus secures the knot, rendering Gratian incapable of biting anyone—at least for now.

"Alright, good. Now tie his hands behind him," Pacious instructs.

Jesse pulls Gratian's arms back, looping the rope from his feet to bind his wrists securely.

"Careful lifting him," Jesse warns as Shamus holds Gratian's head steady, Pacious grabs his knees, and Jesse supports him under the arms. "Head to the stairs. Sariah should be ready with the concoction."

"Hey, can you guys grab my braces on the way back?" Liam

calls as they shuffle past him. His messy brown hair falls over his forehead as he watches from the couch. He describes them, and Pacious nods.

"Yeah, we'll look for them," he says.

With a mix of grunts and muttered instructions, they carefully navigate down the stairs to the main floor and into the basement. Shamus opens the door, flicks on his flashlight, and leads them down into the first room on the right. Jesse lays Gratian on his side so they can untie the temporary restraints, and Shamus secures his ankles to the shackles bolted into the floor.

Jesse frees his hands next, strapping them down with thick bands—like something out of an old insane asylum—securing his wrists, then his head with a forehead strap.

Sariah enters, setting a small bag of supplies on the examination table as Pacious finds the light switch, illuminating the room with a bright surgical lamp. The harsh glow reflects in Gratian's eerie white eyes.

"I just need to find a feeding tube, then we can begin," Sariah says before hurrying out. Moments later, Priya and Honor arrive.

Honor kneels beside Gratian, gently brushing his forehead before pressing a soft kiss to the top of his head. "You have to be strong for me, sweet boy," she whispers. "We're going to give you something to help you feel better."

Jesse moves closer, resting a reassuring hand on the small of her back.

"Look what I found," Sariah announces, reentering the room—this time holding a bundle of dynamite.

"Whoa!" Jesse exclaims, rushing over to take it from her. Old or not, that shit is dangerous. "Where the fuck did you find this?"

"In a tunnel behind the good doctor's office," she explains. "It was hidden behind a filing cabinet. Looks like he dug it out himself and stashed it—just in case. There's a whole boatload down there."

"Fuuuuck," Pacious mutters, sidling up to Jesse to get a better look at the dirt-covered explosives. "What the hell, bro?"

"What was he planning on doing with this?" Jesse wonders aloud, carefully handling the bundle.

"No clue," Sariah admits. "Maybe he planned to blow this place up after he was done? I don't know. But I'm surprised Charlie didn't find it—he would've taken it with him if he had."

"Let's keep it there, then," Jesse decides, handing it back to her. "Save it for a rainy day."

Sariah nods and leaves to return the dynamite. When she returns, she carries the feeding tubes.

"Alright, love, I need you to hold his head still," Sariah tells Honor, who shoots her a tense look. "I'm going to insert this through his nostrils. He might thrash, so boys, be ready. I don't think he's strong enough to break the restraints, but... you never know."

Honor nods, gripping Gratian's head as Sariah inserts the tube. Gratian flails, but Jesse pins his torso while Priya and Pacious hold his legs and Shamus restrains his arms. Once the tube is secured, Sariah hooks it up to the bag and turns the machine on.

"Now, we wait," she says.

"We need to get your medicine going soon too," Priya reminds Sariah.

"Yeah," she murmurs, following Priya out.

"You okay?" Jesse asks Honor as she sinks into a chair beside Gratian.

"No," she admits, stroking his restrained hand. "But I'll be better when I see the brown of his eyes again."

Jesse nods. "I get that. You should rest."

"I'll sleep here with him. I'm not leaving him alone."

"I'll stay too," Jesse offers. "Keep you company. Tell you stories."

Honor huffs a laugh. "You really don't have to. It's boring down here."

Pacious turns to Shamus. "You need to get started on chemo too. C'mon, let's go with the girls and get you hooked up."

"You too, Honor," Jesse adds. "I know you don't think you need it, but it might be worth it—just in case."

Honor sighs. "Let them go first. I don't know how much is left, and if they need it more, I want them to have it."

"How much is left?" Jesse asks, rubbing her shoulders.

"Not a lot last time I checked. We might need another hospital run soon."

A thought hits Jesse. "Have you checked his blood sugar since he turned full Rona?"

Honor's eyes widen. "Shit," she mutters, pushing up from her chair. "That's definitely something we—"

"I'll go with you to get it," Jesse says, letting her lead the way out the door.

As they leave, Honor glances back at Gratian. "I wonder what it'll say."

"I'm not sure," Jesse admits. "I wouldn't think it would be an issue in..." He trails off, the last word catching in his throat. He doesn't want to say it—doesn't want to hurt her with something so final.

"Death," she finishes for him. "It's okay. I know what you were going to say. This is my reality, something I have to face." A small, wry smile tugs at her lips. "I'm lucky there are people like Dr. Mercer who found a cure. Even if it turns people into flesh-eating monsters, it's a cure nonetheless."

Honor laughs, the sound light and unexpected. It fills Jesse with something he can't quite name—something he hasn't felt in a long time. And just like that, he realizes he wants to hear it again.

42

BORROWED DESIRES
PRIYA

"How's that feel?" Priya asks after securing the chemo to the tube already inserted in Sariah's arm.

"It's alright. Nothing to write home about."

"Write home about, huh? That you, or is that the Zane fellow you just ate?"

Sariah smirks, leaning back in the chair. "You know, it's funny—being swarmed by someone else's memories, their thoughts, their personality. It's a trip. I can't even begin to explain it."

As much as Priya doesn't want to know what it's like to consume someone else's brain, she kind of does. "What's it like? Just a wave of new information or...?"

"Yeah, kinda. It's like suddenly remembering something from your past, except it's not yours. A rush of images, memories, even parts of their personality. These memories I absorb, the personalities—they're like puzzle pieces from a dozen different jigsaws, stitched together into something new. There are words in my mind I'd never say, jokes that aren't mine, even... desires." Sariah exhales sharply. "You know I crave pussy, but once, I ate someone who liked dick, and for the first time in my life, I was actually turned on by the thought of one of those ugly things."

Priya shudders at the mental image of the one-eyed monster that straight women and gay men adore. "Yuck. Not my thing."

"Me neither." Sariah laughs.

"Hey, girls, can one of you hook Shamus up too?" Pacious calls, suddenly appearing in the doorway. "We need to get him going before he eats me."

"You'd like that, wouldn't you?" Shamus retorts, throwing him a wink—something Priya has never seen him do before.

"Shame, you good?" she asks, rummaging through the cabinets for another IV start.

"Yeah, I'm fucking fab. You good?"

Priya narrows her eyes, then leans toward Sariah. "Was Zane gay, by chance?" she whispers.

Sariah nods. "I think so. I got really turned on when I saw Jesse's boner just now."

"He had an erection?"

"Yeah, when Honor walked in. The moment he saw her face —boom. Hard as a rock. It was cute, but it made me hot, and I don't like being hot for men. That's not my thing."

Priya hums in thought. "Maybe this will help Pacious finally come out."

"But if Shamus isn't really gay, this might complicate things," Sariah points out. "He's just feeling this way because Zane was."

"But you said the memories, the personalities—they stick with you, yeah?"

Sariah's expression turns serious. "Yeah. They do." She pauses, realization dawning. "Shit. I'm gonna be bi, aren't I?"

Priya chuckles. "Don't worry about that right now. If dicks become your thing, I'm sure we can get a strap-on or something."

Sariah's eyes perk up at the offhand mention of a future together.

Priya clears her throat. "Okay, I gotta go find Krishna. See if she can help with this IV." She looks around. "I'll be right back," she says, hurrying out of the room.

A moment later, she returns with Krishna, who hobbles in beside her, wiping dirt from her hands. "Sorry, I was helping bury Maria," Krishna mutters, leaning against the table for support.

"No worries," Priya says. "Can you help me with this? I need to insert the IV, but I want to make sure I do it right."

Krishna nods, wincing as she shifts her weight. "Yeah, I've done this enough times." She gestures for Priya to come closer, then moves to Shamus, swabbing his arm with alcohol. "Watch —feel for the vein first, like this." She runs her fingers along his arm, finding the right spot. "Then, when you're sure, go in at a slight angle. One smooth motion."

Priya follows her lead, watching closely as Krishna guides her through it. "Okay, deep breath," Priya says. Shamus exhales, and she pushes the needle through his skin, just like Krishna showed her.

"There you go," Krishna says with a tired smile. "Now just secure it."

Priya lets out a breath she hadn't realized she was holding and tapes the IV in place. "Thanks."

"Don't mention it," Krishna replies, rolling her shoulders. "Now, what's next?"

Honor appears through the door, hurrying over to Gratian's wheelchair, where his pokey pack hangs off the back. She digs through it, searching for something.

"Everything okay?" Priya asks, wadding up the trash from the IV insert.

"Yeah. I just came to grab Gratian's glucose monitor. We haven't checked it lately."

"Oh man, you're right." Priya tosses the trash into the bin. "Hope he's okay."

"We have insulin if we need it. It's okay."

Priya nods, looking at Shamus. "I'll need to go mix up your chemo. How much do we have left?" she asks Honor.

"Enough for a few more rounds. We're running low on Methotrexate and 6MP, though. You don't need to give me any chemo if we just want to get Jesus going. Did Juan give him the serum?"

"Yeah, I think so," Liam answers from the couch. "He was looking for one last I remember."

"I'll go check on him," Pacious says.

"See how Michael is doing too," Honor adds. "Do we have any more of the serum syringes left from those fucktards?"

"I don't think so," Priya replies. "Juan was struggling to find one for Jesus. I don't know if he ever did."

"I don't think I can make more," Sariah admits grimly. "Zane wasn't privy to that information."

"Who would've been?" Honor asks.

"Axel was next in line," Sariah answers, "but he's a pile of ashes now, so that's not much help."

"Hells bells," Shamus mutters.

Priya smirks at the uncharacteristic remark.

"We could always rob the jail," Shamus suggests. "We have dynamite. We run in there, threaten to blow the place sky-high if they don't give it to us."

"Okay there, cowboy," Priya says, rubbing his arm. "Let's just hope we don't need any of it anytime soon. As soon as everyone's recovered, we can leave this place and go to that big hospital in Denver—like we originally planned."

"Yes," Honor agrees. "I like this plan."

"Aww, but I wanna blow shit up," Shamus whines, looking at Honor like a child whose dreams were just crushed.

Honor rubs his back soothingly. "I know you do. Don't

worry—you might still get your chance. Don't give up on your dreams just yet."

Priya smiles, then glances at Sariah, who's watching her with a sultry, come-hither stare.

Maybe it's the danger in the air. Maybe it's Zane's lingering personality. Either way, a shiver runs down Priya's spine, heat pooling low in her belly.

She's starting to come around to the idea of Sariah again.

And it's lovely.

43

CATACLYSMICALLY AWAKING A HUNGER

HONOR

As Jesse and Honor sit in the dimly lit underground chamber, unease settles in her chest like a weight. The air is thick with uncertainty, and the sight of Gratian lying motionless serves as a stark reminder of the dangers they face. They've already lost so many, and the future remains uncertain.

Jesse sits across from her, his mind seemingly a million miles away as he idly cleans his nails with the tip of his knife. Honor keeps glancing at Gratian, hoping—praying—that the cloudiness in his eyes will vanish, that he'll look at her again with those wildly beautiful brown eyes, full of childlike wonder.

How long will it take for him to come back to himself?

The moment they returned here, they checked his blood sugar. For the first time in his life, the monitor displayed zeros.

A deep, harrowing sigh escapes Honor, her gaze never straying from Gratian.

"You doing okay over there?" Jesse asks, wiping the blade on his pants.

"Yeah. Just thinking about everything that's happened. Everything feels different now. I feel different."

"I feel it too," he says, standing. "But it's also given us the power to fight back—to understand and use the knowledge we've gained. We can't waste that."

Honor glances at him, her expression softening. "You've really stepped up, you know? Back at that hotel, I wasn't sure what to think. And that whole thing with Lux... but you're different now. You're the leader we needed. You've changed."

His blue eyes bore into her, settling deep in her bones. A flutter stirs in her chest—a sudden, overwhelming urge to rush into his arms, to have him pick her up and kiss her like no one ever has before.

"You think?" he asks softly, his boots echoing on the cement as he stows the knife. His biceps flex beneath the fabric of his black long-sleeved shirt, his eyes glistening slightly with unshed emotion as she nods.

"I appreciate that. Sometimes I wonder if I've changed for the worse, you know? I used to be someone else entirely. Maybe all these Purified are rubbing off on me too."

He's beside her now, resting a firm but gentle hand on her shoulder, giving it a subtle squeeze. She reaches out, covering his hand with hers, then leans her head against their joined hands.

"We've all changed, Jesse. But at our core—our values, our desires—we're still the same. That's what I'm fighting for. It's like a storm raging inside me, trying to hold back the monster clawing at my edges. But I believe we can adapt without losing ourselves. We just have to hold on to our humanity in the midst of all this madness."

Jesse nods, his resolve hardening. "You're right. We can't lose sight of who we are." He kneels, his eyes level with hers, flicking between her gaze and her lips. "We'll find a way out of this. I know we will. We have each other now. I'm not going anywhere."

"You're not scared I'll turn into one of them at any moment?" she asks, her voice barely above a whisper.

He inches closer. "I'm not. I actually think it's kind of hot."

She can't help the laugh that bubbles from her lips unbidden, glancing at Gratian as though he were a sleeping child about to wake. "You think it's hot?"

"Fuck yes, I do," Jesse murmurs, biting his lower lip.

God, those lips.

Then, they're on hers, and the rush hits her like a summer wind knocking over a tree weakened by years in the desert. Determination settles on his breath as he parts her mouth with his tongue, grazing hers before fully devouring it. The kiss is perfect —exactly how she imagined it would be and precisely how she loves to be kissed. No swirling tongue, no swallowing her face— just a perfectly timed, in-and-out rhythm that sets her soul on fire and awakens parts of her she'd forgotten were there. His thumb strokes her cheek while the other hand drifts to her thigh.

The desperation of the moment transforms them, and they cling to each other like lifelines. Weeks of tension, of held-back longing, unravel in an instant. The air between them turns molten.

Suddenly, she's on her feet, and he's pressing her against the wall, his kisses turning frantic, consuming. Aware of Gratian's presence, she shoves Jesse out the door, pushing him into one of the empty cells across the hall.

He grins as his back hits the wall, but then his hands are on her again, roaming, searching. Up her shirt, over her pebbled nipples, making her moan with a need she's fought for too long.

Her hands explore the firm planes of his chest, trailing downward until she finds him hard beneath his pants. The moment her fingers wrap around him, she's gone—utterly undone, her body responding with a sharp, wet ache.

Jesse groans, sliding his hand beneath her pants and dipping his fingers inside her, teasing the depth of her arousal. She fumbles with his belt, unbuckling it, pulling down his zipper. His length springs free, and she gasps as he strokes her with increasing urgency.

She wants to taste him, but she needs him inside her more than she needs air.

He yanks down her pants, and she steps out of them, still stroking him, their mouths never parting. In one swift motion, he lifts her by the knees, pressing her back against the wall. The tip of him grazes her entrance, sending a tectonic tremor of hunger through her.

Then he pushes inside—and it is her ruin.

She clings to him, her nails digging into his shoulders as he fills her, stretching, claiming. He moves in slow, deliberate thrusts, each one unraveling her, setting her ablaze.

She moans, arching into him. "Yes. Yes. Harder."

Jesse growls, gripping her tighter, driving into her with raw, unrestrained passion. His teeth graze her nipple, sending jolts of pleasure through her limbs. The room dissolves around them, leaving only sensation—only this moment.

"I'm gonna come," he gasps against her ear, his voice hoarse with need.

And then he does, shuddering as she follows, her body wracked with waves of pleasure so powerful they leave her trembling.

When he sets her down, her knees threaten to buckle. Jesse steadies her, his breathing ragged, his blue eyes dark with lingering hunger. That damn gap between his front teeth will be the death of her.

"That was..." he starts.

"Earth-shattering," Honor finishes, breathless.

He smirks. "Fucking a monster is the best thing I've ever done." Honor shoots him a look. "Too soon?"

"Too soon," she echoes—though they both know she doesn't mean it. She tugs up her pants as he does the same. "Remember when we fucked against a wall in the death dungeon?"

He chuckles. "Oh, I do."

She exhales, her mind clearing slightly. "Okay, but now I really need to check on Gratian."

Jesse follows her back into the chamber where Gratian still lies motionless, his eyes blank, staring at the ceiling.

Honor swallows hard. "I hope this stuff starts working soon. We need to get the fuck out of here. And soon."

44

UNCERTAIN REMEDIES
PRIYA

"How's Juan?" Priya asks as Pacious returns to the area, where Sariah and Shamus are still getting their chemo.

"I think he's okay," Pacious says, lowering himself into a cold metal chair. "Jesus got the serum, but he looks fucked up. I don't know if it'll work."

"What do you mean, 'fucked up'?" Sariah asks, shifting uncomfortably in her chemo chair.

"Like he's dazed. His eyes aren't milky, but I feel like they could turn at any minute."

"No, that sounds about right," Sariah says, absentmindedly picking at a fingernail. "The serum—it's different for everyone. I've seen people take it. Some take a few days to transition, others minutes, some hours. It all depends on their immune system and how badly CoRona has affected them. Kind of like the disease itself. Some people died right away, others suffered for weeks, some just had a little cold. Such a strange thing."

"I still say keep an eye on him," Shamus says. "You never know who's going to turn into a Jerod."

"Or an Amy," Pacious adds.

Sariah says nothing. She knows she's one of them—a Purified walking among humans, tricking them into thinking she's normal, when in truth, she's a monster in their midst.

"Are there any syringes left?" Priya asks.

"No. Juan gave the last one to Jesus."

"Shit," Sariah mutters. "Those would've been really useful."

"Even more useful to know how to make," Priya adds.

She glances at Sariah, who gives her a knowing smile. Something passes between the two of them, and Pacious isn't sure he likes it.

The moment is interrupted by a crash.

They all turn just in time to see Liam on the ground, one of his makeshift braces flung aside, the other still clutched in his hand. He groans, pushing himself up onto one elbow, his leg braces twisted at awkward angles.

"Shit," Pacious mutters, moving toward him. "You okay, hotshot?"

Liam huffs, clearly embarrassed but grinning up at him. "Yeah, yeah. Just wanted to make sure gravity still works. Spoiler alert: it does."

Pacious snorts and kneels beside him, picking up the broken crutch and inspecting it. "Looks like the strap slipped. Again." He tsks, shaking his head. "What would you do without me, huh?"

"Fall more attractively, I suppose," Liam quips, flashing him another grin.

Pacious rolls his eyes, but a smirk tugs at his lips. "Hold still," he says, tightening the straps around Liam's leg braces and adjusting them until they sit more securely. His fingers brush against Liam's calf, and he tenses slightly—not from pain, but from something else.

"You always take such good care of me," Liam murmurs, his voice lower now, more intimate.

Pacious scoffs, shaking his head as he secures the last strap. "Somebody has to. You're a walking disaster."

Liam grins. "Yet you keep fixing me."

Pacious pauses, meeting his gaze. For a split second, the chaos of the world fades away.

Then he pats Liam's knee, a little harder than necessary, breaking the moment.

"There. Try not to eat dirt again, alright?"

Liam winks. "No promises."

45

THE MONSTER SETTLING IN
HONOR

It's been about a day and a half since Gratian started his rounds of Purification, and he's finally coming around. The milkiness in his eyes has faded, and his brown irises peek through once more. Honor has spent countless hours by his side—reading to him, telling stories, and reminiscing with Jesse about life before the pandemic.

"We're leaving soon to raid that other hospital," Jesse says as she strokes Gratian's hand.

Gratian still hasn't spoken much, but he stirs more often now. Honor knows she won't be able to go with them, and the thought of Jesse leaving without her grates against her nerves. She looks up, and he smiles.

"Hey, it'll be okay. I'll be back before you know it. But we need more of that chemo—especially if you want to keep giving it to Gratian."

"Maaaamaa," a throaty voice rasps from the cot.

Honor's breath catches. She turns to see Gratian looking at her, his head shifting toward her voice.

"Yes, baby, I'm here. Mommy's here," she murmurs,

brushing his unruly curls from his face. "Do you want some water?"

Gratian nods slowly.

Jesse grabs a canteen from the floor, unscrews the cap, and hands it to her.

"Here you go, love. Drink up."

She holds it to Gratian's lips, helping him lift his head. Her heart swells as she watches him drink, as if each sip is washing away the nightmare. When he finishes, she pulls him into a fierce hug, tears slipping down her cheeks.

"How do you feel, baby?" she asks, still holding him close.

"Hungry," he murmurs.

Before she registers his movement, his mouth opens, teeth aimed for her arm. Jesse reacts first, yanking her back.

"Ooohhkay there, buddy," Jesse says, holding up a hand. "None of that, alright?"

Gratian's brown eyes fix on him with an intensity that makes Honor shiver. "But I'm so hungry."

"I know," Jesse says gently. "We'll get you some food. Just... try not to eat people, okay? That's step one."

Gratian nods, but his young mind doesn't grasp the battle waging inside him—the monster curling its claws around his bones.

Jesse pulls Honor aside, his voice low. "We need to give him more chemo as soon as possible."

Honor nods but stiffens when footsteps echo down the stairwell.

"Guys," Pacious says, stepping into the room. "We have a problem."

Honor's stomach clenches. "What?"

"Juan is missing. He took Jesus with him and left a crazy note. I don't think we should stay here."

"What do you mean?" Jesse demands, rising.

Honor stands too. "What did he do?"

Pacious exhales. "He must've overheard Sariah talking about that dynamite. His note says he's going after Charlie—gonna blow up the jail. He wrote, 'Don't follow me. I don't know when I'll be back.'"

Jesse swears, running a hand through his hair. "What the fuck," he mutters, brushing past Honor and booking down the hall.

"I'll be right back, baby, okay?" Honor says to Gratian, who nods and lies his head back down as she follows Pacious up the stairs.

When they reach the apartment, the few who remain are gathered around the kitchen island.

Krishna, hobbling on her makeshift crutch, hands Jesse the letter they found.

Honor leans over his shoulder to read it.

"What do we do?" she asks, her heart pounding.

"We have to stop him," Krishna says.

"He has no idea who he's fucking with," Sariah mutters. "Even if he guesses which part of the jail to hit, he's risking everything. Charlie's people will retaliate."

"How long ago did he leave?" Jesse asks, already gathering his pack.

"I saw him last night after dinner," Michael replies. "He tucked Jesus in near the pool tables."

"So he left in the middle of the night," Shamus says, slinging his bag over his shoulder.

"No one saw him go?" Jesse asks.

Heads shake.

"Where was the note?"

"In the fridge," Michael says. "Sticking out between two beer bottles."

Jesse curses again and shoves more supplies into his pack.

"We have to find him," he says.

Honor watches as the boys gather their things. "How long will you be gone?" she asks, unable to hide her worry.

"I don't know," Jesse admits.

"We can raid the hospital on the way back," Pacious adds.

"Maybe we should all move to the hospital," Sariah suggests. "If Juan's already at the jail, this place might not be safe much longer."

"That's not a bad idea," Jesse agrees. "We can—"

BOOM.

A deafening explosion shakes the building.

Honor's pulse spikes. Without thinking, she bolts for the door, pounding down the stairs. Smoke fills the main floor, and she coughs, waving her arms to clear the air.

She barely registers Jesse and Pacious shouting behind her as she reaches the basement door, flings it open, and races down.

She skids to a stop.

Gratian's cot is empty.

46

FULL RONA

JESSE

Jesse can see the fury in Honor's eyes—she's seeing red, and he's not far behind. But while he's seething, he knows she's losing control, thinking with pure emotion, and he can't seem to pull her back from the edge she's teetering on.

The Rotters are overrunning their space, and it's time to leave—now.

Honor has already yanked out the dynamite stash, packing her things in a frenzy as the rest of them battle the Rotters pouring in by the dozens. There's a gaping hole in their sanctuary—the metal wall-shield and most of the northern wall blown completely to bits—attracting not only Rotters but fast-moving Ronas as well.

"They fucking took him!" Honor's voice is a raw scream, laced with rage and desperation as mayhem erupts around them.

"I know, Honor," Jesse says, his tone steady but tight, shoving everything he can into his pack. When they investigated the explosion and found Gratian missing—his wheelchair gone too—that was all the confirmation they needed.

"But we need to think this through before you blow everything to hell. Gratian's still in there."

Honor's eyes flash, a sickly milky sheen overtaking them as her anger surges.

"Ahhhh, I fucking *know*!" she screams.

She's about to go full Rona.

Jesse takes a step back, instinct telling him to give her space, to avoid provoking the beast within. He keeps his focus on the Ronas, gunning them down as they get too close.

Once the group has gathered their gear, they move fast, clearing out windows and stairwells, knocking Rotters and Ronas aside as they push for the exit. They're on borrowed time —every second matters.

They bolt from the cancer center into the bright sunlight of late May. The harsh winds of winter are finally behind them, and the soft breath of summer is just ahead. Trees are draped in green, a vibrant reminder of renewal—of a new season, a new life. But the Rotters, shambling atop the fresh growth, are a grotesque reminder of how fragile that rebirth truly is. Life and death, clashing in an unholy dance.

Honor is far ahead, driven by a volatile mix of maternal rage and the monster blood in her veins, an unyielding force pushing her forward.

Jesse hangs back with Pacious and Shamus, knowing she needs the space—even if it's just a few feet. Priya and Sariah trail behind, with Krishna, Liam, and Michael bringing up the rear. Krishna, still limping, moves slowly, while Liam, hindered by his braces, isn't much faster. Pacious stays close to him, offering support. Michael, walking beside Krishna, scans the area for danger while helping her maintain pace.

Every step feels like a struggle, and the gap between them and safety stretches with each passing second.

"Think we ought to talk to her?" Pacious asks. "We kinda need a plan before we go barreling in there."

"I know," Jesse replies, his voice edged with concern. "But right now, she's in her 'hell hath no fury like a mother scorned' era. Let her burn off some steam. I'll talk to her before we get to the jail."

"Yeah, Charlie probably did this just to make sure she comes right to him."

"Exactly," Jesse mutters, kicking a rock down the road. "He knew what he was doing."

"He definitely knew," Shamus adds. "I doubt he wants to babysit a rabid six-year-old Rona forever."

Jesse shoots him a glare.

"What?" Shamus shrugs. "That's what he is—a six-year-old monster who wants to eat flesh."

"Yeah," Jesse replies, "but that might be exactly what Charlie wants. A kid in a wheelchair's an easy tool. He could use Gratian to infiltrate other groups. He might not even care about Sariah or Honor anymore."

"Poor kid," Pacious says. "He's probably terrified."

"I don't know," Jesse mutters. "Right before the explosion, he woke up and tried to eat Honor. He's hungry—*really* hungry. And I'm worried this situation is just going to feed the beast inside him."

Pacious nods slowly. "That's very true," he says, then glances at Shamus. "How's the chemo treating you?"

"I feel alright," Shamus replies. "It was... weird. I never went full Rona—just got bit, then took the serum. It felt like dying inside. Then I ate that Zane guy, and *that* was when shit got weird. I got his personality, his memories, his emotions—like waking up from a bad acid trip. But once the chemo kicked in, it was like a switch flipped. The cravings for blood and flesh gone. Kind of like getting hit with Narcan. Instant reset. Three days, three versions of me. Kinda wild. Don't recommend it."

"You were an addict?" Jesse asks, curious.

"In a past life," Shamus says quietly. "My criminal career and the addiction went hand in hand—couldn't have one without the other. But I started getting really good at the criminal shit and really fucking bad at the addict part. OD'ed ten times, maybe more. Lost count. Prison's what finally got me clean."

"What was your drug of choice?" Jesse asks.

"Fentanyl," Shamus answers simply.

"Damn," Pacious mutters.

"Yeah. It was like Russian roulette every time I used. Even after all those ODs, I couldn't stop. The high was the sweetest thing. That blood I ate—it hit me the same way. Like a strong shot of fentanyl."

"I never got into that," Pacious says. "My glory days were fueled by cocaine. Got hooked for a bit, but that's a rich man's drug."

"Same," Jesse adds. "Back in my day, it was all about coke. Tried meth a few times—fuck that noise."

"Yuck. Yeah, fuck that shit," Pacious agrees. "This chick I dated once did it, so I tried it to party with her. She disappeared for, like, eight hours, and all I did was stare out the window, chasing shadow monsters."

Jesse laughs. "Yep. Sounds about right."

"I don't know how anyone could do that shit long-term," Pacious continues. "Makes people lose their minds."

"I wonder what would happen if a Rona got meth," Jesse muses.

"You're a sick fuck," Pacious says, half-laughing. "God, I don't even want to imagine what the world would look like if that happened."

Jesse coughs. "Yeah, I don't want to find out. Just curious."

"What are we gonna do about your girl?" Shamus asks, his tone serious. "We don't want her blowing the whole place up and taking Gratian with it."

"I'm not sure," Jesse admits. "I'm giving her space for now—

let her rage out before we get any closer. I know the monster inside her is close to the surface, and I don't want to get in the way of that."

"Yeah, I wouldn't advise that either," comes Sariah's voice from behind them.

Jesse glances back at her. "What do you think we should do?"

"I'd let her be for now," Sariah suggests. "I know what it's like to feel that monster clawing at you. You do your best to control it, but there were times with Charlie when I just lost it. Someone pissed me off, and all I saw was red. It took everything I had not to tear those idiots apart. If you try to stop her now, you might be the one she tears apart."

"I don't like that," Jesse says, his voice edged with concern. "I like my limbs."

"She likes your limbs too," Shamus jokes.

Jesse slugs him in the arm.

"For real," Pacious says. "You don't want to mess with her while she's all murdery. Just let her be."

"Nah, I'm risking it," Jesse says with a grin, picking up the pace and jogging ahead to catch up to Honor.

She's about a half-mile ahead, her figure a dark silhouette on the horizon. She's already charging down Timberline Road, taking the longer route rather than the highway. Timberline is three miles from the cancer center, and the road to the jail is another four city blocks beyond that. It's a long stretch—but their only option.

Remnants of a forgotten world litter the city. Rusted, broken-down cars line the road—some smashed together, others parked haphazardly. Old Walgreens, restaurants, and gyms lie broken open, glass shattered, belongings strewn across the ground. Moss and weeds climb the abandoned buildings— a hauntingly beautiful reminder of Earth reclaiming its land.

Echoes of a long-gone life remain, Rotters lurking in the shadows around every corner.

Honor, however, doesn't seem to care. Rotters pick up on her scent and begin lumbering after her, but she clutches the dynamite like a precious treasure, her fury propelling her forward.

"Honor," Jesse calls, jogging to catch up. Maybe he can be the calm in her storm. She doesn't acknowledge him, just keeps her relentless pace.

By the time he reaches her, her eyes have gone completely white, her face pale and vacant. She's not blinking. Jesse hesitates, but pushes forward anyway.

"Honor," he says gently. "Babe, I know you're in there. I need you to come back to me. You've got to calm down before you get us all killed... and Gratian. I know you're angry, I get it. But this won't help him."

She slows a bit, the cloudiness in her eyes beginning to clear.

"There you go," he says, cautiously taking her arm. "It'll be okay. I'll let you blow up all the shit you want, but let's get him out safely first, alright?"

She looks at him. Her brown eyes—the color of silky caramel drizzled over toffee—meet his.

She slows almost to a stop, glancing around. "What are we going to do?"

"First, let's keep walking," Jesse says. "The Rotters are catching our scent, and they'll bring Ronas with them. Once we're closer, we'll try to negotiate. Let him know you've got the dynamite and plan to blow the place unless he releases Gratian. But let me handle the talking, okay? I don't want you going full Rona again."

"I was full Rona?"

"Oh yeah." He smirks. "White eyes and all."

"It's funny," she replies with a bitter chuckle. "I didn't feel the craving or anything. Just saw myself tearing Charlie's limbs off."

"You're an angry lioness protecting her cub," Jesse says softly. "Totally understandable."

"He better not have touched one fucking hair on Gra—"

"Shh, Honor, it's okay," Jesse soothes, noticing her eyes whitening. "You're doing it again."

Honor takes a deep breath and focuses on putting one foot in front of the other, her gaze fixed ahead.

Jesse glances back to check on the others. He sees Shamus in the lead, Pacious supporting Liam, followed by Sariah and Priya, with Michael farther behind—maybe four or five city blocks. But Krishna is nowhere in sight. He stops walking, letting Honor continue her march, still gripping the dynamite like it's her child.

When Shamus, Pacious, and Liam catch up, Jesse asks, "Did you see if Krishna got got?" He gestures behind them toward Michael, where a crowd of Rotters have started to follow.

"No, we didn't look," Liam replies. "We assumed Michael was with her."

"Keep walking. I'll check with him."

Sariah and Priya pass by, and ten minutes later, Jesse reaches Michael.

"Hey, weren't you with Krishna?"

"She was with me for a while," Michael answers, his tone steady but reluctant. "She had to rest because of her leg. Told me to keep going, said she'd catch up. I didn't want to leave her, but she insisted. I kept checking—she was keeping up. But then some Rotters started closing in. She hobbled into a gas station. Said she'd wait it out. She knows where we're headed. She's tough—she'll catch up."

"Alright." Jesse nods, turning to leave him behind.

Jesse's never trusted many people. Even before the world fell apart, his circle was small. Most people were fake—fair-weather types who vanished when life got hard. The few friends he had, though, were like stars—always there, even if not always visible.

But in the apocalypse, even stars fade.

Michael isn't one of them. Jesse can't quite place it, but something about him feels off. If Amy hadn't been the one infected, Jesse would've bet Michael was hiding something. Now, with Krishna missing, he can't shake the feeling that she's probably not coming back.

47

THE WEIGHT OF SACRIFICE
PRIYA

Priya tries not to think about what's coming when they reach the jail. She knows Honor is about to unleash chaos, and there's nothing any of them can do to stop her. Gratian is her child—she has every right to be acting the way she is. At this point, Priya just hopes someone finally kills Charlie for good. No matter what they do, he always seems to find a way back.

Sariah hasn't said much during their walk, and Priya can tell she's got a million things on her mind. She must feel terrible from the chemo. She's stopped several times to vomit, her face pale and sweaty, already looking thinner. Priya feels a pang of sadness at that—she likes Sariah's curves.

"What do you think Charlie wants with Gratian?" Priya finally asks, as Sariah wipes her mouth and slowly walks beside her.

"If I had to guess," Sariah says, pulling out a tissue and blowing her nose, "he probably sees Gratian as the perfect pawn to lure people in. The whole 'I'm in a wheelchair and all alone' routine? It's a Charlie classic. He's diabolical like that."

"So you think he's going to turn Gratian into some kind of soldier? To bring survivors back to him?"

Sariah nods, spitting to the side. "Exactly."

"Well... I guess that's better than what I was thinking," Priya murmurs, her voice trailing off as she pushes darker thoughts from her mind.

"What were you thinking?" Sariah asks, frowning.

"A million different things. That he might kidnap and torture Gratian to get to you and Honor. Or tie him up and leave him to rot. Or worse—let him loose to tear people apart. Let the monster inside him come out. That... that would be harder for us to handle later. I didn't even think about the first option." She shudders a little, suddenly queasy herself.

"It'll be okay, Priya. We'll get him back before Charlie can do anything," Sariah says with a small smile. "Even if I have to take his place."

Priya looks at Sariah in disbelief. "What?"

"Yeah," Sariah says flatly. "I've been thinking. Charlie wants me. Now he wants Honor. If nothing else, I'll offer to take Gratian's place—so Honor can have her son back. Charlie gets what he wants, and we get Gratian."

The thought of losing Sariah to Charlie tightens something in Priya's chest, like she's suddenly short of breath. Even though she's been angry with her, the idea of Sariah sacrificing herself again—like she did at the cancer center—makes Priya realize the chemo is working. That Sariah still has a heart. She even took a bullet for her.

"Why'd you get so quiet?" Sariah asks, noticing the shift in Priya's expression.

"I... I just don't know how I feel about all this," Priya says softly.

"About what? Me going to Charlie?"

"You sacrificing yourself. Again. For us," Priya murmurs, her voice barely above a whisper. "Losing you..."

"You're not going to lose me." Sariah stops walking and turns to face her. "Besides, I thought you were done with me. What's this all about?"

Priya meets her gaze, those liquid gold eyes pulling her in, deep into her own emotions. Yes, she's been angry—but only because she cares. Because she loves her.

"I was mad at you," Priya admits, her voice a little shaky. "I still don't know if you're going to eat me in the middle of the night."

Sariah smiles and grabs her hands, and just like that, the sparks Priya's been avoiding ignite again. "Oh, I'll eat you anytime, Priya. For the rest of eternity."

Priya feels heat flood her cheeks, her pulse quickening. "You know what I mean. But... I'd take that kind of eating from you. Anytime."

Sariah giggles and moves closer, slipping an arm around Priya's waist. "I know you were mad. I know I betrayed you. Honestly, I didn't want to eat you. I'd been trying to figure out how to explain that before the chemo started working. Before you, the beast was in charge—but I still had control. I never planned to eat Jesse, Shamus, or Pacious. But you... You're the first person who made me not want to eat anyone at all. I still want to finish the chemo, though. Eating that brain didn't help."

"Was it like taking a hit of something you're addicted to, then trying to quit again? Like it erases all your progress?"

Sariah shakes her head. "No, I don't think so. I've never been addicted to anything hardcore, but it didn't restart the cravings. Actually made me nauseous. Might just be the chemo, though. I don't feel like eating flesh anymore."

She burps and presses a fist to her mouth, swallowing hard. "Ugh. Sorry. Let's talk about something else."

"Yes, let's," Priya agrees, offering her a small smile.

48

PARCELS OF FURY
HONOR

The waves of nausea come faster now, the blinding flashes growing stronger, narrowing her vision until all she can see is the end result—burning it all down. She knows where she's going. The dynamite is cradled carefully against her chest, but every growl from the monster inside her steals precious seconds. The rage ignites it, pulling her closer to the part of herself where the Rona lurks. She can't control it—not when the rage takes over.

Rage at Charlie.

Rage for taking her boy.

Gratian is her world, the center of everything she lives for. His sweet smile. His soft, doe-eyed gaze. That little voice asking her to play, to read to him, to sing, to tuck him in. He's everything. The boy who would say, over and over, just how much he loved her.

"Mama, do you know how much I love you?"
"No, baby, how much?"
"Gillions and gillions and gillions of loves."
"Oh my goodness, GILLIONS? That's so many!"

"Yes. It's way more than you love me."

"No. I don't think that's possible."

"Why? I think it is."

His giggles filled the air as she tickled him.

"Because, baby, while you may love me more, I've loved you longer—and that will always be my winning hand."

"What's a winning hand?"

"In poker, when people play cards, they bet on who has the best hand. The best hand wins."

"So you loving me longer wins our bet?"

"It sure does. But you still have a pretty good hand."

"I do?"

"Yes, my love. Your love for me is immeasurable. The love we have for our mothers is one that will never be surpassed. You'll always feel it, even if I'm not here."

"But where would you go?"

"One day, I'll have to leave you. But don't you worry, my love. That won't be for a long, long time."

Gratian smiled, tucking his little fingers into her hair as he drifted off to sleep in the comfort of their first home, before the world changed.

Now, that memory is all she has. The words. That moment —their moment—is what fuels the fire. What drives her forward with only one thought in mind: how dare he.

How dare Charlie take her baby. Her reason for living. Her whole world.

HOW DARE HE.

The anger swells, like a beast waking from a long slumber. It festers inside her, gathering in every fiber of her being. All the pain, all the fear, all the hurt her boy has endured in his short six years—each injustice, each tear—builds into something unstoppable. Her body trembles with it. The fury collides with her own sense of helplessness, the violence she's locked away for so long surging through her like wildfire. Her blood boils. Her pulse pounds. The pressure builds so high she fears it might break her.

The world fades to black.

The memory surfaces again, tugging her mind back. She sees herself tucking Gration in, late at night, the soft glow of the night-light illuminating his room, casting shadows on the walls as she pulled the blankets up to his chin. He was so small. So fragile. Yet he had the biggest heart. He looked up at her with those wide, trusting eyes, full of love.

"Goodnight, Mama," he whispered, curling into her embrace.

"Goodnight, baby," she murmured, pressing a soft kiss to his forehead. She smiled as she ran her fingers through his hair, the same familiar rhythm she'd followed a thousand times. In that moment, the world was still safe. Just her and him.

Another memory rushes in—just the two of them driving down an old, winding road, their laughter filling the car. Gratian's tiny hand tracing patterns on the seat fabric, glancing over at her with an expression full of wonder.

"Where are we going, Mama?"

"To see the stars," she replied, guiding the car gently down the road as the night sky stretched ahead. "We're going to find a place where we can just look up, no interruptions. Just you, me, and the stars."

He smiled, his eyes lighting up with excitement. "I like that."

"Me too," she said softly, her heart swelling with love.

Those were the moments she lived for. Every word. Every smile. Every tiny hand resting in hers.

Now, it's slipping through her fingers.

The world goes black again. And the rage—blinding,

burning—consumes her. Everything else fades. She doesn't even remember the last time she felt in control.

Time resumes.

And before she even realizes what's happened—

She's biting into someone.

49

MONSTERHOOD

JESSE

It was inevitable.

Honor had been teetering on the edge of something monstrous from the moment they took her baby.

Jesse should've known better than to get too close, should've kept his distance instead of trying to calm her down. Shit, even a normal woman without a monster inside her would be dangerous to fuck with if her child was in danger.

He'd been following her carefully, keeping pace as she moved with purpose. Rotters and Ronas lurked in the shadows, always waiting for a misstep, always hungry. Jesse had just started closing the gap between them when he heard the shift in her breathing. The moment he placed a hand on her shoulder, she spun around, her 'fro brushing against his face.

And then he saw her eyes.

Pale. Empty.

The all-white gaze of the Rona.

Before he could react, she struck—her teeth sinking into his flesh, severing his finger clean off.

Now, as they march toward the jail, Jesse cradles his bleeding hand, his mind reeling. Honor, no longer Rona, seethes—not just at Charlie for taking her son, but at herself for losing control.

"Jesse, I—" she starts, her steps never faltering.

"Honor, it's fine," he says, trying to brush it off. "Didn't need that finger anyway. I'll live... I think. At least it was on my left hand."

She still holds the dynamite, her chin streaked with blood. The moment she realized what she'd done, she spit the finger onto the ground. He tucked it into his pocket on the off chance someone could sew it back on—not that he was holding his breath. If not, maybe he'd make a necklace out of the bones once the flesh rotted off.

"But we don't have any more serum," she says, her voice tight with barely restrained panic.

Jesse keeps a careful distance but stays close enough to be reassuring. He knows better than to push her right now.

"We'll figure it out," he assures her. "Worst case, Sariah Purifies me if I turn full Rona. Not like I haven't always had a knack for monstrous things anyway."

Pacious and Shamus flank him now, a silent precaution to keep Honor from losing herself again.

"I just—I thought I had it under control," she says, her voice breaking. "I can't—"

"You're in a bad place right now, Honor," Priya says gently, walking just behind her. "Once you get your boy back, you'll be able to rein it in. We know you're not yourself. We forgive you."

Honor doesn't respond. The rage pushing her forward only seems to grow, and the group falls silent, keeping pace as she leads them toward Prospect Road.

As they near the old police station, its boarded-up windows and makeshift barricades of abandoned cars cast long shadows across the pavement. Jesse wonders if there are still people holed up inside, watching their approach, already alerting Charlie.

Beyond the police station, apartments stand as hollowed-out reminders of the past. The height of the outbreak must've turned them into feeding grounds, the last stand for whatever officers had been trapped inside. Bodies litter the ground—some nothing more than decomposing husks, others still being picked apart by Rotters. The stench of death forces Jesse to breathe through his mouth as they pass.

They reach Midpoint Drive, where a narrow road leads straight to the jail. It looms ahead, an imposing fortress of steel and concrete.

Honor is already steps ahead, cutting through the remnants of an old halfway house. Jesse catches the slightest movement behind one of the boarded-up windows. Someone is watching.

They're being tracked.

By the time they reach the outer fence, Honor is already at the gate. The red lights of still-functioning security cameras blink down at them. Hands claw through the narrow cell windows, desperate voices screaming for salvation. The place is alive—but not in any way that matters.

Jesse watches as Honor steps forward, holding the dynamite out in front of her.

"CHARLIE!" she bellows at the camera. "Let my child go, or I'll bring this whole fucking place down!"

She grips a lighter in her free hand, the fuse waiting for a single flick to ignite.

Jesse swallows hard. She won't light it. Not yet. Not before she sees her son.

Right?

Charlie's voice crackles through the intercom. "Honor, my dear. So nice of you to visit. Why don't you come in? I'll put on some tea."

"Where. Is. My. Child?" Her voice is low, dark—dangerous.

"He's safe, I promise. Seems to like it here, actually. Says he wants to stay."

"Let. Me. See. Him."

"I will, but you'll have to hand over that little explosive of yours first."

Honor's grip on the dynamite tightens. "Not a fucking chance," she growls. "Show me my son, or I start burning this place down—one building at a time."

Charlie sighs, amused. "Well, well. We'll have to make a deal then, won't we?"

Sariah steps up beside Honor. "Cut the bullshit, Charlie. What do you want?"

His laughter echoes, sending a chill through the air.

Jesse notices the red dot before anything else.

A sniper.

It hovers over the back of Honor's head, shifting slightly but staying locked onto her.

Then—movement in the distance. Rotters creeping closer.

Gunfire rings out, and they drop.

Jesse barely registers the snipers in the towers as he turns to Honor.

"Hey," he whispers. She doesn't respond. "Honor," he tries again, as Sariah negotiates with Charlie.

Still nothing.

Jesse reaches out, his fingers pressing gently—urgently—against her shoulder. "Come back to me."

Her eerie, milk-white Rona eyes flicker—then fade back to brown.

"There are snipers," he says quietly. "They're going to shoot if you're not careful. You dying won't save Gratian."

Honor's breath steadies. Slowly, she lowers the dynamite and lighter.

A red dot shifts, landing on her forehead.

Jesse glances up at the towers, gives a small nod—a silent plea to hold fire.

Pacious steps closer. "Dude. You see it?"

"Yeah," Jesse murmurs.

"What's the plan?"

Shamus cracks his knuckles. "I'll take care of the bastards."

Jesse exhales sharply. "We didn't think this part through."

"Let's see what Sariah can work out first," he says, keeping his eyes on Honor.

Sariah steps forward. "Open the door," she calls. "Let us in, and we'll talk this through."

Charlie's voice comes from the other side. "I'm afraid I won't be doing that. It's not worth the risk."

"Then let me in," Sariah counters. "Leave Honor and the others out here. I'll come in alone and talk."

"Sariah, baby," Charlie says smoothly, "I have you all surrounded. My snipers have their beads on you right now. You haven't won, my love—you've lost. You'll surrender your dynamite and weapons before stepping inside, or there is no deal. You come to my house, you play by my rules. That's all there is to it."

Sariah glances back at Honor, who is trembling—barely holding something dark and dangerous at bay.

Her gaze shifts to the doors.

And in one swift motion, she snatches a stick of dynamite, flicks the lighter, and hurls it straight at the front door.

50

BURN. IT. DOWN.

PRIYA

Panic settles deep into Priya's bones as Sariah grabs her hand and pulls her in the opposite direction—away from the dynamite.

Gunfire erupts. The snipers open fire, and the group scatters like startled ducks in a cornfield.

Then—boom.

The explosion is deafening, a shockwave that rattles Priya's skull and sets her ears ringing. She stumbles, clutching her head as they dive behind a brick enclosure meant to house industrial-sized dumpsters.

"What the fuck were you thinking?" Honor demands, her voice sharp over the sound of crumbling brick and shattering glass. The blast must've snapped her out of whatever trance she'd been in—her Rona-tainted, milk-white eyes are gone, replaced with their usual dark mahogany.

"I know the building," Sariah says, breathless but firm. "If Charlie was talking to us through the intercom, he wasn't in that front room—he's way in the back. When this place was a working jail, officers in the rear had to buzz people in. The entrance is just a counter with cameras. Nobody sits there unless they're monitoring something. Unless he had prisoners in that room, it was empty."

Priya peeks around the brick barrier. The blast ripped a gaping hole into the front of the jail. The entrance—and whatever had been directly behind it—now lies exposed, open to the elements.

Pacious, Shamus, and Jesse had taken off in the other direction, likely hunting down the snipers.

She ducks back behind the enclosure and looks at Sariah. "Okay, what the fuck is the plan now?"

Sariah shrugs. "I dunno. I just wanted him to shut the fuck up."

Honor lets out a sharp laugh, but there's no humor in it. "Great. You blew up the intercom, so now we have no idea where he is." The anger in her voice is a thick, tangible thing, rolling off her in waves. "What the FUCK am I supposed to do now?"

"Give me a second to think," Sariah mutters.

Priya isn't sure if this was a brilliant move or a catastrophic mistake. They may have just lost their only advantage—the element of surprise.

"Wait—I got it," Sariah says suddenly, turning to Priya.

"What?" Priya asks, impatience creeping into her voice.

"How many sticks of dynamite do we have left?"

Honor answers without hesitation. "Nine. It was a bundle of ten."

"Good." Sariah snatches a branch from the ground and starts drawing in the dirt. "Okay. This is the intercom." She marks a square for the jail, then places an X toward the back. "These are the jail cells and common areas." She marks more X's along the west and north sides. "This"—she drags squiggled lines along the middle and south—"is where the kitchens and dining halls are. Ad-seg used to be here—" She taps a spot near the back. "That's where Charlie keeps his labs and the most volatile Ronas. Also where he locks up soldiers who don't obey."

Her finger traces the plan. "We each take a stick, spread out, and start blowing up sections. Bit by bit. Make him come out with Gratian. Force his hand instead of going in blind."

Honor glares at her. "What if my baby is in one of those rooms?"

"She has a point, bae," Priya says, testing the word. Sariah grins a little before glancing back at her crude map.

"There's no way to know for sure where he's keeping Gratian."

"SARIAH."

The booming voice from the jail makes Priya's heart lurch into her throat.

"Or maybe he'll just come to you," she mutters.

"Gimme another," Sariah says to Honor, tucking a stick of dynamite into the waistband of her pants as she stands up.

"What are you gonna do?" Priya asks, her blood running cold.

"I don't know yet."

Then, before Priya can react, Sariah cups her face and kisses her. "But whatever happens, just know—I love you. I love you, Priya Singh. And I will burn this whole fucking world down before I let anything happen to you."

Tears sting Priya's eyes. She kisses her back, fierce and desperate. "I love you too, Sariah. Please—be fucking careful."

Sariah nods once, then steps out from behind the brick wall.

"Yes, Charlie?"

Priya and Honor huddle behind cover, peering around the edge.

Charlie limps forward, bloodied and beaten. He must've been behind a wall that took the brunt of the explosion. His eyes are milky, but he's still human. And he's dragging something behind him.

Priya's stomach drops.

Gratian.

He's limp, his small body nothing but dead weight in Charlie's grip. But he isn't crying. He isn't struggling.

His eyes are milky white.

He looks feral.

Honor surges forward, ready to charge, but Priya grabs a fistful of her shirt and yanks her back.

"Not yet," she hisses. "I know you want to, but let's see what Sariah does first."

Honor is full Rona again, barely leashed, her fury a tangible force crackling in the air. Priya edges back, giving her space, while straining to listen to Charlie's voice.

Sariah is close now, standing in the wreckage, smoke and debris swirling around her like a battlefield ghost. Priya sees movement behind Charlie and searches the shadows for Jesse, Pacious, or Shamus.

Charlie's voice slithers through the air. "What did you think that little trick would do, Sariah—other than piss me the fuck off?"

Sariah tilts her head, casual, fearless. "Oh, Charlie. I just wanted to see your pretty face again. Figured this was the best way."

Before Priya can hear more, there's a scuffle behind her. She whips around—Jesse and Pacious drop down into their hiding spot.

"Gimme some of that dynamite," Jesse says, breathing hard.

"What's the plan?" Honor demands. Pacious flinches at her milky gaze.

Jesse grins. "Blow this fucking place to hell. He's got Gratian out here—we take our shot now. Hurry."

Honor hands each of them two sticks. "Where's Shamus?"

Jesse smirks. "Oh, he's got his own brand of fucked up planned." He jerks his chin toward the rooftop. "Snipers are down. Just wait."

Priya's pulse hammers. Terror and adrenaline tangle in her chest.

"When you hear the blasts," Jesse says, "charge him. Get Gratian. We'll handle the rest."

Honor nods. Jesse leans in, kisses her fast—probably worried she'll bite him—then jumps back over the wall, Pacious at his heels.

Priya grips her gun. "When shit hits the fan, run for Gratian."

"What about you?" Honor asks.

Priya cocks the pistol. "I'm gonna kill some dirty fucking Purifieds."

51

SHIT HITS THE FAN
HONOR

Honor knows one thing and one thing only.

Save her fucking son.

The rest is just meaningless bullshit.

She waits for the blasts, straining to listen to Sariah and Charlie's conversation, but the storm inside her has already broken loose. It's a full-blown maelstrom now, a hurricane of rage and hunger clawing its way through her bones—thriving, alive, and out for blood.

The minutes drag like hours, and the itch under her skin turns into a scream she can't silence. She hasn't lived with this monster for long, but surrendering to it feels natural—like taking off a bra after a long day. Suppressing it is agony. Letting it out would be so much easier.

Before she even realizes it, she's running for Charlie.

No explosions. No signal. Just the raw, relentless pull of instinct.

Charlie sees her coming and bolts toward the buildings, but Sariah is faster. She pounces, her own monster unleashed, landing on his massive shoulders and sinking her teeth into his neck. He screams, thrashing to throw her off, while Honor zeroes in on Gratian.

Explosions rip through the air, heat licking at her skin as echoes of war and ruin slam against her eardrums—but none of it matters.

Gratian is still being dragged, Charlie's grip tight on his shirt. He doesn't look afraid, his milky eyes blank, his body full Rona. But the sight of Charlie's hands on him shreds Honor apart. He could bite her—turn her—but she doesn't care. She's already in her monster era.

She doesn't think. She lunges.

Her teeth sink into Charlie's arm, tearing flesh, putrid brown blood spilling into her mouth. She fights back the urge to vomit, rips deeper, and he finally lets go of Gratian, flailing wildly to shake her off. She stumbles on the rubble, but before she can steady herself, Gratian strikes—biting into Charlie's calf, right through the filthy fabric.

Charlie kicks him, sending him flying.

The fury in Honor surges, hot and violent. She regains her footing, ready to tear Charlie apart, but he grabs Sariah first. His fingers twist into her locs, yanking her up, then slamming her down against a pile of shattered cinder blocks. The sickening crunch that follows turns Honor's blood to ice.

She lunges again, teeth bared, but Charlie is faster. His hands clamp around her throat, lifting her off the ground. Her lungs seize, her vision darkening at the edges. She claws at his grip, but it's ironclad.

And then—more of his monsters spill from the broken jail.

Milky eyes. Hollow expressions. Moving as one.

Michael finally appears, Shamus right behind him, weapons drawn. Liam takes position, crossbow steady against his shoulder. He looses an arrow. It strikes true. Another follows. More bodies drop—but not enough.

They just keep coming.

Jesse and Pacious circle back, fire and debris marking their path. The jail's walls are collapsing, explosions ripping through its structure. Maybe it helped. Maybe it just made things worse.

They've kicked an anthill, and now the swarm is upon them.

Jesse fires arrows into the horde. Pacious wields his Viking spear like a reaper's scythe. Shamus tears through bodies, biting when he can't shoot. Priya wields a sword, severing heads and faces with brutal precision.

Sariah writhes on the ground, moaning, her eyes seeping to milk.

Gratian bites at any ankles that come too close.

Honor's strength wanes. Her vision narrows to a pinprick.

Then—an arrow slices through the air and buries itself in Charlie's neck.

It's not enough to take him down, but his grip falters.

She crashes to the ground. The impact jolts through her spine, pain splintering up her back. She gasps for air, the burn in her lungs sharp and raw. Her vision clears just enough to see—

Gratian.

Lost in the chaos.

Bodies clash and fall, shadows shift and lurch. Rotters and Ronas tear into anything that moves, their hunger mindless, insatiable. She sees Juan and his son, Jesus, shuffling among the dead, their decayed faces slack, their empty eyes searching.

She pushes forward.

Just a little farther.

Then—Michael emerges from the fray.

There's a glint of silver.

A sharp, sudden pain.

And then—darkness.

52

WHAT THE ACTUAL FUCK

JESSE

Jesse watches in horror as Michael buries a knife into Honor's skull. Her body goes slack, lifeless, crumpling to the ground like a marionette with severed strings.

Anger. Chaos. Rage. Vilification. Vengeance.

They don't just rise inside him—they detonate. A volatile hurricane colliding with a tsunami and an earthquake, obliterating every rational thought. His heart slams against his ribs like a war drum. His breath saws in and out of his lungs.

He *sees red*.

A snarl rips from his throat as he lunges forward, tearing through the battlefield, shoving bodies aside like they weigh nothing. The world is a blur of screaming, snarling, and the wet, meaty sounds of flesh being torn apart.

Honor.

He drops to his knees, scooping her limp body into his arms. She's still warm, but her eyes—fuck, her eyes. That empty stare makes something inside him break.

"No, no, no, no, NO," he growls, hauling her against his chest.

His hands tremble as he carries her to the brick barricade,

laying her down with a gentleness that contradicts the chaos raging inside him.

Then—

Gratian.

Jesse twists, scanning the battlefield for the kid. He spots him—teeth bared, body thrashing like a wild fucking animal, snapping at anything that moves. A feral thing, driven by pure instinct.

Jesse doesn't hesitate. He charges in, weaving through the mayhem, dodging flailing limbs and gnashing teeth. A Purified lunges at him, but he doesn't stop—just lifts his pistol and blows its fucking brains out mid-step.

Gratian is too far gone to recognize friend from foe. When Jesse grabs him by the collar, the kid lunges at him, teeth snapping inches from his face.

"Calm the fuck down, kid!" Jesse snarls, shaking him hard. "I'm gonna save the fucking day—just chillax!"

For a second, Gratian keeps fighting. Keeps snarling. Then something in Jesse's voice—maybe the certainty, maybe the rage, maybe just the sheer fucking insanity of it—reaches him.

Gratian's breathing slows. His body twitches once, twice— then goes still.

That's all Jesse needs.

He tightens his grip and hauls Gratian toward Honor, firing with pinpoint precision, each bullet finding a Purified's skull. One. Two. Three. They drop like sacks of rotting meat, but more keep coming.

Jesse can't fucking stop now.

He's not losing her.

Not like this.

Not to *him*.

As he reaches the barricade, a shadow moves in his periphery—Michael.

Standing over them. Watching. Smirking.

And that's when Jesse snaps.

He reaches into the back of Honor's pants and pulls out the remaining dynamite, then fishes his lighter from his pocket. Peeking over the barricade, he spots Pacious and jerks his head in a quick summons.

Pacious doesn't hesitate—he sprints over.

"There are five sticks left," Jesse says, his voice low but electric with urgency. "Let's blow this place the fuck up."

Pacious nods.

"What about Sariah, Liam, and Shamus?"

Jesse exhales sharply. "Casualties of war, man." He hands Pacious two sticks of dynamite. "Get to the roof. When I nod, light 'em up."

Without a word, Pacious takes off, vaulting over the wall and vanishing into the chaos.

Jesse turns to Gratian, who's staring at his mother's body, eyes vacant, shoulders heavy.

"It's gonna be alright," Jesse says, his voice softer now. "Just stay here, okay?"

Gratian doesn't respond. Doesn't even blink.

No time to push.

Jesse moves, slipping over the wall and creeping along the side of the building. He peeks around a corner and spots Sariah locked in combat with Charlie, Shamus fending off a pack of Purified—then Michael, creeping up on him, blade raised, ready to tear into his back.

Before Jesse can react, a blur bursts from the fray—Krishna, a Rona, latches onto Michael's arm and bites down hard. Michael stumbles, howling, his knife clattering to the ground. He scrambles, searching for another weapon—but the Rotters find him first.

One drops to its knees and sinks its teeth into his leg. Another tears into his throat, ripping away flesh in wet, slopping chunks. Another gnaws at his stomach.

And as the blood spills from him—it isn't red.

It's brown.

Michael was the Purified all along. Not Amy.

But there's no time to dwell on it.

Jesse's heart is a war drum in his chest, pounding so hard he swears it'll burst. He spots Pacious on the roof and takes a deep breath—then sprints straight for the chaos.

"Hey, motherfuckers!" he roars, his voice cutting through the carnage like a siren.

Sariah and Charlie whip their heads toward him. Shamus glances up, spotting Pacious on the roof—his face twists in realization, and he bolts away from the crowd.

The Ronas and Purified turn—focus on Jesse.

Perfect.

He locks eyes with Pacious and nods.

Jesse flips open his Zippo, flicking the wheel.

Nothing.

He tries again.

Nothing.

Pacious, on the rooftop, gets his lighter going on the first try. A spark blooms into flame, licking at the tip of the fuses like a Fourth of July sparkler.

Jesse grits his teeth, rolling the flint along his pant leg.

Come on.

The horde is closing in.

Pacious throws his dynamite into the fray.

Sariah sees it, grabs Liam—runs.

Jesse flicks his Zippo again. Fails.

A Rona woman is almost on him.

One more time—a spark, a flame.

Shaky hands. Steady aim.

He touches the fire to the fuse. The first stick ignites.

He throws it into the mass of bodies.

Flicks the Zippo open again for the last one—

Nothing.
A Rona woman is at him now.
Too close.
He flicks again.
It doesn't fucking light.

53

WHEN THE WORLD SPLINTERS
PACIOUS

Pacious watches from the rooftop as the first stick of dynamite detonates. The explosion is deafening—a violent, gut-punching roar that shakes the earth and makes the building beneath him shudder like it might collapse right then and there.

Shattered body parts—both putrid and fresh—burst into the air, raining down in a grotesque display. A firework show of flesh and bone. The air fills with a hellish symphony of sound: the guttural moans of the undead, the agonized screams of the living, the eerie static of the reprogrammed.

Jesse is still below, struggling with that damn Zippo, the horde of Ronas and Purified mere feet away from tearing him apart.

Then—BOOM.

The second stick goes off. This time, it's dead center in the throng.

Right where Charlie and Sariah were.

Pacious sees her—sees the exact moment she realizes what's happening, grabs Liam, and tries to run. But did they make it? Did they get out in time? He has no way of knowing, because the explosion isn't just a blast—it's a goddamn inferno.

This one was packed with more firepower. Way more.

A fireball erupts, shooting thirty feet into the sky. An angry, pulsing wave of destruction that doesn't just spread—it devours. The heat slams into him even from up here, and the force of the blast sends a shockwave outward, ripping through everything in its path.

The world splinters.

Bodies. Carnage. Cement. Brick. Asphalt. Glass. All of it—every last bit—goes airborne, rocketing upward in a chaos storm of debris.

The building beneath Pacious trembles.

Then it begins to fold in on itself.

Panic grips him. *Run*. He has to run.

He pivots, sprinting for safety—but it's too late.

The shockwave hits like a ripple effect, the impact traveling through the structure, fracturing its integrity with every second.

One by one, the supports beneath him give way.

The entire rooftop buckles.

And then . . .

It swallows him whole.

54

AMONGST THE CARNAGE
PRIYA

There are bodies everywhere, and Priya's head is ringing. The smoke is thick, the stench unbearable, and the scene is nothing short of gruesome. A headless body lies on top of her, another across her legs, and three more surround her. She doesn't know if her legs are even still there. . . she can't feel them.

Priya strains to move the carnage off her, listening for any signs of life—regular people, Purified, Ronas, or Rotters. But all she hears are distant fires and the sound of falling rubble. Finally, she manages to shove the headless corpse—Rona, Purified, or whatever it is—off her chest. Her legs are still intact. She clears the others away with effort.

There's wetness on her face. She raises a hand and finds brown blood mixed with red, but no pain. Not yet. The air is thick with smoke, ash, dust, and debris.

She struggles to stand, her vision obscured by the haze, and she can't see more than a few feet ahead. A massive crater gapes where the jail once stood, and she can't tell if any part of it is still standing.

She remembers where Jesse left Honor and Gratian—

behind her—and she stumbles in that direction. But with the devastation all around, there's no way to know if she's heading the right way.

Then she hears a groan in the distance. Part of her wants to follow the sound, hoping it's one of her friends, but all she can think about is Gratian. The little boy. Whether he's okay.

She trips over debris, her body aching everywhere. Her head pounds, her leg feels broken, her arm is twisted, and her stomach is in knots. The pain is overwhelming. She doesn't know how much longer she can keep moving.

Up ahead, the alcove that used to stand ten feet tall is now reduced to rubble. Bricks and shattered concrete are everywhere. Her heart races as she limps toward it, praying that Gratian made it through the blast.

But when she reaches the alcove, it's empty.

No one's there.

Where the hell is he?

Frantic, she scans the area. Gratian couldn't have gotten far; he can't walk, and he's still weak from transitioning. She stumbles toward the crater's center, where the damage is worst. Kicking bodies aside, she searches for Honor's familiar 'fro or Gratian's small frame.

Nothing. Just bodies—some still alive, writhing in agony.

One woman catches her eye.

If Priya were thinking clearly, she might notice how beautiful she is—long black hair, tattoos covering her arms, neck, and face. Her black hoodie is torn and stained with dirt, blood, and bits of rubble and flesh.

"Help me," the woman gasps. Her voice is shaky, raspy, a mixture of fear, pain, and something like defiance.

Priya crouches and pulls the hoodie from her face. "Why should I help you?" she asks bluntly.

"Please," the woman begs. "I didn't want this life. I just want to be free."

Blood pours from her nose and eyes. Priya feels a flicker of sympathy, but she knows better than to trust a Purified.

"I don't trust you," she says. "I need to find my friends. Sorry."

She turns to go, but the woman grabs her ankle.

"Please. I can help you. Don't leave me. I can help."

Priya hesitates. "What's your name?"

"Reverie. Please. I won't hurt you. I didn't ask for this—whatever the hell he made me into. I was trying to escape when I got blown back. I never did what he wanted. He beat the shit out of me. I think he was going to have me killed."

"What do you mean?" Priya asks warily.

Reverie struggles to sit up, wincing in pain. "After he... Purified me, or whatever it was, I started fighting back. He didn't like that. So he used me like a lab rat, torturing me with all kinds of concoctions. I don't even know what I am anymore. But I'm sure as hell not one of *them*."

Priya wants to believe her, but she's been lied to before.

"Look, I get it," Reverie says. "You don't trust anyone. That's smart. But think about it—if I were one of them, why would I be begging for your help? I could just wait for you to leave, then find another group to blend into. But I don't want that. I want to be with people like you. People who are *against* all this shit. I've got friends too, who fought the change. One of his concoctions actually helped. I don't know if they're still alive, but I want to try to find them."

What does Priya have to lose?

She offers a hand and helps Reverie to her feet.

"Okay. I'm looking for my friend Honor—dark skin, 'fro—and her son Gratian. He's six. Same skin tone, small 'fro, can't walk. He'll be crawling or dragging himself. And... they're both Purified."

She hesitates, unsure how much to reveal, but Reverie's expression is cautious, not predatory.

"Actually," Reverie says, starting to back away, "I'll take my chances somewhere else."

"No. Wait." Priya grabs her arm. "We found a way to reverse it. Long story. My girlfriend was Purified and had leukemia after she ate someone who had it. She didn't tell us what she was at first, but we started giving her chemo, and the hunger stopped. It's weird, but it works."

Reverie stares like Priya's grown a second head.

"I know," Priya says. "You don't trust me, and I don't trust you. Maybe we should just part ways now."

"No, wait. If that's true, I need this. I *need* the affliction gone. I can't handle it. Even though I fight it, it's still there. I'd do anything to silence it."

Priya nods, the doubt still there but softening. "Well, I can only help you if my girlfriend is still alive. I have no idea where she is in all this mess."

"Let's start looking, then, shall we?"

55

NEW FRIENDS
PRIYA

Priya's breathing is shallow, panic creeping in.

She's rolled over countless bodies, each in various stages of carnage. Some are missing limbs. Others have their entrails spilling out. Some have no faces at all. The gore is endless. She's covered in guts, blood, and dirt, and has no idea how she'll ever sleep again.

"Hey, Priya—help me?" Reverie's voice cuts through the chaos.

Priya finds her struggling to lift large cinder blocks off a dark-skinned woman with short black hair—hair like Priya's own.

"This is my friend Oviana," Reverie says. "I think she's still alive."

Oviana is bloody and beaten, her eyes shut, buried beneath debris. Priya helps Reverie clear the rubble until Oviana stirs, her head rolling from side to side.

"Ovi?!" Reverie shakes her. "Ovi, can you hear me?"

A weak cough escapes Oviana's lips as they remove the last chunk of debris from her chest.

"Rev?" she rasps, her eyelids fluttering open. "Is that you?" She blinks, unfocused. "I... I can't see anything."

Priya leans in, studying her eyes. A foggy mist clouds what should be a deep mahogany brown.

"Maybe it's just from the explosion," Priya offers gently.

"Who is that?" Oviana asks, trying to sit up with Reverie's help.

"That's Priya. She's one of the good ones. She's gonna help us."

Priya shakes her head. "I need to find Sariah first. I can't help anyone without her."

Reverie turns to Oviana. "Stay right here, okay? We'll be back."

Oviana nods weakly, and they continue the search.

Thirty minutes later, Priya spots a small puff of black hair sticking out from beneath a pile of cinder blocks.

"Honor?!" she shouts, sprinting toward the mound of debris.

There's at least four feet of wreckage on top. How she even noticed that tiny tuft of hair is beyond her—but there it is. It has to be her.

"Honor?" she calls again, her voice trembling.

Silence.

Reverie appears, having heard the shout. "Is this her?"

"I don't know yet," Priya murmurs, already pulling chunks of concrete away.

Reverie helps. After a few agonizing minutes, Honor's clothes come into view.

Priya swallows hard. "Yeah... it's her."

It doesn't look good.

When they finally uncover her, Honor is facedown, draped over other bodies. Priya grabs her under the arms and drags her free from the carnage. She collapses onto her back, Honor limp in her arms.

Her face is melted on one side—skin, hair, everything gone —exposing bone and teeth through what used to be her cheek.

"Oh, Honor," Priya whispers, smoothing back what's left of her hair.

Honor doesn't move.

How is this possible? Priya saw Michael stab her through the head. Saw Jesse take her away with Gratian. How did she end up here?

"Hey, Priya?" Reverie calls.

Through blurry eyes, Priya looks up. Reverie is still by the pile, pulling a small child into her arms.

"Is this your boy?"

Priya's heart stops. "Gratian?"

She sets Honor down gently and runs to Reverie. But as she reaches him, Gratian's head lolls to the side. His milky white eyes lock onto her, and he growls, snapping at Reverie's arm.

"Gratian, NO!" Priya yells, grabbing him. She sets him down in front of her. "Gratian, are you in there? Come back to me. Please. Follow my voice."

His white eyes flicker—just a hint of recognition.

Reverie crouches beside them. "Is he gonna bite you?"

"I hope not," Priya mutters. "I'm still unbitten, and I'd like to keep it that way—especially since we just blew up our only means of curing this."

"Even so," Reverie murmurs, watching Gratian closely, "I don't know that you'd want this life. Honestly."

A strangled noise rumbles from the debris pile.

Priya reaches for her gun—but her waistband is empty.

"Shit. You got a weapon?" she asks, scanning the area.

Reverie scrambles to a corpse and yanks a machete from its stiff fingers. Priya spots a pistol jutting from the rubble—right where Gratian had just been. But the grunting is coming from there too.

She moves toward it, cautiously stretching out her hand for the gun.

A hand latches onto hers.

She freezes.

She doesn't need to look to know—it's Jesse.

But when she does, his eyes are milky white. His features are slack and gray.

He's gone to the Ronas.

And he's trapped under the rubble.

Priya swallows hard, prying the gun free with her other hand, stepping back slowly. Her chest tightens. She wishes she could help him.

"What do we do about him?" Reverie asks, eyeing Gratian, who's still crawling around like he's not sure if he's human or not.

"I don't know yet," Priya admits. "We started Purifying him, gave him the chemo, but he's stuck in between. He could go either way."

A voice cuts through the haze.

"Priya?"

Priya's heart leaps.

"Sariah?" She whirls around. "Sariah, where are you?"

Dust and smoke still hang heavy in the air, turning the landscape into a post-apocalyptic wasteland. Priya stumbles toward the voice, Reverie close behind.

"Priya!" Sariah calls again. "I can hear you. Come to me. I'm over here."

Priya breaks into a run, then trips, slamming face-first into the ground.

She turns her head, and there she is.

Sariah is pinned beneath rubble, a thick metal pole protruding from her chest. Blood pools at the corner of her mouth.

"Oh my god, Sariah!" Priya scrambles toward her. "Shit, what do we do?"

Sariah's breath comes in sharp gasps. "First... get this off my leg. I have to do something before it's too late."

"What do you have to do?"

"Charlie." Her voice is urgent. "He's over there. I have to kill him and eat his brain. Now, Priya—hurry."

"Charlie's still alive?" Reverie asks.

Sariah's gaze flicks to her. "Who the fuck is this?"

Priya answers quickly, yanking bricks off her legs. "Sariah, Reverie. Reverie, Sariah."

"Nice to meet you," Reverie says, helping with the bricks.

Sariah ignores her.

"Where is he?"

Priya follows her gaze. Two legs, still clad in pants, stick out from the wreckage, severed clean at the waist.

"Fuck," Priya whispers.

As soon as Sariah is free, she staggers to her feet—pole still sticking out of her chest—and stumbles toward the remains of the jail.

A thick, bloody trail snakes across the rubble. A body is dragging itself forward.

Charlie.

Sariah strides toward him. "Charlie."

He glances over his shoulder, his face twisted in pain.

"Fuck you!" he spits, frantically clawing ahead.

Sariah yanks the pole from her chest. She reaches him in seconds, stomping on his entrails to stop him.

"Look at me when I kill you, motherfucker."

Charlie's arms buckle. His chest hits the ground.

Sariah climbs onto his back, her boot pressing into his neck.

"Any last words?"

Charlie only flips her off.

Sariah takes the sharp end of the pole and jams it into the base of his skull, from the back of his neck upward. It splices through with a wet, sickening crunch—one of the most grotesque sounds Priya has ever heard. Charlie twitches once, twice, then is still.

When she's sure he's dead, she smashes the pole into his head again and again until it cracks open like a watermelon.

Once his brains are spilling across the cement, she looks up at Priya.

"Please don't watch this."

"Oh, like what I just witnessed was any better." Priya smirks.

But Sariah is right—she doesn't want to see her girlfriend consume the brains of the mastermind behind the Purified.

56

BREAK WHAT'S LEFT OF THE WORLD
PRIYA

Priya and Reverie are still searching through the dead, hoping to find any surviving friends, when Sariah finally catches up to them.

"Have you found anyone else?" she asks, wiping blood from her chin. It doesn't help. There's still so much of it covering her.

"We found Gratian," Priya says solemnly.

Sariah's expression darkens. "And?"

"He's still kinda Rona. He was under Honor. It looks like she saved him and Jesse—or was trying to—when the last blast hit."

"But I thought she was already dead?"

"So did I. But maybe the Rona in her kept her going? I don't know. We stabbed Charlie in the head and he still got away. But this time... I don't think she's coming back. And Jesse's Rona too."

They make their way back to where they left Gratian and Honor. Jesse is still grumbling beneath the pile of bodies, Honor lies motionless on the ground, and Gratian—he's gone.

"Shit!" Priya swears. "Where the fuck did he go?"

"I'll look for him," Reverie says.

Sariah, however, is still fixated on something else. "Seriously, who the fuck is that?" she asks again, nodding toward Reverie.

"I found her while I was looking for you guys. She asked for help. She said she didn't want the life Charlie had planned for her, so he threw her in ad-seg."

Sariah looks doubtful.

"I know," Priya sighs. "I don't know either, boo, but what else do we have to lose? She doesn't trust us, we don't trust her. Whatever. I just want to get the fuck out of this place."

Sariah doesn't argue. Instead, she slings an arm around Priya, pulling her close as they reach Honor's body.

Priya kneels beside her fallen friend. Her eyes are closed, but deep wounds mar her head, black hair matted to her skull with blood. Half her face is melted to the bone, and her chest is completely still.

Priya sinks to the ground, cross-legged, and gently lifts Honor's shoulders into her lap. Silent tears spill down her cheeks as she strokes her friend's face.

"Oh, my sweet friend," she whispers, her voice breaking. "I don't know how I'm supposed to go on without you. You were my rock. You fought so hard for G, and now... I just—" A choked sob cuts her off.

Sariah kneels beside her, rubbing her back in quiet support.

"Why isn't she coming back?" Sariah murmurs. "I don't get it. I died, like, five times today."

Priya wipes at her tears. "I don't know. Maybe it's because of the chemo she had a long time ago?"

Before Sariah can respond, Reverie returns, Gratian in her arms.

"Found your little monster," she says, setting him down beside Priya and Honor.

When Gratian looks up at Priya, his eyes are clear.

"Auntie Pree?" he says, his voice small.

Priya's heart clenches. "Oh, Gratian! I'm so happy you're with us," she breathes, pulling him close as he settles beside her and his mother.

"Why is Mommy sleeping?"

The question shatters her.

Sariah is the one to answer. "Mommy is…"

But before she can finish, Gratian speaks, his voice barely above a whisper.

"She saved me," he says. "I 'member she jumped on me and Jesse. He was holdin' me and runnin' after throwin' that sparkly thing. But the other one that Pacious threw went boom first, and we fell. Then I saw Mommy runnin' from over there, and she jumped on us."

Gratian wiggles out of Priya's arms, crawling to Honor and hugging her tightly. He rests his head on her chest, tiny hands clutching at her still form.

"Please wake up, Mommy. Please."

His sobs pierce the air—raw and devastating. They echo into the void, loud enough to level the decaying ground they walk upon, sad enough to break what's left of the world.

Priya has no idea how to comfort him.

"I'm going to look for more of my people," Reverie murmurs, slipping away.

Sariah stays, wrapping Priya in a firm embrace, letting her sob into her shoulder.

A low, guttural sound rumbles nearby.

Sariah stiffens. "What was that?"

Priya blinks away tears. "Oh. Yeah. Jesse's over there. He's Rona."

"Shit," Sariah mutters. "Guess we'll have to tie him up and drag him with us so I can fix him."

"You're really gonna do that?" Priya asks, surprised.

"Of course. I love that dude. You haven't seen the other two shitheads anywhere, have you?"

Priya shakes her head. "I haven't seen either of them in the mess."

Sariah exhales. "I'll let you grieve for a bit. I'm gonna go find something to tie Jesse up with."

Priya barely acknowledges her, watching Gratian sob against his mother's still chest.

AFTER SOME TIME, Reverie returns with Ovi and two others—a blond woman with a faux-hawk, the sides of her head shaved while the remaining tresses, streaked with faded pink, blend with some locs. The other is a massive Black man, built like Mr. T and bearing a striking resemblance to him.

"Priya, this is Crimsynn," Reverie says, gesturing to the blond. "And this is Ocho. They're my friends. Like me, they're Purified, but we were all in ad-seg together for refusing to comply."

Priya nods slightly, feeling too drained to do much more. "Nice to meet you. I'm Priya, and that's Gratian." She gestures toward Gratian, still curled up against his mother, sobbing.

At that moment, Sariah appears, dragging Jesse behind her on a makeshift leash. His hands are bound with rope, and his mouth is gagged to keep him from biting.

"The fuck?" Ocho blurts out.

"That's Sariah. And Jesse," Priya answers flatly.

"Y'all some sick and twisted motherfuckers, ain't ya?" Ocho mutters.

"No, it's not what it looks like," Priya starts to explain.

"They know a cure," Reverie interjects.

"What?" Oviana stares, stunned.

"Yeah, so it would seem," Priya confirms.

Sariah stops before them, pressing a firm finger to Jesse's forehead to halt him. Her face is still covered in blood, making her look even more imposing. She squints at the newcomers, her eyes full of skepticism. "Who the fuck are these people?"

"Oviana, Ocho, Crimsynn," Reverie says, pointing to each in turn.

Sariah narrows her eyes, studying them. "Uh-huh. And why are they here?" she asks, motioning to the ground.

"Babe, chill," Priya says. "Listen, we've got a lot to explain, and if they want to come with us, we'll figure it out. But we can't stay here. We need to move before dark. Just know this—Sariah here is the only one who knows how to Purify."

A tense beat passes before Sariah exhales sharply.

"Yeah, about that..." she mutters.

Priya frowns. "What?"

Sariah nods toward Honor's lifeless body.

"She was the only one who knew exactly what chemo to use."

57

A NEW LEVEL OF FUCKED UP
PRIYA

F uck.

Sariah is going to have to eat Honor's brain.

Priya's eyebrows knit together. "You sure you don't know the regimen?"

"I never finished mine, remember? I still need to."

"Fuck," Priya breathes.

Gratian looks up at her as if he understands what they're contemplating. But there's no way they can do to Honor what Sariah just did to Charlie.

"There has to be another way," Priya insists.

Sariah shakes her head. "Not one that I know of. Unless we find another leukemia survivor who happens to know the chemo regimen."

"But it was working for the others we treated, even though they didn't have leukemia," Priya points out. "Maybe any chemo works."

Sariah pulls her aside, out of Gratian's earshot. Jesse stumbles as the rope tugs him forward. "Is that a risk you really want to take? Especially with Gratian? We need to finish Purifying him. I think this is our only option."

Priya's stomach twists at the thought of her girlfriend cracking open Honor's skull and eating the brain of Gratian's beloved mother. The horror of it is too much.

"I don't know. Do whatever you have to, but I won't be here to watch."

Sariah's gaze softens. "I know, love. I wouldn't expect you to."

"I'll take our new friends and Gratian and start heading toward the hospital on Prospect and Lemay. Meet us there when you can."

"Okay."

Sariah pulls her into a deep kiss before Priya turns back to Gratian.

With the wheelchair likely blown up along with the rest of the jail, she's going to have to carry him the whole way.

Luckily, he's not that heavy.

"Gratian," she says gently.

He lifts his head from his mother's chest, his eyes red and puffy, streaks of clean skin cutting through the dirt on his face where tears have fallen.

"Yes?"

"We need to go to our next stop. We have medicine for you there, okay?"

"What about Mama?"

"Sariah's going to stay back and see if there's anything she can do for her, alright?"

She hates lying to him, but there's no way she's telling him what's really going to happen to Honor. She and Sariah will have to come up with a story—one that will live in his memory for the rest of his life.

It has to be a good one.

"Okay," he says softly.

Priya picks him up, settling him on her left hip.

"Alright, everyone ready?" she asks, glancing at her new entourage.

"Ready," Reverie replies.

By the time the sun begins to sink behind the ruins of Fort Collins, hours have passed, and Priya is shifting Gratian to her other hip. He's getting heavier, sluggish. She stays on high alert, bracing for the moment he turns Rona again—she can't let him bite her. The last thing she wants is to go through Purification or endure chemo herself.

"Which hospital are we heading to again?" Crimsynn asks, her brown backpack bouncing as she hops over a pile of rubble.

"Poudre Valley. They have an infusion wing for cancer treatments. Should have everything we need for Purifying and cleansing."

"And you're sure you can fix... us?" Ocho asks, using the walking stick he picked up along the way to flick a leaf off the ground.

The only sounds are the crunch of gravel beneath their boots and the distant shuffling of Rotters. So far, the undead haven't noticed the group slipping through the back alley toward the hospital.

"Yes," Priya says. "It was working for Sariah. She said her cravings were getting weaker."

"You really had no idea she was Purified?" Oviana asks.

"No." Priya's voice comes out sharper than she intended. The question feels like an insult, as if she was too oblivious to realize the woman she's been sleeping with was a Purified Rona. "She never gave me any indication."

They're almost at the hospital when a gunshot shatters the air, pinging off a car next to them.

"Shit!" Priya shouts, diving for cover.

The others follow.

Another shot rings out, shattering a shed window above her. Glass rains down, and she scrambles back with Gratian on her back, ducking behind a dumpster.

"The fuck?" Ocho yells from across the alley. "Who's shooting at us?"

"Whoever took up residence in the hospital," Priya answers.

"What do we do?" Crimsynn hisses from behind her.

"I don't know yet," Priya admits. "Maybe if I go out there with Gratian and wave a white flag, they'll see we're not a threat."

Another shot hits the gravel inches from her.

"Why are they wasting bullets?" Crimsynn mutters. "They're shit shots too."

"Well, we better figure something out soon—Rotters are coming," Ocho warns.

Priya looks up the alley. A horde, at least fifty strong, is closing in fast. More shuffle in from the right and left, blocking the road near the hospital.

"Auntie Pree," Gratian says.

"Yes?"

"I feel low."

Shit.

Okay. Fantastic. Everything is going to shit at the same time.

"There's candy in my pack," she says, setting him down. "Get something to eat. I'm going to try to get the people inside to stop shooting at us."

"Priya!" Reverie whisper-shouts from across the alley.

More gunfire. A rotter drops. Someone inside the hospital is sniping.

"Priya!" Reverie calls again, louder.

"What?!" Priya snaps.

"I don't think they were shooting at us."

"I feel like they are though," Priya retorts. The horde wasn't close enough when the first shots were fired.

"We gotta do something fast," Crimsynn urges.

"Auntie Pree," Gratian says.

"Priya," Reverie calls.

"Yo, Priya," Ocho chimes in.

"You guys," another voice joins in from the alley, but she can't tell who—too many people are demanding too much when there's no time to think.

Her patience snaps.

"WHAT THE FUC—"

A sound like nothing she's ever heard before rips through the air—a screech, high-pitched and unnatural. It's like a banshee's wail.

And suddenly, the horde of Rotters behind them is running.

What the actual fuck?

Priya whips her head around. The Rotters that had been closing in from behind? They're fleeing.

She looks toward the hospital. The ones in front of them are still shambling forward.

But the ones behind? They're running away.

Fucking.

Running.

The Rotters don't run. Only Ronas do.

Before she can process it, something leaps into the fleeing horde.

Her stomach turns.

It was human once. Now, its skin is pitch black, cracked with glowing red fissures. No facial features remain except for burning red eyes and a mouth that stretches far too wide for its head.

Then it screeches again.

Priya's blood runs cold.

The thing lunges at a rotter, jaws unhinging to reveal rows

of jagged, serrated teeth. It tears through one, slicing it clean in half with claws the size of butcher knives. Guts spill across the dirt. Another rotter barely has time to turn before the creature's maw clamps down, shearing off its arm in a single, sickening gulp.

A new level of fucked up.

Priya's heart pounds as she locks eyes with Gratian.

Crimsynn is staring too, mouth agape, her face pale with horror.

Movement ahead draws Priya's gaze—more Rotters shuffling toward them, cutting off their escape to the hospital.

Behind them, that thing is still tearing through the horde.

And now...

There are two of them.

58

ROTWRAITHS

PRIYA

More shots ring out from the hospital, and several Rotters in the horde ahead collapse.

Priya scans the alley, glancing between Reverie and Ocho, then Crimsynn and Ovi. Gratian has that faraway look in his eyes—the telltale sign he's either about to turn into his own Rona or pass out from going low.

"What the fuck do we do?" Crimsynn demands.

Another shot. More Rotters fall.

"Whoever's in the hospital is clearing a path for us," Ovi observes.

Crimsynn repeats, more urgently, "What do we do?"

"We run," Priya says.

She hoists Gratian into her arms and stands, whistling to get Reverie's attention across the way.

"Hey!"

"Yeah?"

"Let's fucking run."

Reverie nods, and Priya takes a deep breath before she bolts.

As she sprints, her feet pounding the pavement, the gunfire

intensifies. More Rotters drop, but there's still a thick cluster—twenty, maybe thirty—blocking their path. No choice but to fight their way through.

Priya draws her weapon, as do the others. Gunshots crack through the air, blades slice through decaying flesh. Priya smashes one in the skull. Crimsynn's machete fells another. Reverie empties her rounds into the oncoming horde, while Ocho swings his reaper scythe, carving a path through the chaos.

The alley ends at the hospital parking lot, enclosed by a towering chain-link fence. The exit is in sight.

Priya's muscles burn. Gratian is getting heavier, his small hands clamped over his ears against the relentless gunfire. The Rotters keep coming, drawn by the noise, and worse, the screeching wails of Ronas echo from behind.

A fresh horde crests the hill behind the hospital, fast and relentless.

They aren't going to make it.

Priya reaches the fence first and lifts Gratian. It takes everything she has to get him high enough.

"Okay, you're gonna fall hard on the other side. Try to land on your bum, not your face, okay?"

"Okay," he says, gripping the top with trembling hands and using what strength he has left to pull himself over.

"Hurry! Drop!"

"But Auntie Pree—"

"Just fucking do it, Gratian! Drop now!"

He lets go, landing hard on his side with a yelp.

Priya jumps, gripping the fence, but a rotter snags her pant leg. She kicks violently.

"Get. The. Fuck. Off. Me!" she snarls, each kick more desperate than the last.

A gunshot cracks. The rotter's head jerks back, and its grip loosens.

"Got him," Sariah calls, Jesse on a leash behind her.

Priya nearly kisses her on the spot.

"No time," Sariah says, catching the look on her face. "Get over. Now!"

Priya nods and hauls herself up and over.

"How are you getting Jesse over?"

"I'll have to go around."

"What if whoever's in there doesn't let you in?"

Sariah, a Purified, doesn't rush. The Rotters sniff her, sense what she is, and move on. She's safe. Priya isn't.

The Ronas are closing in.

"I'll be right there, okay? Trust me."

Priya presses her lips to the fence, and Sariah meets them before running off in the opposite direction, leading Jesse away from the chaos.

The banshees' shrieks grow deafening. The Rotters scatter, but the Ronas—fast, vicious—swarm the fence.

Sariah slips past them, Jesse in tow.

Priya sprints toward the locked hospital doors, Gratian in her arms. The others are already there, pounding on the entrance.

"They're not letting us in!" Reverie shouts.

Priya sets Gratian down and steps back, scanning the windows where the gunfire had come from moments ago.

"Hey!" she yells.

Nothing.

She grabs a rock and hurls it. It smacks a redheaded girl square in the forehead.

"Ow! What the fuck?!"

"Oh god, sorry! So sorry."

"Bitch!" the girl shouts, pulling up a rifle.

Priya throws up her hands. "Please don't shoot! We have a kid! He's diabetic, he's going low. We just need to get inside."

She braces for the gunshot. It doesn't come.

An older redhead steps into view, peering down at her.

Priya waves.

A shriek—too close. She whirls. The creatures have scaled the fence.

"Please! Let us in!" she screams.

One lands on the ground, another just behind it.

Priya grabs Gratian and turns to run.

The doors crash open.

They rush inside.

The doors slam shut just as those red eyes reach them.

A boy, young, maybe seventeen, slides a massive siege-style bolt into place, securing the entrance.

Priya sets Gratian down and rests her hands on her knees, gasping for breath.

"What the fuck was that?" she pants.

"No fucking clue," the boy replies. "But I don't wanna find out. That's the fifth one we've seen. They're the only things the Ronas and Decayers are scared of." He nods toward Gratian. "C'mon. Let's get your kid some sugar, then you can be on your way."

Great. A kid thinks he owns the hospital just because he and his siblings are holed up in it.

He's lanky, with bright red curls and freckles, his dirty white T-shirt and ripped jeans hanging loose on his frame. A shotgun rests in his hands, strap dangling.

Priya straightens. "Wait—my girlfriend's coming around the other side."

The pounding on the door intensifies. Priya flinches.

"There's more of you?" the boy asks.

"Just my girlfriend." She hesitates. "And Jesse."

The boy narrows his eyes. "Who's Jesse?"

Priya exhales sharply. "We found a way to cure a Rona bite."

The boy freezes. "You what?"

"It's a long story. Let's get my girlfriend in, and I'll explain."

"Not so fast." He lifts the shotgun. "Who the fuck are you people?"

"I'm Priya. This is Gratian. He can't walk. My girlfriend, Sariah, has Jesse with her. He looks like a Rona, but we can help him."

The boy scoffs. "You wanna bring one of those fucking dead things in here? Hell nah, dawg. Ain't happening."

Ocho stiffens. "I'm one of those fucking dead things, you half-wit."

Before Priya can react, Ocho slams his forehead into the kid's face. Blood spurts from his nose as he stumbles back, scrambling for his gun.

"Ocho, what the fuck—" Priya starts, but Ovi and Crimsynn are already on it, kicking the gun away.

"Chill! CHILL!" the kid shouts, hands raised in surrender.

Priya steps forward as Crimsynn levels the shotgun at him.

"Now, look here, kid," Priya says as Crimsynn keeps the gun trained on him. "We're not here to hurt you. We just need to find some medicine, make our concoctions, and then we'll be on our way. Okay?"

The kid looks up at her, hands still raised, blood dripping from his nose onto his shirt. He nods. "Just don't hurt us, okay? My little siblings are upstairs. I've been through hell trying to keep them safe. Please."

"We don't want to hurt you," Priya reassures him. "But we do need to let my girlfriend in. And she has a Rona with her. He's a friend."

"Okay. Yeah. No worries."

Crimsynn nods, and the kid slowly gets to his feet. His eyes flick to Priya. "What did he mean when he said he's one of those dead things?"

"We've been Purified. Long story." Priya waves a hand. "Now, where's the other door to let Sariah in?"

Still looking bewildered, he gestures. "This way."

They follow him in silence through the dark hallways, turning left, then right, then left again.

"It's up there," the kid says, stopping in front of a set of heavy double doors. "Through those doors."

"You first," Ocho orders, pressing his scythe lightly against the kid's chest.

The kid swallows hard and nods, inching forward. When he pushes the doors open, Priya half expects something to lunge at them. But nothing happens.

She exhales, then hands Gratian to Reverie before hurrying to the exit door. Pressing her ear against the cold metal, she listens.

Silence.

"I don't think she's here yet," Priya murmurs.

"So... who are you guys?" the kid asks Ocho, watching them warily.

Ocho just grunts.

"Shh," Priya hushes them, straining to hear.

Then—a faint tapping at the door.

Quickly, she unfastens the heavy siege-style lock, sliding back the bolts. When she pulls the door open, Sariah is there, out of breath, with Jesse bound, still on his leash.

"Oh, what the fuuccckkk," the kid mutters as Sariah hurries inside.

Priya slams the door shut just as distant screeches and guttural howls echo through the night.

Sariah leans against the wall, panting, terror still written across her face.

"Are you okay?" Priya asks.

"Yeah, I think so."

"What were those things?"

"Charlie called them Rotwraiths," Sariah answers grimly.

"Rot-what-the-fucks?" Ocho asks.

"You mean Charlie never told you guys about the Wraiths?"

"Um, no."

Sariah swears under her breath. "Shit. That's a huge part of his operation."

"What do you mean?" Priya presses.

Sariah exhales, her expression dark. "The Rotwraiths—or just Wraiths—are what happens when Purified don't eat brains. When they refuse to partake. Their bodies necrotize, turning them into those things. Awful, evil fucking things that even the Rona are afraid of."

"What the fuck," Ovi mutters.

Priya's stomach tightens. She turns to Reverie. "Didn't you say that you four were in ad-seg because you refused to eat brains?"

Reverie nods. "Yeah, that's right."

"And how long had you been in there?"

"A couple of days. Why?"

Priya meets her gaze. "Because he put you there for a reason. Because that's what you're turning into."

59

ECHOES OF WAR
SARIAH

"Will someone please explain to me what the fuck you all are talking about before my head explodes?" the kid exclaims, throwing his hands up.

Sariah eyes him. "Who's this?"

"Uh..." Priya glances at him. "I don't know your name."

"I'm Bracket," he replies.

"Bracket?" Sariah snorts. "That's a funny name."

"Uh... thanks?" Bracket says, clearly unsure how to take that. Ocho chuckles beside him.

Sariah folds her arms. "Who's with you?"

"My little brother and sister are upstairs."

"That's it?"

He nods. "Why?"

"Because we need to get our shit going and don't need any interruptions." Sariah pushes past him, Jesse stumbling along behind her, barely restrained.

Bracket hesitates, then follows. "What are you guys gonna do with him?"

"We're going to fix him," Sariah answers without looking back.

Priya sighs. "We need to start the chemo immediately."

"Chemo?" Bracket repeats, completely lost. "I'm sorry, what?"

"Yes, Brody, keep up," Sariah says flatly.

"Bracket."

"Whatever. Where are your siblings?"

"Upstairs. Why?"

Sariah stops so suddenly that Bracket nearly runs into her. Before he can react, she draws her sword and presses it lightly against his throat.

"I'm sorry, ginger boy," she says coolly. "Did I stutter?"

Bracket's Adam's apple bobs as he swallows hard. "N-no."

"Good. Now... go get them."

He nods frantically and scurries off.

"Someone go with him," Sariah orders. "Meet us in the pharmacy."

"On it," Ocho says, jogging after Bracket.

Priya watches Sariah resume walking, still exuding that no-nonsense, take-no-shit energy. "You good, babe?"

"Yep. Peachy."

Priya shudders, knowing the sheer amount of brains Sariah's consumed is messing with her. But, oddly enough, the way she's acting now? It's kind of hot.

She leans in. "You're gonna have to take this wicked attitude to bed with me later."

Sariah smirks, her eyes glinting. "You like that? Just wait and see how wicked my tongue can be."

A rush of heat floods Priya's face, but before she can respond, hurried footsteps echo down the hall.

Bracket returns, two more redheaded kids trailing behind him. The boy is tall and lanky like Bracket, while the girl is smaller, her sharp eyes darting between everyone like she's memorizing escape routes.

Bracket hands Priya a candy bar. "For the kid."

She takes it gratefully. "Thanks."

Sariah crosses her arms. "Who do we have here?"

"My little brother, Conner. And my little sister, Jade."

Both kids look hardened, their childhood long swallowed by war.

"Alright," Sariah says, turning. "Try to keep up."

As they move through the hospital, she explains everything —the Purification process, the lethal Purified hunting humans, how chemo somehow helped her suppress her own ravenous urges. She tells them about how Charlie's group kidnapped Gratian, leading them here.

When they finally reach sublevel four, Bracket exhales sharply. "So you guys basically figured out a cure for CoRona."

Sariah glances at Priya. "Yeah. Pretty much."

"What about those things outside?" Ovi asks. "The, uh... Wraiths?"

"We have no idea how to kill or cure those," Sariah admits. "Once they go black like that, there's no way to reverse it."

"So even if we stop the Rona, those things are gonna stick around?" Crimsynn mutters.

Sariah doesn't answer. Instead, she approaches a locked glass door—the pharmacy. Through the dusty glass, rows of untouched medicine line the shelves.

Priya exhales, relief washing over her.

Sariah grips the hilt of her sword and swings it at the glass. Bang. The impact vibrates through the air, but the glass holds.

She scowls and tries again. Bang. Still unbroken.

Ocho clicks his tongue. "We'll have to shoot it out."

The group plugs their ears as Ocho fires three shots, shattering the glass. Sariah steps through, scanning the shelves.

"Alright, for the three who need chemo, we need

Methotrexate, Vincristine, Cytarabine, and 6MP. For Jesse, I need Altretamine, Cisplatin, Dacarbazine, and Busulfan. Grab as much as you can."

The group disperses, gathering the necessary drugs. The air is thick with tension.

Jesse, still bound and gagged, thrashes weakly. His eyes, clouded by the Rona infection, burn with feral hunger and rage. A guttural snarl tears from his throat, spraying spit through the gag.

"We need to start his Purification now," Priya urges, panic in her voice. "If we wait any longer—"

Sariah stiffens.

A jolt of electricity sears through her skull. Not her own thought. Not her own memory.

Charlie's.

Syringes. Formulas. Ratios of chemicals measured to the microliter. A whole lattice of medical knowledge that shouldn't exist inside her brain crashes down in a dizzying flood.

Her knees buckle, hands flying to her temples. She tastes copper. Breath hitches. "I can... I can make it."

Priya blinks. "Make what?"

"The serum," Sariah whispers, the words alien on her tongue yet certain in her bones. "I know how."

Ocho narrows his eyes. "That's insane. How the hell—"

"Charlie's brain," she gasps. "When I ate it—his memories, his skills—they... stuck. I shouldn't know this, but I do. I can make the serum. But I don't know if it'll cure him or kill him."

The silence that follows is thick, broken only by Jesse's low, strangled growls as he bucks against his restraints.

Finally, Priya snaps. "Then stop wasting time and do it. Before there's nothing left of him to save."

Sariah swallows her fear and turns toward the dimly lit pharmacy. The air smells faintly of antiseptic and mildew. Her hands shake as she tears open drawers, pawing through vials, labels half-peeled and faded. Cabinets screech when she yanks them open, rattling with bottles no one has touched in years.

"Take him upstairs," she orders, breathless. "Infusion center. Level four. Get him strapped into a chair before he tears someone apart."

Ocho hesitates. "And leave you here alone?"

"GO." Her shout cracks through the pharmacy.

Priya and Ocho exchange a look, then wrestle Jesse down the corridor, his body jerking like a rabid animal's, guttural noises echoing off the sterile walls.

The second they disappear, the silence presses down on Sariah.

She works by instinct. Pour. Measure. Stir. Neutralize. The formulas aren't hers—Charlie's ghost rides her veins, guiding her every motion—but even with his knowledge, her hands falter. Twice the mixture smokes violently, once it curdles into black sludge. She curses, dumps it, and starts again, heart pounding.

Sweat beads on her brow. Her knuckles ache from how tightly she grips the syringe. She doesn't know how much time passes—minutes? hours?—but when the liquid finally glows faintly green, something inside her screams that this is it. This is as close as she'll ever get.

Her throat is dry. Her legs barely hold her as she bolts up stairwells and empty halls, clutching the loaded syringe like it might detonate.

In the infusion center, Jesse is already strapped into a chemo chair, his body straining against leather restraints, head whipping side to side like a trapped animal. His veins bulge and blacken. His chest rises in ragged, shuddering gasps.

Priya looks up, eyes wild. "Sariah—"

"No time." Sariah drives the needle into Jesse's neck before anyone can stop her.

His body seizes instantly. A muffled scream rattles his gag, echoing sharp and guttural through the sterile room. His muscles convulse, locking so violently his bones look ready to splinter.

Priya stumbles back, horrified. "Sariah... what the fuck did you just do?"

Sariah grips the arm of the chair, her own chest heaving, unable to look away from Jesse's writhing form.

"I guess," she whispers, voice breaking, "we're about to find out."

60

A DOSE OF DESPERATION
PRIYA

As they watch Jesse, and marvel at how the concoction swirls under his skin, lighting up the dark room, Gratian makes a strange sound—a sharp inhale, followed by a stumble. His face suddenly pales, and his body lists to the side.

"Shit—!" Priya rushes to him, catching him before he hits the ground. "He's out," she says, pressing her fingers to his neck. His pulse is weak.

"He needs sugar," Sariah says.

She runs to the nurses station, going through cabinets as a distant explosion causes a picture to fall off the wall.

Ocho and Crimsynn look at each other, dashing out of the infusion center to go investigate, Bracket hot on their tail with his twelve gauge.

The explosion rattles the building, sending dust cascading from the ceiling. A sharp crack echoes down the hall, followed by a deep boom

The others barely register their departure.

Sariah rushes back over to Priya, handing her a packet of glucose gel. Priya rips it open with her teeth, tilts Gratian's head back, and squeezes the gel into his mouth, rubbing his throat to make him swallow.

Gratian's frail body is as light as a leaf as she lifts him from the ground, rushing him over to bed. His chest rises and falls in shallow, unsteady breaths, his skin clammy and pale.

"Come on, kid," she mutters.

The pallor of his already dark skin is almost a mocha color, but as the glucose gel enters his system, it shoots his blood sugar up.

Sariah kneels by Jesse's side, her eyes darting over his still, unmoving body. His breathing is slow and steady, but there's a faint twitch to his fingers, a sign of life flickering just beneath the surface. His skin is cool to the touch, and the black veins crawling along his arms seem to be fading ever so slightly, the Rona quality beginning to lose its grip. She presses a hand to his forehead, murmuring softly. "Come on, Jesse. You're stronger than this."

The door bangs open again, and Ocho, Bracket, and Crimsynn show back up with a battered and disheveled Pacious, whose glasses are broken, and he's dirty with black soot streaking his face. Liam, who has leg braces and crutches, is helping Pacious to walk. He looks worse for wear too, his hair matted with sweat and grime.

"These guys say they're with you," Bracket announces, looking thoroughly unimpressed. "They blew a hole through one of the walls, so. Thanks for fucking up our home, assholes."

"Holy shit," Priya breathes, eyes widening. "You two look like hell."

"We crawled through hell to get here," Pacious replies, wiping dust from his face.

Sariah and Priya help Liam and Pacious into the room, guiding them toward the nearest seats.

"I'm so sorry," Pacious blurts out, his voice filled with guilt. "We didn't have a choice. We were being swarmed by Ronas and Rotters—everywhere. We had one stick of dynamite left, and... the other entrances were all boarded up. We tried every way in, but time was running out. We found a run-down part of the hospital that didn't look used, so..." He trails off, guilt weighing heavily on his features.

"We blew the hole," Liam finishes, his voice low and apologetic. "We had no other option."

"Should we be worried about the hole?" Ocho asks, concern etched into his face.

Bracket shakes his head, a small wave of relief passing over his otherwise irritated demeanor. "No. It was in a wing that's not accessible by foot. They had to climb up the wall on a ladder to get to the floor above. Whatever's out there can't get in that way."

"Good," Priya mutters, finally exhaling.

Pacious rubs the back of his neck, looking down at the floor. "We didn't mean to mess things up for you guys. We just... had to get here."

"Relax," Sariah murmurs, her tone softer now. "You're here. That's what matters.

HOURS LATER, while they're waiting for Jesse's purification to work, Bracket, Jade, and Conner show them to a little area that used to be for families with kids in the hospital. There's a living room, a small kitchenette, and chairs and tables everywhere. Bracket is making something on a stove propelled by gas, Ovi, Reverie, Sariah talking amongst themselves.

Pacious clears his throat.

"Priya, got a sec?"

Priya nods and gets up, letting the blanket she had over her lap fall to the ground.

"What's up?" she asks as they enter the dark hall.

"I found more of these," he says, pulling his backpack off his back and unzipping it.

He hands her a dozen syringes filled with the purification serum.

"Why are we whispering about it?" she asks, taking them and fanning them out.

His face folds in worry. "Because I don't know if they are what they had at the cancer center. I found it in a fridge in a pile of rubble," Pacious says. "The fridge was labeled 'experimental' so I have no idea what it will do."

Priya hesitates, glancing at the syringes in her dark and elegant hands.

"Who should we try it on? Crimsynn, Ovi, and Ocho are already Purified, so they don't need it. And Sariah ate Honor and Charlie's brain, so she can make the serum."

Pacious shifts, hesitantly. "What if we tried it on Gratian?"

Priya scoffs. "No. Absolutely not. We already lost Honor and everyone else I care about. I'm not about to do some experiment on Gray."

Pacious nods, taking the syringes back. "I'll just hold on to them for a rainy day then."

THE GROUP SITS GATHERED around a makeshift fire. Since ventilation is nonexistent, the flames are fake—an old space heater crackling in the center of the room, casting long, flickering shadows against the walls.

The atmosphere is calm, almost peaceful. They talk, reminiscing about a life before the world collapsed. Priya and Sariah lean into each other, sharing quiet conversation and stolen glances over their meal. Ocho and Ovi continue their debate over the logistics of mass-producing the cure Sariah carries in her blood.

None of them notice Pacious slipping away into the dark.

None of them see him creep back to the infirmary, where Gratian lies curled beneath a thin blanket, his breaths even but his body still weak.

And none of them witness the moment Pacious uncaps one of the syringes, pressing the needle to the soft flesh of Gratian's arm.

He hesitates.

Then—his jaw tightens.

And he pushes the plunger down.

61

EPILOGUE

WHEN MONSTERS KNEEL

GRATIAN

Heat rushes through Gratian's veins like liquid fire. His body hums—pulses—like he's being remade from the inside out.

His eyes snap open.

For a moment, the ceiling above him doesn't feel real. He can see the cracks in the paint, the way dust particles float in the dim light. Every sound is amplified—the crackle of the fire in the next room, the murmur of voices, the faint wind howling through the broken hospital corridors.

Then he realizes—

His legs.

He feels his legs.

Gasping, Gratian sits up. He's breathing too fast, his heart pounding in his chest. This has to be a dream. A hallucination.

But when he swings his legs over the side of the bed, they move.

Not weakly. Not sluggishly. But with power.

His feet touch the cold floor.

He stands.

And he doesn't fall.

His breath catches in his throat. His hands shake as he looks down at himself, flexing his fingers, curling his toes against the ground.

He feels weightless.

Like he could fly.

A wild, euphoric laugh bubbles up in his chest, but he swallows it down. He's not supposed to be walking. He should be in bed, barely clinging to life.

But he's not.

He knows what this means.

And he knows what he has to do.

Silently, he slips out of the room, his movements smooth—almost too graceful. His senses stretch far beyond what they should. He can hear Jesse's heartbeat before he even reaches the infusion room.

Jesse is strapped to the chair, his body still bound, his golden-glowing eyes flickering open. His breath comes in short, sharp gasps. He looks normal, but Gratian knows he isn't.

Jesse isn't human anymore.

And neither is he.

Gratian moves without thinking, his hands working the straps loose. Jesse jerks, his teeth bared.

Gratian doesn't flinch.

He steps forward, presses his hands to Jesse's shoulders—then bites him.

Jesse lets out a sharp, strangled sound, but the moment Gratian's teeth sink into his skin, something shifts between them.

Their bodies jolt with an unseen energy. Their blood connects.

And suddenly, they understand.

Jesse's eyes snap fully open, glowing like twin suns in the

darkness. His breathing evens out. He looks at Gratian, and for the first time since his transformation began, he smiles.

Together, they walk down the dark, crumbling hospital halls, past the hole in the wall, out into the night where the creatures wait.

The Rotters. The Ronas. The Purified. And the Rotwraiths.

The Wraiths are the first to react. Their massive, blackened bodies reel back, hissing and screeching in a chorus of pure rage. Their many eyes gleam in the night, their claws twitching.

They are ready to kill.

Gratian steps forward.

They lurch, shrieking, their bodies coiling.

Then, suddenly…

They stop.

One by one, the Rotwraiths lower their heads, their voices turning into something else. Something like a chant—an eerie melody of whispers in a language no human should understand.

Jesse and Gratian do understand.

The words hum in their bones.

The creatures bow.

Not just the Rotwraiths.

All of them.

The Rotters. The Rona. The Purified.

They lower themselves—their heads touching the ground, their bodies still as statues.

Jesse exhales slowly. Gratian watches, his pulse steady.

This is right.

This is how it was meant to be.

A sound breaks through the quiet.

Footsteps.

"Gratian!"

He turns.

Priya is standing just outside the hospital, her chest rising and falling in rapid breaths, her face pale in the moonlight.

Her wide, terrified eyes lock onto him.

And he smiles.